CAUGHT
IN THE ACT

The ladder was steady beneath my feet. I started down, one rung at a time. As my shoulders and head descended into the basement, I could see the room was nearly empty, lit by the glaring glow of a bare bulb.

One foot was on the floor and the other was still on the ladder when the heavy door to the coal chute suddenly slammed shut over my head. At the same instant, the light went out, plunging the room into total darkness. Scrambling hand over hand, I raced back up the ladder only to crash headfirst into the door just as the lock clicked home.

"We got him," a voice said in triumph. "We got him."

They sure as hell did.

Other Detective J. P. Beaumont Mysteries by
J.A. Jance
From Avon Books

J·A·JANCE

A MORE PERFECT UNION

AVON BOOKS
Library of Congress Catalog Card Number: 88-91258

A MORE PERFECT UNION is an original publication of Avon Books.
This work has never before appeared in book form. This work is a novel.
Any similarity to actual persons or events is purely coincidental.

AVON BOOKS
A division of
The Hearst Corporation
1350 Avenue of the Americas
New York, New York 10019

First Avon Books Printing: November 1988

AVON TRADEMARK REG. U.S. PAT. OFF. AND IN OTHER COUNTRIES, MARCA
REGISTRADA, HECHO EN CANADA.

Printed in Canada.

UNV 10 9 8 7 6 5 4

To J. L. and her quarter century
and
To Bill B. whose career as a technical advisor
was also short but brief

Chapter 1

"CASSIE, for God's sake! What the hell's the body doing out there already? I didn't call for the body. We're not set up yet."

Speaking through a megaphone from his perch on a raised boom, movie director Sam "The Movie Man" Goldfarb's voice echoed through the wooden maze of Lake Union Drydock like God himself speaking from the mount.

Cassie was Cassie Young, a punk-looking young woman who served as Goldfarb's right and left hands. She scurried toward the base of the director's boom as she raised a hand-held radio to her lips.

Because I'm a homicide cop, my ears pricked up when I heard the word "body." For the past two weeks I'd been trailing around Seattle, dutifully mother-henning a Hollywood film crew. Officially, I was on special assignment for Mayor Dawson's office, acting as technical advisor to His Honor's old Stanford roommate and buddy, Samuel Goldfarb. Unofficially, I was doing less than nothing and felt as useless as tits on a boar.

My short venture into the moviemaking business had certainly stripped away the glamour. As far as I can tell, movies are made by crowds of people who mill around endlessly without actually doing anything. I mean nothing happens. They take hours to set up for a scene that takes less than a minute to shoot, or else spend hours shooting a scene that amounts to two seconds of film footage. The whole process was absolutely stultifying. I hated it.

My initial spurt of "body"-fueled adrenaline disappeared quickly. After all, movies are totally make-believe. On a film set, nothing is really what it seems. I naturally assumed that this was more of the same. Leaning back against a workbench in the pipe shop, I shifted my weight to one foot as I attempted to ease the throbbing complaints of the recently reactivated bone spur on my other heel.

I had been whiling away the time by chatting with a

1

garrulous old duffer named Woody Carroll. Woody was a retired Lake Union Drydock employee on tap that day to keep a watchful eye on the cast and crew of *Death in Drydock*. His job was to make sure we didn't do any damage to company property in the course of our Saturday shoot.

Woody told me that he had worked as a carpenter for Lake Union Drydock both before and after World War II. He had been there steadily from the time he got home from a Japanese POW camp in the Philippines until he retired in 1980. He was full of countless stories, and his tales had kept my mind off the bone spur for most of the day. Hiding out from a blazing sun, we had retreated into the gloomy shade of the pipe shop. Seattle was sweltering through an unusually hot, dry August. People who live in the Northwest aren't accustomed to heat.

"I don't know what to think of these young 'uns today," Woody Carroll drawled, picking up his train of thought and resuming our conversation as though nothing had happened. He had been complaining bitterly about the quality of some of the younger employees around the drydock. "They'd rather buy and sell stuff to put up their noses than do an honest day's work. It just beats all."

Outside I could see Cassie Young returning her radio to her pocket. Now, shading her eyes with one hand, she called up to Goldfarb where he remained enthroned on the boom.

"The shop says they're still working on the body. It isn't ready yet."

"Well, what the hell do you call that? It's right in the way of the next shot. Get it out of there, for God's sake! What do you think I pay you for? And where's Derrick's stuntman? I need him. Now!"

Goldfarb had pointed toward a spot in the water near where steep wooden steps led up the wingwall of the drydock. They had been using the boom to shoot a fight scene on the narrow steps with the navy minesweeper *Pledge* looming in the background. Two of the movie's name-brand stars, Derrick Parker and Hannah Boyer, still clung to two-by-four handrails some twenty feet above the solid planking of the pier.

As the entire crew jumped in response to Goldfarb's barked commands, Cassie Young carefully picked her way across a snarled tangle of electrical cords toward the place Goldfarb had indicated.

I didn't much like Cassie. She was a scrawny, red-haired, postadolescent who went in big for the spiked, new-wave look. She wore a thick layer of white pancake makeup. Her eyelashes dripped with heavy, black mascara. She could easily have been mistaken for a refugee from a school for mimes. Looking at her made me grateful she wasn't my daughter, although she and Kelly were probably much the same age.

Cassie and I had crossed swords on numerous occasions during the course of my two-week stint of involuntary servitude on the set of *Death in Drydock*. I had a tough time taking her seriously. The feeling was mutual.

According to Captain Powell, my main assignment as technical advisor was to make sure Goldfarb didn't portray the Seattle Police Department as "a bunch of stupid jerks." I had quickly learned, however, that trying to tell Sam Goldfarb anything he didn't want to hear was like talking to a brick wall. Every time he had his pretend cops doing something unbelievably stupid, I squawked bloody murder. For all the good it did me. Cassie Young didn't mince any words in letting me know that I was to keep those opinions to myself. I was a technical advisor all right. In name only.

For the past week, I had called Captain Powell every morning at eight o'clock, begging him to let me off the hook and pull me from the assignment. No such luck. He kept telling me that the mayor wanted me on the set, and on the set I'd stay.

Still mildly interested in whatever had plucked Goldfarb's nerves, I watched as Cassie reached the edge of the dock and knelt down to peer over the side. Her knees had barely touched the wood when she sprang back as though she'd been burned. She covered her mouth with one hand, but still the muffled sound that escaped her lips was as blood-curdling a scream as I'd heard in years. The wrenching sound echoed back and forth through the otherwise eerily silent wooden buildings.

For days I had lurked in the background of the process, staying out of the way of cameras and equipment. Now, the sound of Cassie's scream galvanized me to action. No matter what, I'm first and foremost a cop. In emergencies, we're trained to react. It's a conditioned response as natural as breathing. Without giving it a second thought, I started toward Cassie on a dead run, ignoring the quick stab of pain in my injured heel.

"Quiet on the set," someone boomed through a megaphone, but Cassie kept on screaming, pointing hysterically toward the water. I reached her and grabbed her by the shoulders just as the megaphone boomed again. "For God's sake, somebody catch Hannah! She's going to fall."

Cassie barfed then. I managed to swing her away from me just in time, then I held her by the waist while she heaved her guts out on the dock.

Between barfing and screaming, I prefer the latter.

At last Cassie straightened up and leaned heavily against me while her whole body quivered with terrible shudders. I held her, patting her gently on the back, soothing her as best I could, while I attempted to peer over her shoulder and see into the water, but we were too far from the edge of the dock. The angle was wrong.

"What is it?" I demanded finally, holding her at arm's length. "What's down there?"

Shaking her head from side to side, she seemed totally incapable of speech, but as soon as I took a step toward the edge of the dock, she came to life and fought me tooth and nail. Her ability to speak returned as well.

"No, no!" she protested, twisting her wrists to escape my grip. "I can't look again. Please don't make me look again, please."

By then, one of the electricians was standing beside us. I handed Cassie off to him, then went to the edge of the pier to see for myself.

As soon as I did, I understood why Cassie Young had fought my attempt to drag her back.

A corpse floated there in the water, or rather, what was left of a corpse. Although Lake Union has no natural currents to speak of, heavy boat traffic on the lake creates a lot of water movement. This movement, mimicking current, had left the body with its legs straddling a wooden piling.

I could tell the corpse was that of a man, but I could make out little else. The bloated body floated low in the water. What was visible could hardly be called a face. His features were distorted and out of focus where skin slippage and feeding fish had done their ugly work. His hair, slicked down against his scalp, was dark and shiny, matted with oil from the lake.

Horror movies manufacture phony death masks all the time. Cassie Young was in the movie business. I found it surprising that she took it so hard, that she was so shocked and shaken, but of course horror-movie masks are done in the name of good clean fun. This wasn't fun or make-believe.

This was real—all too real.

I turned around to assess the situation. It was as though everyone on the set was frozen in place. Nobody moved. Nobody said a word. On the top surface of the wingwall stood a cluster of men, grouped in a tight circle around what I assumed to be a stricken Hannah Boyer. I was grateful someone had managed to catch her and drag her to safety. If a twenty-foot fall doesn't kill you, it cripples you up real good.

The first person to move was Woody Carroll, who hurried toward me as fast as his seventy-year-old legs would carry him. He stopped beside me and looked into the water.

"Call 911," I ordered. "Have 'em send an ambulance for Hannah and a squad car for him." Without a word of protest, Woody nodded, turned, and hurried away toward a phone which was visible near the base of the wingwall.

Lake Union Drydock consists of some 500,000-odd square feet, all of it sitting over thirty-five feet of water. Walking or driving, you have to cross a city-owned moat to get there. The various shops and docks are thrown together in a crazy-quilt, hodgepodge pattern. The company has been in continuous existence and use since 1919. Buildings and docks have been added whenever and wherever the spirit moved, giving the whole place a haphazard, thrown-together appearance.

Looking now at the maze of buildings and docks, I

wondered how emergency vehicles would ever manage to find us. We were clear out near the base of the largest drydock.

Woody picked up the receiver of the phone. No sooner had he spoken into it than a shrill whistle sounded, sending five short sharp blasts into the air. Woody put the phone down and hurried back to me.

"You'd better go meet them and direct them here to us," I told him. "Otherwise they'll never be able to find us."

Woody laughed. "'Those other guys I told you about are already on their way. That's what the whistle's for. Don't worry. They'll find us."

Woody had informed me earlier that a skeleton safety crew was playing cards upstairs in an employee locker room. I hadn't thought we'd need them. Now I was more than happy they were there.

Goldfarb, down from his overhead perch, stormed up behind me. "What's going on, Beaumont?" he demanded. "We've got a movie to shoot. We're losing the light."

In the days I had been on the set I had found Goldfarb to be an altogether disagreeable little man who put his bad temper on a pedestal and called it "Artistic License." I had watched over and over as the whole crew leaped to satisfy his slightest whim. But that was movie business. This was police business, my business—maybe homicide.

The crew suddenly came unstuck. They edged forward, trying to catch sight of whatever was under the dock. I shooed the nearest ones away.

"Get your people out of here, Mr. Goldfarb. We've got emergency vehicles on the way." Even as I spoke, I heard the thin wail of an approaching siren.

"Cops?" Goldfarb screeched, his voice becoming shrill. "You mean somebody's called the cops?"

"That's exactly what I mean, Mr. Goldfarb," I returned.

Goldfarb wasn't my boss, and I had developed a certain immunity to the director's ravings. He was a chronic complainer, always bitching and moaning, always at the top of his lungs.

"You can't do that, Detective Beaumont," he roared

back. "You can't bring cops in here and order me to clear out my people."

"Watch me," I said. I turned to Woody. "Do it."

He did, quickly and effectively, leaving Sam "The Movie Man" Goldfarb hopping from foot to foot in total frustration.

"Cassie, can't you stop this?" he wailed. From bellowing one minute, Goldfarb was reduced to whining the next. "Robert Dawson's going to hear about this," he continued to me. "I'll see you fired before the day's over."

Hizzoner can stick it in his ear, I thought. I said, "Be my guest. You do that."

Seattle's Medic One has some of the best response times in the country. An aid car was the first emergency vehicle to appear on the scene. It rattled noisily over the wooden planks and jerked to a stop. I hurried to meet it and directed the medics to the stairs. "The woman's up there," I said, pointing. "On the wingwall."

"Great," the driver replied, shading his eyes and evaluating the perpendicular wall with its steep wooden staircase. "What's wrong with her?"

"Fainted probably."

He drove the aid car as close as he could to the bottom of the steps. He and his partner leaped from their vehicle just as a Seattle P.D. squad car pulled up on the dock behind me. Two uniformed officers got out, a man and a woman.

The man was a guy named Phil Baxter. I had seen him around the department before, although I had to check his name tag before I could remember his name. The woman was a young black with the name "Jackson" pinned to the breast pocket of her blue uniform. She was new to me.

"What's going on here?" Baxter demanded of no one in particular. "Who's in charge?"

"Looks like he is," Goldfarb said disgustedly, pointing at me.

I answered with no further prompting. "A body," I told Phil. "Over there. In the water."

Baxter walked to the edge of the dock and looked down. Sheer force of habit made me follow. It was still there, slapping against the wooden piling as the wake of a landing float plane rippled across the lake.

As the body rose and fell, a large decorative brass belt buckle glinted briefly in the sun, just under the water's surface. There was a design on it of some kind, and some printing as well. I squinted my best middle-aged squint. Try as I might I couldn't make out the letters.

"Can you read what it says on that buckle?" I asked Baxter.

He too squinted. "Not from here," he answered.

I hadn't noticed, but his partner, Officer Jackson, had followed us. "It says 'Ironworker,' " she remarked quietly.

I glanced back at her in some surprise. She was several feet farther away than I was, and she was able to read it when neither Baxter nor I could. "My vision's twenty-ten," she explained with a smile that made me feel ancient.

For the first time Officer Baxter looked me full in the face. "Why, excuse me, Detective Beaumont. I didn't recognize you. How'd homicide get here so fast? I was just getting ready to call you guys."

"Go ahead and call," I told him. "I'm not here representing homicide."

"You're not?"

I didn't want to go into all the gory details of why I was there. "Trust me on this one," I said. "Call Harbor Patrol and have them send somebody out."

Baxter turned to his partner. "Do that, would you, Merrilee?"

With a nod, Officer Jackson headed back toward the patrol car.

I felt a tap on my shoulder. When I turned, there was Derrick Parker. "Hey, Beau. What's going on?" he asked tentatively. "Hannah really got an eyeful. She fainted dead away."

"How is she?"

"Hyperventilating. She was coming around, but she had a relapse as soon as the medics showed up. Hannah's got the hots for guys in uniform."

Derrick Parker wasn't the least bit fond of his female costar. He and I had chummed around together some while he had been in Seattle. We shared similar tastes, although his ran to Glenlivet rather than MacNaughton's. He seemed to enjoy slumming in some of my favorite watering holes. The waitresses at the Doghouse still hadn't tumbled to the fact that he was a genuine celebrity. Parker said he wanted to keep it that way.

"Who was he?" Parker asked, nodding toward the water.

"The dead man?" I shrugged. "That's up to the medical examiner and the detectives on the case."

"But you're a detective, aren't you?" Parker objected.

"This isn't my case. I'm doing a movie, remember?"

Officer Jackson came back to where we were standing. She gave Derrick Parker a small, tentative smile. I'm sure she recognized him, but when she spoke, Merrilee Jackson was strictly business. "They're all on their way."

"All?" I asked.

"Someone's coming from the medical examiner's office. So are two detectives. Davis and Kramer."

It wasn't exactly by the book, but Officer Jackson had taken a little initiative, and calling everybody at once would probably save time.

I nodded. "Good," I said. "By the way, we haven't been introduced. I'm Detective J. P. Beaumont, and this is Derrick Parker."

She held out her hand. "Merrilee Jackson," she said, shaking my hand, but flashing Parker a wide grin. "I'm glad to meet you."

Merrilee Jackson didn't comment aloud on Derrick Parker's star status, and neither did Baxter. They had other things to worry about. A crowd of movie crew members was edging closer. "We'd better get these people moved back out of the way," Baxter said. "The M.E.'s van will need to pull up close to the water."

They had barely turned their attention to crowd control when another car with lights flashing and siren blaring pulled onto the dock. Detective Manny Davis got out on the rider's side and strode over to me while Detective Paul Kramer stopped to talk with Officers Jackson and Baxter.

"How's it going, Beau?" Manny asked with a chuckle. "How soon are we going to see your name in lights?"

"Cut the comedy, Manny."

"But I heard you were enjoying the movie business."

I glowered at him.

"Okay, okay," he said. "No big. What have we got, fish bait?"

"That's right. A floater."

Manny sauntered over to the edge of the dock and looked into the water. "He's been in the water awhile," Manny observed. As if to confirm his words, the wind shifted just then and the pungent odor of putrid flesh wafted over us like an ill-smelling cloud. Fortunately, Goldfarb had led Cassie away by then. Had she been within range, I'm sure she would have barfed again.

One whiff and Derrick Parker's engaging smile vanished completely.

"Jesus," he said with a grimace. "That's awful." He started to back away, but Manny stopped him.

"Hey, wait a minute. Aren't you . . ." Manny paused, searching for the name, then broke off, embarrassed.

"Derrick Parker?" Parker finished for him. He sighed. "Yes, that's me," he said, and held out his hand.

Manny shook it wonderingly. "You know, my wife's crazy about you, your pictures, I mean," he said. "She was pissed as hell that Beau got this assignment and I didn't." Manny groped in his pocket for the small notebook he carried there. He found it at last and tore out a page which he handed to Derrick. "Could I have your autograph? For my wife, I mean. She'd be thrilled."

Obligingly, Derrick took the paper. Using the back of Manny's notebook as a writing surface, he scrawled his name. He was just giving the autographed sheet of paper back to Manny when Paul Kramer showed up.

Manny Davis has been around the department for years. The last time I had worked with him had been several years earlier on a bum-bashing case. Paul Kramer was the new kid on the block, and I use the word kid advisedly. He was thirty years old and had just moved up to homicide from robbery. His rise to detective had been meteoric, but word was out around the squad that working with Kramer was a royal pain in the ass.

Kramer arrived just in time to see Manny taking the piece of paper from Derrick and stuffing it in his pocket. He looked from Derrick to Manny and back again.

"Witness?" Kramer asked.

Manny glanced in my direction then shook his head. "It's nothing," he said. "I was just lining Beau and his friend here up for a friendly game of golf."

Partnerships, like some marriages, aren't always made in heaven. Manny and Kramer's working relationship was evidently an uneasy one.

I understood the situation. So did Derrick. We both had sense enough to keep our mouths shut.

Chapter 2

CRIME-SCENE investigation is an exact science, complicated by the countervailing demands of accepted protocol and a need for swift, definitive action. What may seem absolutely straightforward in an artificial laboratory situation or in a case study at the police academy becomes less clear-cut in the real world. At crime scenes, hard-and-fast rules of evidentiary procedure often fall victim to jurisdictional disputes and personality conflicts. After all, cops are people too.

In this particular instance, the infighting started immediately after the arrival of an investigator from the Medical Examiner's office. Her name was Audrey Cummings, and she turned up almost on the heels of Detectives Kramer and Davis. As soon as Paul Kramer noticed her, he took offense and attacked.

"Who called you in?" he demanded. The question and the way he asked it were both only one step under rude.

Officer Merrilee Jackson had followed Kramer down the dock. Now she stepped forward, ready to accept full responsibilty. "I did, Detective Kramer. It seemed like a good idea."

"That decision is supposed to be left up to the detectives," Kramer snapped, irritation sharp in his tone.

"Sorry," she answered.

"Don't worry about it," Manny put in quickly to Officer Jackson. "You were right. We do need her, and it's a good thing she's here. It'll save time." He turned to Kramer. "Don't get your bowels in an uproar, Paul," he said.

The admonition came too late. Detective Kramer is one of those intense, territorial individuals who can't stand having other people set foot on his private turf. As far as I'm concerned, he's in the wrong business. Murders seldom come posted with "No Trespassing" signs. In fact, at that very moment, Seattle's media clan, alerted by the sudden surge of mid-afternoon activity, was beginning to gather in a disorderly knot just outside Kramer's line of vision. Woody Carroll was doing his best to keep them herded together behind a blockade of police vehicles.

The lady from the medical examiner's office, a midfifties dame who had been around more than the barn, remained cool and collected in the face of all the wrangling. Audrey Cummings' studied disinterest made it clear that professional squabbles were old hat to her.

Waiting until the fireworks died down, she finally tapped one foot impatiently. "Well, do I get a look or not?" she asked.

Manny grinned and made a low bow, stepping aside with a gallant sweep of his arm. "Please be our guest, milady," he declared.

Smiling at Manny's courtly gesture, Audrey Cummings marched past us in a suitably regal manner. In the world of homicide, where death and disaster are daily companions, we tend to take our laughs wherever we can find them.

Audrey good-naturedly joined in Manny's joke, but only up to a point. The fun ended the moment she reached the edge of the dock. There she knelt down on one knee and took a long, careful look at the body in the water below her. At last she stood up and walked back to where we waited.

"I'll have to have one of the assistant medical examiners come take a look at this," she said. "I think Mike Wilson is on call."

"Any obvious wounds?" I asked, as she started to walk away.

She shrugged. "Possible homicidal violence."

The words "homicidal violence" constitute a catchall phrase that can mean anything or nothing.

Paul Kramer frowned, jerking his head in my direction. "Wait just a damn minute here. How come he's asking questions, Manny? I thought this was our case."

Manny made little effort to conceal his growing annoyance. "Professional courtesy," he answered curtly. "Beau was here when they found the body."

"Oh," Kramer replied. He didn't sound convinced.

I tried my best to give Detective Kramer the benefit of the doubt. After all, being a novice on the fifth floor of Seattle's Public Safety Building isn't any bed of roses. I thought maybe having a seasoned homicide veteran like me peering over his shoulder was making him nervous. Whatever was bugging him, Paul Kramer was creating a bad first impression as far as I was concerned.

Not wanting to escalate the situation further, I changed the subject. "That's one good thing about being called out on a Saturday," I said jokingly. "At least you won't be stuck with Doc Baker."

Manny snorted. "You got that right, Beaumont. Compared to Baker, Mike Wilson's a piece of cake."

On several different occasions in the past it had been my personal misfortune to summon Dr. Howard Baker, King County's chief medical examiner, away from a social engagement of one kind or another. Irascible under the best of circumstances, Baker could be a real pisser late at night or on weekends. Around homicide, a place where consensus on anything is virtually impossible, there seemed to be almost total agreement that Mike Wilson, Baker's newly appointed assistant, was a big improvement.

Wilson had a pleasant, easygoing way about him that was a breath of fresh air compared to his hard-assed boss. A recent transplant to Seattle, Wilson was an energetic man in his mid-thirties. Rumor has it that one of his undergraduate degrees is in philosophy, although that's probably something he wouldn't want advertised around in the law-enforcement community.

Mike Wilson arrived at Lake Union Drydock a few minutes later, still dressed in casual tennis togs. He went straight to Audrey Cummings. The two of them conferred briefly before going over to view the body, squatting together side by side on the edge of the dock.

"How long do you think he's been in the water?" I heard Wilson ask.

Audrey cocked her head to one side as if giving the matter serious consideration. "A week, maybe?"

Wilson glanced up at the metallic blue sky above us and nodded in agreement. "Pretty good guess. Maybe longer than that, but in this kind of heat, a week is probably right on the money. That's about how long it would take for him to float to the surface."

Getting up, Wilson helped Audrey to her feet then ambled back to where the bunch of us still stood in a quiet circle—Manny Davis and Paul Kramer, Officers Baxter and Jackson, Derrick Parker and I. Mike glanced around the group, trying to figure who was in charge.

"We'll need a boat," he said finally to the whole group in general. "A boat and a body basket. Has anyone called Harbor Patrol?"

"They're supposedly on the way," Manny told him. He turned to Officer Jackson. "See what's holding them up, will you?" Merrilee Jackson nodded and left, slipping quickly through the assembled group of reporters, a few of whom had, despite Woody Carroll's best efforts, managed to work their way inside the perimeter of vehicles.

Meanwhile, Derrick Parker slipped away from us long enough to edge his way to the side of the dock and steal a curious glance at the body. He turned away, groaning. "I think I'll go check on Hannah and Cassie," he said, hurrying off without another word to anybody.

Manny watched him go. "Some hero, huh?" he said, shaking his head. "But my wife thinks he's the greatest thing since sliced bread."

"Come on, Manny," Kramer said shortly. "Quit stalling. Let's get this place cordoned off for a crime-scene search."

I couldn't believe what I was hearing. Crime scene? When a floater has been in the water as long as that one had, there's no way it would come to the surface the same place it went down. Not even someone as new to homicide as Kramer could be that stupid. It was a grandstand play, pure and simple, but I was in no position to call him on it. Mike Wilson did.

"Are you sure you want to bother, Detective Kramer? It looks to me as though the body's at least a week old. My guess is he died somewhere else and got carried here by the water. Not only that, we have no way of knowing whether or not it's homicide."

"But you can't say for sure one way or the other, can you?" Kramer insisted.

Wilson shrugged. "No," he agreed mildly. "I suppose not, but even if he went in the water on this very spot, look around. There's been a whole lot of activity on this dock. How can you expect to find any useful physical evidence in a place like this after that long a time?"

What Wilson was saying should have been clear to the most casual observer. Lake Union Drydock, already working overtime to get a series of naval minesweepers back in working order for duty in the Persian Gulf, was one busy place even before you factored in Goldfarb's moviemaking army. In fact, the naval repair contract schedule was so overloaded, they had been forced to cut back our on-site shooting from two weekends to one. During the previous week when I had stopped by the drydock with the location manager, the place where we were now standing had been a beehive of activity cloaked in a cloud of sandblasting dust.

Wilson was right, of course. No physical evidence could possibly have survived a week in that kind of turmoil, but Detective Paul Kramer wasn't buying any of it, and he was the one calling the shots.

"We're still going to look," he said shortly. He motioned to Officer Baxter. "Go get some tape," he ordered.

Baxter left, reluctantly, with Kramer right behind him.

I turned to Manny. "That's one arrogant asshole," I told him. "What Mike said made all kinds of sense."

Manny gave a long-suffering sigh. "Just because something makes sense to the rest of the world doesn't mean it will to Paul Kramer. He marches to a different drummer."

"But Goldfarb and his crew are going to need to go back to work here. They've only got today and tomorrow to finish filming this sequence."

Manny shrugged. "You're welcome to try to talk some
sense into him, Beau, but don't hold your breath. Once
Kramer gets a wild hair up his butt, you can't change his
mind for nothing."

I started after Detective Kramer. Sam Goldfarb and
Cassie Young intercepted me before I could catch up.

"What's happening?" Goldfarb wanted to know. "When
are they going to clear out of here so we can get back to
work?"

"I'm checking on that right now," I told them.

Kramer was removing a roll of Day-Glo crime-scene
tape from the trunk of his unmarked patrol car when I
caught up to him. He handed the tape to Baxter. "You and
that partner of yours start roping off the area," Kramer
directed. He pointed toward the minesweeper towering in
the drydock. "Start from that boat over there and go all
the way to the end of the dock."

"Come on, Kramer," I said. "Isn't this a little prema-
ture? Why rope off half of Lake Union when you still
don't know whether or not you've got a homicide? You
know as well as I do that you're not going to find anything. There've been dozens of people all over that dock
today. There've been dozens of people on it all week long,
and nobody saw anything."

I was stepping on toes, but Kramer needed to be taken
down a notch.

"It's my case, Beaumont, and as far as I'm concerned,
this is a crime scene," he insisted stubbornly. "If I say we
do a search, we do a search." He slammed the trunk lid
closed for emphasis.

"Are you aware they're trying to shoot a movie here
this afternoon?"

"What of it?" he asked. "I'm a police officer."

"So am I, Detective Kramer. Like it or not, my current
assignment is to help these folks get their movie finished."

He stared at me, his long look critical and appraising
before he finally replied. "And my assignment is to find
out how this dead bastard in the water got that way. That's
just what I'm going to do. Get off my back, Beaumont.
I'm not in the habit of taking advice from playboy cops."

With that, he stalked away. I stood there in a fury after

he left, with explosions of light blurring my vision and blood pounding in my temples.

Playboy cop my ass! I was aware that there had been some idle comment around the department about my change in lifestyle. The red Porsche 928 and my penthouse condo in Belltown Terrace had been the subject of mostly congenial ribbing, especially on the fifth floor where some of the guys regularly asked me if I was still on the take. There may have been more serious gritching going on behind my back, but Kramer was the first one ever to tackle me about it head-on.

I wanted to wring his neck. Unfortunately, Kramer is built like a Marine, with a thick neck that goes straight from his chin to his broad shoulders with barely an indentation. Ripped as I was, though, I think I could have handled him.

Officer Jackson got out of the patrol car and came over to me while I was still fuming. "I've called Harbor Patrol," she said. "They say it'll be awhile. There's been an accident in the locks."

My legs still quivered as misdirected adrenaline burned off through my system. I had to really concentrate before Merrilee Jackson's spoken words penetrated the fog of anger and made any sense.

The Hiram Chittenden Locks form a narrow bottleneck between Lake Union and Shilshole Bay. The lake is freshwater and the bay is salt, a part of Puget Sound. The locks raise and lower boats to allow access between the two bodies of water. On sunny summer days, mobs of amateur water-jockeys and serious drinkers simultaneously attempt to maneuver their boats through the locks. It can be tricky under the best of circumstances, because currents in the locks behave far more like those in rivers than they do those in lakes. Which is how Seattle ends up with weekend watercraft traffic jams that can rival any freeway.

If that was what this was, we could be in for a long wait. "Great," I muttered. "That's just great."

As Officer Jackson headed toward the dock once more, Cassie Young came up to me in a blind panic. "Why's that guy fastening tape to our boom?" she asked. "What's going on?"

"We've got a hotshot detective here who thinks the sun rises and sets in his ass."

"What's that supposed to mean?" Cassie demanded.

"That he needs to be taken down a peg or two." I left her standing there fuming and went looking for Woody Carroll. I found him in the midst of the bunch of milling reporters.

"Where's the nearest phone?" I asked.

"That one I used, down on the wingwall." He pointed, but that phone was already well inside Paul Kramer's barricade of Day-Glo tape.

"That one won't work. Are they any others?"

Woody shrugged. "Go on into the administration building. The girl in there will let you use one."

As I walked toward the office I remembered Ralph Ames, my attorney in Arizona, complaining that what I really needed was a car telephone in the 928. Ames is a gadget nut, especially when it comes to telephones. For the first time, I thought maybe he might be right about a car phone.

The "girl" in the Lake Union Drydock office was probably pushing sixty-five. "It's not long distance, is it?" she asked in response to my request for a phone.

I shook my head and she pointed me toward a conference room where a high-tech push-button phone sat on a battered wooden desk. I went so far as to pick up the receiver and punch the first three digits of Sergeant Watkins' home phone number. Then, stopping in mid-dial, I stood there holding the phone.

The socialization of little boys includes very strong interdictions against carrying tales. My first lesson came when I was five. I've never forgotten it. My mother's alteration shop in Ballard was next door to a bakery owned by a friendly old man. One afternoon I overheard several older boys bragging about how a whole group of them would go into the store at once. One or two would occupy the baker's attention while others smuggled doughnuts out from under his nose.

Offended by their blatant dishonesty, I told my mother who in turn told the baker. He caught them in the act the very next day. Two days later, the older kids waylaid me in the alley behind the shops. I don't know how they found out, but they accused me of being a tattletale and a sissy. They dumped me out of my Radio Flyer wagon and proceeded to beat the holy crap out of me. When it was over, my shirt was so badly torn it had to be thrown away before my mother saw it. I cleaned myself up as best I could, and when my mother asked what happened, I told her I tipped over in the wagon.

But I had learned my lesson. Permanently. And some forty years later, that lesson was still there, its taste as strong and bitter in my mouth as the dirt and blood from that long-ago alley.

I put down the phone without ever finishing dialing Watty's number. I'd take care of Paul Kramer myself, one way or the other.

"Nobody home?" the receptionist asked as I came back past her desk.

I shook my head. "Nope. I'll try again later," I said.

The aid car was just leaving as I walked back outside. I waved them down. "The lady's all right?" I asked.

The driver nodded. "Like you said, she just fainted. No big deal."

His partner leaned forward and grinned. "Yeah, we'll be happy to come back and administer first aid to her anytime."

Maybe Derrick Parker didn't like her much, but Hannah Boyer was obviously a hit with Seattle's Medic One.

By the time I collared Manny, my temper was fairly well back under control. "If that asshole Kramer wants a search, let's give him one, but let's get it over with now while we wait for Harbor Patrol to show up."

So for the next forty-five minutes, while we waited the arrival of the police boat, we diligently combed every inch of the area Kramer had cordoned off. It didn't take long, and it wasn't tough, either. The creosoted wooden planks yielded nothing useful. The whole dock was clean as a whistle. By the time Harbor Patrol got there, even Kramer was ready to admit defeat.

Harbor Patrol Three arrived along with two Seattle P.D. old-timers, Jim Harrison and Ken Lee, both of whom are contemporaries of mine. They brought their thirty-eight-foot Modu-Tech alongside the dock and gently eased in close enough to reach the corpse with a body hook.

That particular piece of police equipment is very much like a ten-foot-long question mark. The long handle has foam floats to help keep it on the surface of the water. Despite its name, the implement is neither pointed nor sharp. The curve at the end, formed by one continuous U-shaped piece of tubing, is about the size of a basketball hoop.

Harrison gently maneuvered the metal half-circle around the midsection of the corpse and pulled it toward the boat while Ken Lee untied the body basket from where it was stowed on top of the cabin. The basket, a man-sized frame of galvanized tubing lined with small-mesh chicken wire, was dropped into the water and positioned under the corpse. Once the body was tied in place, they hefted it into the boat.

All this was done with absolutely no discussion. Lee and Harrison worked together quickly and efficiently, the way good partners are supposed to.

Only when they were finished and had covered the body with a disposable paper blanket did Harrison look up. "Sorry it took so long for us to get here, Manny," he said. "We were stuck in the locks. Do you want him here on the dock, or should we take him back to Harbor Station?"

Kramer answered before Manny had a chance. "Here," he said.

That's when I hit the end of my rope and bounced into the fray. "Wait a minute," I said, turning to Wilson. "Is it going to make any difference to you if you look at him here or there?"

"None whatsoever," Wilson replied. "Either place is fine with me, although I think the dock over at Harbor Station is a little easier to work from."

"Then how about doing it there?" I suggested. "That way these people can get back to work."

Kramer started to object, but for a change Manny beat him to the punch and backed me up. "Good deal," he said to Harrison. "Take him down to Harbor Station and off-load him onto your dock. We'll meet you there in a couple of minutes."

"Okay." Harrison nodded. "You're the boss."

Kramer's face turned beet-red. With a little help from his friends, J. P. Beaumont had won that round fair and square. I motioned for Officer Jackson. "Do you see those two people standing there with Derrick Parker?" Derrick was standing in a tight little threesome with Sam Goldfarb and Cassie Young.

Officer Jackson looked where I pointed and nodded. "I see them," she said.

"Go tell them to start getting their people lined up. Now that the body's leaving, we'll be able to get back to work."

Merrilee Jackson flashed me a smile. "I'll be more than happy to do that," she said.

Jim Harrison finished securing the body to the deck and straightened up. Catching sight of me, he gave me a half-assed salute. Naturally, he was wearing surgical gloves.

In the good old days at homicide, we wore gloves only when dealing with bloated and decaying flesh, bodies like this one. We wear them more often now. They're considered essential equipment, right along with our badges and our guns.

I wondered suddenly if the good old days really had been that good, or if I was just an antique.

The real answer was probably a little of both.

Chapter 3

BY the time they resumed filming that afternoon, we had indeed lost the light. Goldfarb got in a huge shouting match with several members of his crew. As usual, the director carried the day. Over strenuous objections, Sam "The Movie Man" decreed they would reshoot the fight scene while somebody rewrote the script so the body could be found at night rather than in daylight. Meantime, techs scurried this way and that, bringing in more equipment, including a tractor-trailer rig containing a huge whispering generator to provide the juice to run the carbon arc lamps required for a night shoot.

Screwed up and incomprehensible as it may seem to a rank outsider, making a movie is a lot like living life. You work with little bits and pieces without ever getting a look at the big picture. It comes together gradually, in order or out of it, with no discernible pattern. No rhyme or reason, as my mother used to say.

I was doing my best to follow the story, but it wasn't easy. From scattered fragments, I had managed to determine that *Death in Drydock* was nothing more or less than an old-fashioned melodrama.

According to the story, Hannah Boyer, playing a somewhat less than virginal heroine, inherits a failing family business—the drydock company of the title. While attempting to turn the business back into a money-making proposition, she becomes romantically involved with a land-grabbing developer. The developer turns up dead in the water, and naturally the sweet young thing is a prime suspect. The lead detective on the case, played by Derrick Parker, is totally smitten once he encounters his gorgeous suspect.

The story itself was nothing short of ridiculous, and the idea of a cop falling for his suspect sounds like an overused cliché. It may be overused, but it does happen on occasion, even to the best of us. I should know.

The crew reshot the fight scene first, then they began working on the scene where make-believe cops pull the make-believe corpse out of the water. At least the water was real.

The retrieval scene was enough to make me want to turn in my technical advisor badge. Permanently. For one thing, Goldfarb couldn't be bothered with a boat. They dragged the body out of the water and dumped it directly onto the dock. For another, the dummy, fresh from the prop shop, had suffered none of the damage real corpses do. When they dropped it on the dock, the makeup was still totally in order, and all hair, fingers, and toes were still completely intact.

In addition, despite having seen a real body hook in action that very afternoon, Goldfarb insisted on using a sharply pointed metal hook to retrieve the body. All my pleas for realism fell on deaf ears. I tried to explain to

Cassie Young that sharp hooks were used only for dragging the bottoms of rivers and lakes. I even offered to call Harbor Patrol and ask to borrow a real body hook to use in the scene. No dice. Cassie didn't pay any attention. She told me Goldfarb wanted a sharp point on the end of his body hook. That was what the script called for and that was the way it would be.

The reason Goldfarb wanted a sharp hook was soon obvious. Part of the retrieval scene included a special-effects sequence in which the sharp end of the hook is pulled free from the make-believe skin of the make-believe corpse. I took Cassie aside and attempted to explain that real human skin is amazingly tough, that body hooks catch on clothing, not on skin, but unrealistic or not, Goldfarb liked that ugly scene. He climbed down from the boom and crawled around on all fours to lovingly direct the cameras in capturing the sharp end of the hook as it came loose from the all too lifelike plastic skin.

For some reason, neither Cassie Young nor Hannah Boyer found any of this pretend gore the least bit distressing. So long as I live, I never will understand women.

In the end, the scene stayed as is. I didn't. I left the whole bunch of them to their own devices and went in search of Woody Carroll. If I had walked off the set completely, if I had pulled up my pants and gone home, there would have been hell to pay. I didn't need to have both Captain Powell and Mayor Dawson on my back. I was mad, but not that mad. Not yet.

After all, orders are orders. Instead, I hid out with Woody Carroll and some of the Lake Union Drydock employees. We settled down in the employee locker room and played several friendly hands of Crazy Eights on sickly green wooden lunchroom tables while Goldfarb went right on having his stupid cops do stupid things.

No matter what I did and no matter what Captain Powell wanted, the fictional Seattle cops in *Death in Drydock* were going to be a bunch of incredibly asinine jerks.

I stuck it out until almost midnight when Goldfarb finally called it a day. By then, even though I'd been off my feet for the last couple of hours, my heel was hurting like hell. The mobile canteen folks had brought dinner

hours earlier, but it was that so-called nouvelle cuisine—
the kind of food that looks real pretty on the plate but
you're hungry again by the time you finish chewing the
last bite. As I limped toward my Porsche parked five
blocks away on Fairview Avenue East, I was craving a
hamburger—a nice, greasy, juicy hamburger.

Derrick Parker hailed me from behind before I opened
my car door. "Hey, Beau. Are you going straight home,
or do you feel like stopping off for awhile?"

"What have you got in mind?" I answered. Parker
waved away a limo driver who had been following, waiting
for him to get in. "I guess you want a ride," I added.

Parker was already climbing into the car. He leaned
back into the deep leather seat with a grateful sigh. "I've
got to get away from these people. They're driving me
crazy." As I started the car, he glanced slyly in my
direction. "Let me guess," he said. "What you need is a
chili-burger and a MacNaughton's from the Doghouse,
right?"

I laughed. "Right, although I hadn't gotten to the chili
part of it yet. If they run you out of the movies, Derrick,
maybe you could get work as a mind reader."

"That's a thought with a whole lot of appeal," Derrick
Parker replied. "This has been a hell of a day."

He didn't get any argument from me about that. We had
put in a good, solid eighteen hours, and although I was
tired, I wasn't the least bit sleepy. Neither was Derrick. I
drove us straight to the Doghouse at Seventh and Bell.

In all of Seattle, it's my home away from home. The
place has changed little over the years. The walls are still a
dingy, faded yellow. Stray electrical cords still meander up
the corners of the rooms. The duct-taped patch in the
carpet has yet to be replaced. It's the kind of place where a
guy can really relax. You can sit there and see what work
needs to be done and revel in the fact that you personally
don't have to do any of it.

Parker and I went directly into the bar. The only pleasant part of my moviemaking experience had resulted from
Cassie Young asking me, half seriously and half in jest, to
keep an eye on Derrick Parker. Her thought was that I
would keep him out of trouble, make sure he showed up

on the set on time, that sort of thing. The whole thing was a joke. Leaving J. P. Beaumont in charge of Derrick Parker was like the blind leading the blind. We were either very good for one another or very bad, depending on your point of view.

From a strictly business view, the Doghouse loved it. Not that many people in their lowbrow clientele of drinkers consume Glenlivet on the rocks, and certainly not in Derrick Parker's prodigious quantities.

The night waitress in the bar was a seasoned veteran named Donna. It was late in her shift and her feet hurt, so she was moderately surly. On that score, she had my heartfelt sympathy. When my feet hurt, it's hard for me to be civil, let alone cheerful.

Donna took our dinner order at the same time she delivered our drinks. Derrick blessed her with one of his engaging, boyish grins, but Donna wasn't impressed. Derrick Parker might be a household name all across America, but not in Donna's household, and not in the Doghouse, either.

Whenever that happened, whenever a waitress didn't recognize him or throw herself at his feet, Derrick acted both pleased and mystified. He liked to experience that rare sensation of anonymity, but it bothered him too, made him uneasy.

Derrick picked up his drink and took a long pull of Scotch. When he put down the glass and turned to look at me, the smile he had used on Donna was gone. "Do you know that's the first time I've ever seen a real dead body?"

"Is that so?" I responded. I was surprised. I think people hold the idea that movie stars have been everywhere, done everything. Derrick's comment was remarkably ingenuous.

He nodded. "I've just never been around when someone died. My grandmother passed away years ago, but my family's into cremation. We don't do funerals with open caskets and all that jazz." He shuddered. "Do they all look that way?"

"What way?"

"That . . ." he paused, looking for a word. ". . . gross," he added finally.

Gross did pretty much cover it.

"The floaters usually look like that," I told him. "Sometimes better, sometimes worse."

He seemed shocked. "And that's what you guys call them? Floaters?"

I nodded.

"That's terrible. I thought that was just in scripts." Derrick sat quietly for a few minutes letting that soak in. "How do you think he died?" he asked eventually. It was as though the dead man held a terrible fascination for Derrick Parker, as though he wanted to know all about him and yet, at the same time, he wanted to think about something else. I have a more than nodding acquaintance with that compulsion myself. It's what makes me a detective instead of a stockbroker.

"I can tell you one thing. He didn't jump," I said.

"He didn't? How do you know that?"

"The jumpers end up with their clothes all screwed up. Either they're torn to shreds or wrapped around their necks, depending on how they hit the water. If they go off one of the high bridges, the Freeway or Aurora, their clothes are usually torn to pieces on impact."

Derrick signaled Donna and ordered another round. With the drink in hand, he stared moodily into it, shaking his head. "Jesus. That's what you call them really, jumpers and floaters?"

"You got any better ideas?"

"No."

There was another pause when Donna brought our food. For late on a Saturday night, the place was practically deserted except for a few sing-along types gathered around the organ at the far end of the room. Derrick waited until Donna walked away.

"So what happens next when you find a body like that?"

"We try to determine how he died and get a positive identification. Then we notify the next of kin."

"You have to do that?"

I nodded.

"How old do you think he was?"

I shrugged. "I don't know. Thirtyish. Somewhere around there."

"And how do you go about finding next of kin?"

"What's with all the questions, Derrick? Have you decided you want to be a cop when you grow up?"

Derrick shook his head. "Nothing like that. I don't know what it is. I can't seem to get him out of my mind. It must be awful, having to talk to families like that, having to find them and tell them."

"It's no picnic," I said. "You're certainly right about that."

The conversation had set me to thinking about the dead man too. I remembered the sunlight glinting off his brass belt buckle. "He was an ironworker," I remarked offhandedly.

Derrick looked thunderstruck. "One of those guys who builds tall buildings? The ones who walk out on those high beams? How in the hell did you figure that out—his build maybe?"

I laughed. "His belt buckle," I said. "He was wearing one that said 'Ironworker' on it."

"Oh." Derrick sounded disappointed, as though he had wanted my answer to be more exotic or complex, something brilliant out of Sherlock Holmes. It occurred to me then that Parker was getting his eyes opened about the reality of being a cop the same way I was learning about the reality of movies and movie stars. The lesson was clear: nobody has life completely sewed up. Not even Derrick Parker.

There was another lull in the conversation. I was thinking about Paul Kramer and about what an arrogant bastard he was, when Derrick interrupted my train of thought.

"You must really like it," he said.

"Like what?" I asked, puzzled. He had lost me.

"What you do. I mean, I've seen your place, your car. You're not stuck being a cop because you have to be. You must get a kick out of tracking things down, out of figuring out what really happened."

His comment made me laugh out loud. It was the other side of the coin, the same thing Kramer had said only turned around so it was a compliment instead of an insult. I had never given the matter much thought, but Derrick was right.

"I do like it," I told him. "When I finally break the code and know who did what to who, when I figure out how all the pieces fit together, I'm on top of the world. Not even a screw-up prosecutor losing the case later in court can take that away from me."

Derrick got up abruptly and signaled for the waitress. "I'm paying tonight," he said.

Donna brought the check and Derrick Parker paid for both our meals. He left a sizable tip on the table when we walked out. "It's nice to go someplace and not be hounded for autographs," he said.

The cast for *Death in Drydock* was staying in the Sheraton at Sixth and Pike. I dropped Derrick there and went home to Belltown Terrace. I was alone in the elevator all the way from P-4, the lowest level of the parking garage, to the twenty-fifth floor. Late at night, riding alone in the elevator is like being in a decompression chamber. I could feel the residue of the day's hassles dropping away from me. By the time I opened the door to my apartment, I was home. And glad to be there.

The red light on my answering machine showed there had been a number of messages while I was out, but it was after one in the morning, far too late to return any calls, so I didn't even bother to play them back. Instead, I poured myself a nightcap and settled into my recliner.

I was as bad as Derrick Parker. My mind was restless. No matter what, it kept coming back to the dead man in the water. The fact that he was none of my business didn't make any difference. It's not your case, Beaumont, I tried telling myself. He's not your problem. But the dead man wouldn't go away.

Ironworker. What was it about ironworkers? There was something about ironworkers that had been trying to nose its way into my consciousness ever since Merrilee Jackson had read the word to me off the glinting belt buckle. The thought had been there, poking around the edges of my mind, but with all the hubbub of the afternoon and evening, I hadn't been able to make any connections.

Now though, as I sat in the comfortable silence of my living room with the icy glass of MacNaughton's in my hand, it finally came to me.

Someone in my building. Someone from the ironworkers' local across the alley had rented a unit in Belltown Terrace. I knew it because, as one of the members of the real-estate syndicate which owns the building, I am apprised of comings and goings of tenants. I remembered the lady who handles rentals laughing and telling me that the new renter's vertical commute would be longer than his horizontal one since his office was in the Labor Temple across the alley at First and Broad. I tried to remember what else she had said about him. He was one of the union bigwigs, a business agent or something, not one of the regular working stiffs.

I felt better then, relieved somehow. It was a bit of information I could pass along to Manny and Kramer. Well, to Manny, anyway. Paul Kramer was a prick. I wasn't going to lift a finger to help him.

After two weeks it was good to know that no matter how long my exile in La-La Land might last, I was still a detective at heart. My mind would still work away at solving puzzles, even when it wasn't supposed to. With that knowledge, my body finally began to unwind.

I was going to have one more drink, but I never got around to it. I fell asleep in my chair without bothering to get up and pour that last MacNaughton's.

And without having anyone there to tell me it was time to wake up and go to bed.

Chapter 4

RON PETERS woke me at seven o'clock on Sunday morning. It was a good thing, but not quite good enough. I was supposed to be on the set by six-thirty.

Peters and I were partners until a car accident broke his back and put him in Harborview Hospital on a semipermanent basis. By then he had been confined there for five long months and had finally worked his way onto the rehabilitation floor. The doctors said there was no way he'd ever be a detective again, but the department had cleared the way so that whenever he was ready to come back to work, on either a full- or part-time basis, a place would be waiting for him in the Public Information Office. Try as I might, I can't remember to call it Media Relations.

Despite his injury, things were starting to look up for Ron Peters. He had fallen hard for Amy Fitzgerald, his physical therapist. Fortunately, the feeling was mutual. The two of them were busy planning a late September wedding that would include Peters' two daughters, Tracie and Heather, as dual flower girls. They were all four counting the days.

While Ron was hospitalized, I had installed the girls along with their live-in baby-sitter, Mrs. Edwards, in an apartment on the eighteenth floor of my building. It was a lot easier for me to keep an eye on things with them seven floors down than it was to trundle back and forth across ten miles of bottlenecked Lake Washington bridge traffic.

"What are you up to?" Ron asked cheerfully. He is disgustingly bright-eyed and bushy-tailed early in the morning.

"Still asleep," I muttered. I'm not a rise-and-shiner, never have been, never will be. "What time is it?"

"Seven," he answered. "Aren't you working this morning? I thought they were scheduled to shoot all weekend long."

"Shit! You're right. I'm late." I struggled to sit up. The foot of the recliner dropped with a resounding thump.

"This won't take long," he said. "I need a favor."

"What's that?"

I paused long enough to let my head clear, more than half resenting the fact that Peters sounded bright as a new penny. That's one thing about hospitals that has always puzzled me. If patients in hospitals are supposed to be there to rest and get well, how come nurses wake everybody up at the crack of dawn, feed them, take their temperatures, and then leave them to spend the rest of the day doing nothing? At least they get an early start on it.

Peters had taken to this regimen like a duck to water.

He's been an early riser for as long as I've known him, and once the morning hospital routines were completed, he would invariably give me a call. I was his connection to an outside world of work and family that was otherwise closed to him. His calls were so regular that I had almost quit bothering to set my alarm clock.

"The girls have been bugging me about Bumbershoot," he said. "It's next weekend, you know. They're dying to go, but Amy's going to be out of town at a convention, and Mrs. Edwards just can't hack it by herself. Having the girls in a crowd like that would be too much for her."

Bumbershoot is an end-of-summer celebration, a four-day extravaganza that takes place in Seattle over Labor Day weekend. It's held at Seattle Center, the site of the 1962 World's Fair. Bumbershoot is like a gigantic medieval fair, complete with food booths, fortune-tellers, street musicians, jugglers, name-brand entertainment, and a crowd of approximately 250,000. I could well believe Mrs. Edwards couldn't hack going there with two little kids. I wondered if I could.

Peters continued. "I told the girls the only way they could go was if you'd agree to take them, but that I'd have to check with you first, for them not to get their hopes up."

"Sure, I'll take 'em." I couldn't believe I was saying it. Maybe it was guilt about my own kids that made me say yes. I remembered back when Kelly and Scott were little. I had worked event security at Bumbershoot for two of the three days. When I woke up Monday morning and Karen said that she wanted to take the kids and go Bumbershooting, she and I got in a hell of a fight. We ended up not going at all.

Did I say maybe it was guilt? Of course it was guilt. Who am I trying to kid?

"Thanks, Beau," Peters said. "I figured you would." I didn't tell him why I was such a pushover.

"They'll be thrilled," he continued. "I was afraid Heather would try to get to you before I had a chance."

"Nope," I said, glancing at the still-flashing light on my answering machine. There were at least five messages waiting to be replayed. "This is the first I've heard anything about it."

"Good. I'll tell Mrs. Edwards to get in touch with you to make arrangements.

"How's the movie going?" he asked, changing the subject. "Were you anywhere near where they pulled that body out of Lake Union yesterday?"

I glanced at the clock. I was already late. It didn't much matter if I got there later still. I took the time to tell Peters some of what had gone on the day before. As soon as I got to the part about the buckle, Peters stopped me short.

"Hey, wait a minute. Remember that guy whose boat blew up last week out in the middle of Lake Union? I seem to remember the papers saying the owner of the boat was an ironworker. He was missing afterwards. They had divers down and were dragging the lake, but they didn't find a body."

Peters' more than adequate memory had been honed even sharper by the months of hospital confinement. He would devour newspapers, remembering almost verbatim everything he read. His comment jarred my memory as well. I had heard about the case and the missing body. I had forgotten that the missing victim was an ironworker.

"I'll bet you're right, Peters. I wonder if Davis and Kramer have made the connection?"

"Kramer?" Peters asked. "Paul Kramer from robbery?"

Wanting to avoid going into detail about my hassle with Kramer, I had neglected to tell Peters the names of the homicide detectives assigned to the case. It was nobody's business but my own, one I didn't care to advertise.

"That's him all right," I said. "What about him?"

"He's a first-class son of a bitch," Peters growled. "When I was still in robbery, he almost caused me to quit the force. What's he doing working in homicide?"

Knowing I wasn't the only one bothered by Paul Kramer made me feel less like the Lone Ranger. "He transferred up just in the last couple of weeks. What's his problem?"

Peters paused for a moment. "Paul Kramer wants to be Chief of Police someday, Beau, and he doesn't give a shit who he has to step on to get there."

Suddenly, Detective Kramer's actions made a hell of a

lot more sense to me. "Thanks for the info, Peters," I said. "I'll bear that in mind."

"You want me to call Manny and tell him about that boat?"

I thought about that for a minute. And I thought about the guy in my building as well, the one who worked for the ironworkers' local. "No," I said finally. "I don't think so. If this Kramer character is so goddamned smart, let him figure it out for himself. If it looks like they're going to miss it altogether, then we can tell them. For all we know, somebody from Harbor Patrol has probably already passed the word."

"Just the same," Peters said. "I think I'll call the library and check out that story on the boat. I'd like to know more. For me."

I didn't try to stop him. I was still so delighted to see Peters showing an interest in the world outside the confines of his hospital room that I refused to discourage him in any way. Besides, I wanted to know myself. After all, I'm a detective. I've been one of those a helluva lot longer than I've been a technical advisor.

When I hung up the phone, I played back the messages on my machine. There was one message from Peters asking me to call him back, and four from Heather asking if I would please, please, please, please take them to Bumbershoot. The brat. She knows she has me wrapped around her little finger. I erased the messages and decided not to tell Peters that Heather had done her best to beat him to the punch.

I went slinking onto the set a little after eight. I thought I could sneak in unobtrusively. No way. Cassie Young caught sight of me and lit into me before I was within ten feet of her.

"Where the hell did you and Derrick go last night? He's late this morning, too. We're waiting to film the last fight sequence, the one between Derrick and the banker, and he shows up looking like something the cat dragged in."

"I didn't do it," I said. "I'm innocent. Parker was in perfectly good shape when I dropped him off at the Sheraton last night."

She glared at me and sniffed. "As if you'd know good

shape when you saw it.'' With that, Cassie Young turned
on her heel and marched away. Woody Carroll eased up
behind me. He was holding a styrofoam cup of steaming
coffee.

"She's not having a very good day,'' he said. Woody
Carroll had truly mastered the fine art of understatement.

I glanced enviously at his cup. "Where'd you get that?"
I asked.

He nodded toward a table near the stairs leading up to
the locker room. "They've got coffee and doughnuts over
there. You look like you could use some.''

"Thanks,'' I said, but I was getting tired of all the
editorial comment, of everyone implying that I looked like
I'd been run over by a truck. I did look like it, actually,
but it had far more to do with working an eighteen-hour
day than it did with anything I'd done after Goldfarb had
finally closed up shop.

Woody followed me to the table where I helped myself
to two fat doughnuts and a cup of thick, black coffee. "Is
she always like that?" he asked.

"Who?'' I returned.

"That woman—what's her name?''

"You mean Cassie Young?''

Woody nodded.

"As far as I can tell,'' I told him. "I've known her
exactly two weeks, and she's been on a rampage the whole
time.''

"That reminds me,'' Woody said. "Speaking of unreasonable people. Yesterday, when all those reporters were
here, one of them wanted to talk to you. Insisted on it.
Said he knew you, that you and he were old friends.''

"Let me guess. His name was Maxwell Cole.''

"So you do know him. I've read his column in the
paper a couple of times. I guess I should have let him
come to talk to you. I thought he was just giving me the
business.''

"He was. Max and I are old acquaintances. Fraternity
brothers, not old friends. He was giving you that line so
you'd let him on the set.''

"You don't mind that I didn't let him through?" Woody
asked, still unsure of my reaction.

"Not at all."

"He said he wanted you to introduce him to some of the movie people so he could do a story about a real murder showing up at the same time they're filming a fake one."

"If Maxwell Cole wants to be introduced to Cassie Young or Sam 'The Movie Man' Goldfarb, he'll have to get somebody else to do the honors."

Woody looked at me closely. "You don't like Cole much, do you."

"You could say that," I replied.

I couldn't believe that worthless asshole Cole would try to pass himself off as a bosom buddy of mine, but then, after all these years, nothing Max does should surprise me. Once an asshole, always an asshole.

The film crew had moved away from the wingwall area to another part of the drydock. They were out on a long, narrow wharf where a series of moored houseboats would provide the basis for a crashing climax in which Derrick Parker was supposed to track down the crooked banker, the real-estate developer's killer.

Houseboats had been collected from all over the city. There was to be a carefully orchestrated fight in which the stuntmen for both stars, Parker's and the movie's heavy, were to leap from boat to boat in a climactic chase scene.

Once more I had tried, unsuccessfully, to include a hint of realism in the process. The scene had been written to include two gun-toting characters, a good guy and a bad guy, crashing through groups of innocent bystanders. At one point in the script, they were to barge through a deckside family dinner, fatally wounding a child in a barrage of cross fire. In the real world that's called reckless endangerment. Cops who do it don't stay cops very long.

I had done battle over this segment when I first saw the script, and now I thought it worthy of one last-ditch effort.

I tracked Cassie Young down during a break in the filming. "Why does the little kid have to get shot?" I asked. "Police officers can't do that. They can't go shooting their way through groups of civilians that way. It's a joke."

"It's no joke, Mr. Beaumont," Cassie retorted, pointedly dropping the word "Detective." I had been summarily demoted. "We're making a movie here. We want people to care about what happens."

"And you don't give a shit if it's accurate or not."

She smiled sweetly. "That's right. Accuracy doesn't sell tickets. Emotions do."

Her remark made me wish that I *had* introduced Maxwell Cole to Cassie Young. They were two of a kind, a matched set, only he sold newspapers instead of movie tickets.

I made one final attempt. "But your cops look like jerks," I protested.

Cassie crossed her arms and looked up at me. "So?" she said.

The implication was absolutely clear. In Cassie Young's book, cops were jerks. At least the drydock cops would be generic. There was nothing whatever to connect them to Seattle P.D. Except me.

"I'm going home," I said.

"Can't stand the heat?" she asked demurely.

"Won't," I replied. "There's a big difference."

I left Lake Union Drydock, but I didn't go home. There wasn't a cat to kick, and in my frame of mind, I was mad enough to break up furniture. Instead, I made my way up Eastlake all the way around to the other side of Gasworks Park where I paced back and forth along the water until my blood pressure returned to normal. I started for home, but when I drove past the entrance to Harbor Station, something made me turn in. Force of habit, I suppose.

The City of Seattle covers an area of ninety-two square miles. What most people don't realize is that there's a whole lot more to the city than meets the eye—parts that are underwater. As a consequence the Harbor Patrol, based in Harbor Station, has jurisdiction over some ninety-three miles of shoreline, all within the city limits. Seattle operates a fleet of six boats and boasts the only twenty-four-hour municipal marine unit in the state. When King County's and Mercer Island's police boats aren't working, Seattle P.D.'s Harbor Patrol handles all of Lake Washington on an emergency basis.

Originally the unit was a separate police organization

under the jurisdiction of the Port of Seattle, with a warden in charge. Later, it was part of the Seattle Fire Department. In the late fifties, Harbor Patrol became a branch of the Seattle Police Department. Some of the officers stayed with the fire department while others went through the police academy and became police officers.

Jim Harrison wasn't one of those originals, but he was close. I found him drinking coffee in the Harbor Station kitchen when I got there.

"Hey, Beau, how's it going?"

"Can't complain," I said. "How about you?"

He grinned. "I'm counting the days until I'm outta here," he said. "Then I'm going fishing."

I laughed. He sounded like a kid waiting impatiently for summer vacation to start. "After all these years, haven't you had enough of boats?" I asked.

"Working on boats, yes. Playing on boats, no."

I shook my head. Boats hold no fascination for me. I'm a believer in the old saw that boats are just holes in the water you pour money into.

"So what are you up to today?" Without asking, Harrison filled a cup with coffee and handed it to me. "From what Manny said yesterday, I was under the impression they were still going to be filming today and that J. P. Beaumont was stuck for the duration."

"I took a powder," I told him. "I'm playing hooky."

He shook his head and clicked his tongue. "Couldn't that have long-range repercussions? Isn't the director some kind of buddy-buddy with the mayor?"

I shrugged. "Let 'em fire me. I'm supposed to be there to give them technical advice, but they won't take it when I do, so what's the point?"

"Beats me," Harrison said, then, with a sly grin, he added, "Is that what you're here for, to cry on my shoulder?"

"Actually, I came by to ask you about that boat fire last week."

"Which one?"

"There was more than one?"

"Three by actual count. It was a bad week on the water."

"Peters told me it blew up."

Harrison nodded. "Oh, that one. It blew all right, to kingdom come. We're still not sure we've found the body. We had divers down for two days straight. They came up empty-handed."

"Where was it when it exploded?"

"Out in the middle of the lake. If the boat had been in a marina when it blew, we wouldn't have any trouble finding the body, but it wasn't. That's the way it goes."

"Any idea what caused it?"

Harrison paused thoughtfully. "Stupidity mostly. That's my guess. It was a gasoline-powered Chris-Craft. One of those old fiberglass jobs from the early seventies. We got there as fast as we could, but it burned all the way to the waterline. The boat's a total loss."

"What kind of stupidity?" I asked.

Harrison shrugged his shoulders. "We see it all the time. These goddamned landlubbers buy boats, keep them for less than two years, and then sell them again without ever learning a damn thing about the boat or how to use it. They don't bother to maintain their equipment properly. My guess is either his fume-sensor system wasn't working or his blowers weren't. The engine room filled up with gas fumes. You know all about low flash points."

"One spark?" I asked.

He nodded. "It must've popped him right out the top of the wheelhouse like a goddamned champagne cork."

"You're saying it's an accident?"

"That's right. It's a joint investigation, us and the Coast Guard. We're pretty much agreed on this one. The boat was called *Boomer*, incidentally, and it sure as hell did."

"How about the missing owner? Does he have a name?"

Harrison walked into the other room, plucked a file folder out of a drawer, and brought it back into the kitchen with him. "Tyree," he said. "His name's Logan Tyree. I told Manny and Kramer about him, just in case."

"And this Tyree character. Did he happen to be an ironworker?"

Harrison ran his finger down the file then peered at me over the top of his glasses. "As a matter of fact, he was. How'd you know that?" he asked.

"Just lucky," I told him. "What happened to the boat? What did you call it, the *Boomer*?"

"Like I told you, the fire was out there in the middle of the south end of the lake. We couldn't leave it there, what with float planes landing and taking off. We had it towed back to Tyree's moorage at Montlake Marina, over here by the bridge. The owner says the rent is paid through the end of the month." Harrison's eyes narrowed. "How come you're so interested in all this, Beau? You're not working this case, are you?"

"Curiosity more than anything else," I answered. I put down my cup, thanked Harrison for the coffee, and took off before he had a chance to ask me any more questions. I couldn't have given him a better answer, because there wasn't a better answer to give.

I got back in the Porsche and sat there for a moment without starting the engine, trying to sort out exactly what was going on. No, I wasn't working the case. Playing was more like it.

When I finally started the car and got going, I pulled up to the stop sign at North Northlake Way. I had two choices. I could go right and go back home, or I could turn left and drive past the Montlake Marina.

I turned left.

Chapter 5

ONCE you've seen a burned-out fiberglass boat, you don't forget it in a hurry. It's a scary sight.

Just as Harrison had told me, Logan Tyree's Chris-Craft *Boomer* had burned right down to the waterline. Most of the wheelhouse had disappeared, melted into a gaping hole in the deck. What little was left of the superstructure was lined with an eerie fringe of blackened icicles which were actually melted fiberglass. It had obviously been one hell of a fire.

If Logan Tyree had been blown clear by the force of the explosion, he must have died instantly. On that score, I

counted him among the lucky ones. To my way of thinking, instant death is preferable to enduring the well-meaning
tortures of a burn unit's intensive care. If that ever happened to me, I'd want to go quick.

"Were you a friend of his?"

Startled by the sound of a voice, I turned from studying
the charred wreckage to see a wizened old man limp onto
the dock from a peeling junker of a boat that looked more
like a derelict tug than anything else. The deck was clut-
tered with an odd assortment of mismatched patio furniture
and the unassembled parts of several bicycles. Two lines
of clean laundry hung lifeless from wires strung between
the cabin and the bow.

"I'm a police officer," I said, flipping open my identification wallet to show him my badge.

"Your friends have already come and gone if that's who
you're looking for," he said. He was smoking a cigarette.
He finished it and tossed the stub into the water between
the two boats, where it disappeared with a minute sizzle.
At first I thought the man was entirely bald, but closer
inspection revealed his head was covered with a thin fuzz
of iron-gray hair. The unshaven stubble on his jaws was
much more plentiful. If he owned a set of dentures, he
wasn't wearing them.

He ran one hand over the top of his head and then
reached quickly for a baseball cap which stuck out of a
frayed hip pocket. "Chemotherapy," he explained self-
consciously, covering his scraggly head. "The name's Red
Corbett." He held out his hand in greeting. The jutting
toothless chin evidently didn't bother him the way his bald
head did. His handshake was firm and thorough enough to
belong to an old-time politician.

"Those other guys told me to keep everyone away, but I
suppose it's all right for you to be here. After all, you're
one of them."

Not exactly, but I didn't disabuse him of the notion.
"Who told you to keep an eye out? Detective Davis or
maybe Detective Kramer?"

The old man nodded. "That last one. At least I think
that was his name." He reached in his pocket, pulled out a

bedraggled package of unfiltered Camels, and offered one to me.

"No thanks," I said. "I don't smoke."

He paused long enough to extract a cigarette and light it with a match from a book stored inside the cellophane wrapper. "I figure they can't hurt me any more than they already have. Why give 'em up?" He took a pensive drag on the cigarette. He seemed to have forgotten me completely.

I reminded him. "You were telling me about the detectives."

"That's right. They said it would only be for a day or two, until his family decides what to do with it. Logan's ex isn't going to be wild about payin' the moorage fees. I expect she'll get out from under 'em just as soon as ever she can."

"She'll get rid of the boat?"

Red Corbett nodded vigorously. "You'd better believe it. She'll take the insurance money and run. That broad's a lulu. Logan was right not to have nothin' to do with her after they split up. She's the jealous type, you know, one of them screamin' Mimis. And jealous of a boat besides. If that don't beat all. Anyone who hates boats the way she does has to have some kind of problem."

"Tyree and his wife were divorced?" My question was calculated to prime Red Corbett's pump. It worked like a charm.

"Separated," Corbett replied. "His wife gave him a choice between her and the boat, and he took *Boomer*. As far as I'm concerned, he made the right decision. That Katherine's nothin' but a ring-tailed bitch."

"Where does she live?"

Red Corbett shrugged. "Who knows? Down around Renton somewhere, I think, but I don't know for sure. Poor Logan was all broke up when Katy—he called her Katy—when she told him she was actually filing for a divorce. He come creeping onto that there boat of his with his clothes in a box and his tail tucked between his legs. I felt sorry for him. He acted like it was the end of the world. I told him not to worry, that there were plenty of other fish in the sea. It didn't take him no time at all to figure out I was right, neither."

"He found someone else?"

Corbett nodded. "That little Linda ain't no bigger 'an a minute, but she'd make two or three of those Katherine types easy. I'd pick Linda over Katy any day of the week."

"Linda's the girlfriend?"

He nodded.

"Do you know her last name?"

"Decker. Linda Decker. I told those other guys all about her just this morning. Don't you work together?"

For a change, a plausible lie came right to my lips. "One of the two detectives is pretty new on the job," I said casually.

Corbett gave me a sharp look then nodded sagely. "And you're backstoppin' him to make sure he don't miss nothin'?"

"That's right," I answered. My logical-sounding reply not only placated Red Corbett, it gave me some real pleasure. In actual fact, it wasn't that far from the truth, but Detective Paul Kramer would shit a brick if he ever got wind of it. "Tell me what you can about this Linda Decker," I urged.

Corbett eyed me uneasily. "She's a nice girl. Don't you go gettin' no funny ideas about her. The way I understand it, Logan met her in an apprenticeship class down at his union hall. He was teaching welding. She needed to be a certified welder in order to work as an ironworker." Corbett stopped short and looked at me with a puzzled expression on his face. "You got any idea why a cute little gal like that would want to work at a job like ironworking? I mean it's hard work, and dangerous too, walking them beams way up in the air and such."

"I can't imagine," I said, although I suspected that money had something to do with it.

"Anyways," Corbett continued. "They met there in that class. He came by here that night to have a beer and tell me all about this lady he had met. You'da thought it was love at first sight, I swear to God. He was grinnin' from ear to ear like the cat that swallowed the canary. And it went on from there. She was real nice to him, helped him work on his boat on weekends. And he idolized those two little kids of hers. He would have been a good father. Katy refused to have any kids, you know. Just out and out refused.

"So like I was sayin', Linda and Logan got along great. My wife and I looked after the kids a few times for them when they went out. You forget how hard it is to find a baby-sitter once you don't have to use 'em anymore. The wife and I figured they'd wind up married sooner or later—I mean, as soon as the divorce was final. I was real sorry when they broke up."

"When did that happen?"

He shrugged. "Not long ago, I guess. Week before last maybe. Linda came over and they had a hell of a row. I heard 'em yellin' back and forth. As long as they'd been together, I'd never heard 'em exchange so much as a cross word. When they left, Linda's kids was both cryin' fit to kill."

"Did he say what the fight was about?"

"Not really. He was real upset about it. I figured it had something to do with work, but he never said what. All he told me was that sometimes a man has to do what's right no matter what."

"And Linda Decker hasn't come back around?"

"No. Not even after the article about the fire was in the paper. That kinda surprised me. I expected to see her. I mean, they'd had a fight and all, but I woulda swore she'd care about what happened to him. Course, she mighta been out of town and just didn't hear about it. That could be it."

"So you haven't seen her at all?"

"Nope. Not since the night they had that fight."

"Do you know if anyone from the department has talked to her?"

Corbett shook his head and blew a cloud of smoke into the air. "I doubt it. You know how it is. After the fire some guys came around lookin' for the next of kin, and Linda wasn't that. I gave 'em his wife's name, and Linda's too, although I got the feeling that there wasn't much chance anybody'd be interested in talkin' to an ex-girlfriend. I was gonna give it to your detective friends this morning, but they said the same thing, that the wife's name was enough. Said they'd get Katherine to identify the body."

"Kramer and Davis didn't bother to take Linda Decker's name?"

"Maybe they wrote it down. I don't recollect exactly, but they said that with an accident like this the wife would be all they'd need."

An accident. Jim Harrison at Harbor Station had called it that too, but that was a Coast Guard finding made in a vacuum with no knowledge of an ex-girlfriend and an ex-wife. A jealous ex-wife.

"Somebody already mentioned that to me," I said. "Something about the gas-fume sensor or the blowers being out of commission. What do you think?"

Red Corbett tossed the butt of the second cigarette into the water with a contemptuous shake of his head. "Well sir," he said finally. "It sure don't sound like the Logan Tyree I knew."

I had been chatting easily with Red Corbett, but that remark put me on point. He had my undivided attention. That kind of comment is a shot in the arm for homicide detectives. It's what makes them go combing through whole catalogs of victims' friends and acquaintances. Something in the circumstances surrounding the death that doesn't fit, something that isn't quite right.

"What do you mean?" I asked.

"Logan loved that boat. He worked on her and tinkered with her every spare minute. He kept her shipshape."

"You mean if something wasn't working right, he would have noticed right off and gotten it fixed."

"You're damn right!"

"Did you tell Detectives Davis and Kramer that?"

Corbett laughed. "Are you kiddin'? I didn't tell them two nothin'. They didn't ask."

I felt like I had stumbled into something important, and I didn't want to let it loose. "You wouldn't happen to have this Linda Decker's address and phone number, would you?" I asked.

Corbett gave me a wily toothless grin. "I sure do. Like I said, me and the wife looked after her kids a couple of times. Linda lived with her mother and she left us her mother's name, address, and phone number just in case there was an emergency. We never had any call to use it, but it's still written down inside the cover of the phone book. You want it?''

I nodded. Corbett turned and walked unsteadily back toward his boat. In a few minutes he reappeared on deck, trailed by a woman who appeared to be several years older than he was and in equally bad shape. She stopped on the deck long enough to gather up the laundry while Red tottered over to me with a ragged phone book clutched in his hand. "Leona Rising," he read, gasping for breath. The phone number and address he gave me were in Bellevue, a suburb across Lake Washington from Seattle.

As I finished jotting the information into my notebook, the woman stepped forward, stopping at her husband's side. She looked at me quizzically. "Red said you wanted Linda's number. Will you be seeing her?" she asked.

"Probably," I said.

"Well, you tell her Doris and Red are thinking about her. Tell her we're real sorry about the way things worked out."

"I'll be sure to do that," I said. Turning, I walked away, leaving the two wizened old folks standing side by side. When I reached the car, I was still holding my open notebook with the scribbled name and address plainly visible. Looking down at them I knew I had stepped off the dock at the Montlake Marina and onto the horns of a dilemma.

What the hell was I going to do about that name and address? Look into them myself? Why? It wasn't my case. Turn them over to Manny and Kramer? Fat chance. They were already working on the assumption that Logan Tyree's death was an accident. I might be totally convinced that their assumption was wrong, but any contradictory suggestion from me was bound to cause trouble.

In the end, I decided to talk the whole situation over with Ron Peters. Young as he is, he's got a cool head on his shoulders. What's more, he has the ability to see several sides to any given argument.

I glanced up at the sky. It was almost afternoon. Over the past few months, I had made a habit of spending Sunday afternoons with Peters' two daughters, taking them to visit their father at the hospital and then messing around with them for the rest of the day. Our Sunday outings gave their baby-sitter, Maxine Edwards, a much-needed break. It was good for her, good for the girls, and good for me too.

I wondered briefly if I should go back to Lake Union Drydock and see how things were going, but even thinking about Cassie Young and her moviemaking cohorts filled me with a flood of resentment. It only took a moment to make up my mind. The day was an unauthorized day off, but it was still a day off, a jewel to be treasured. I hadn't had a break in over two weeks, and neither had Mrs. Edwards.

Maxine wasn't just relieved when I offered to take the girls off her hands. She was downright overjoyed. Less than forty minutes from the time I called downstairs to extend the invitation, the girls were at my door ringing the bell—freshly showered, shampooed, and dressed to go visit their father.

I looked them up and down and gave a low whistle. "Why so dressed up?" I asked.

Tracie's answer was serous. "Amy said she has our dresses ready to try on, so if we came over today we should wear our good shoes and stuff."

Amy Fitzgerald, Peters' fiancée, had been busy sewing wedding clothes for herself and for both of the girls as well. With the wedding less than a month away, activity was definitely switching into high gear. Women are like that. If men know what's good for them, they keep their heads low and go along with the program.

"So that's how it is. If Amy wants you dressed up, dressed up you'll be," I told them.

I traded my two-seat Porsche for Peters' rusty blue Toyota sedan. It was a considerable sacrifice on my part, but I believed in kids using seat belts long before the State of Washington made it a law. Once the girls were securely belted in, we headed for Harborview Hospital on First Hill—Pill Hill according to long-term Seattlites.

Peters' room was on the fourth floor, the rehabilitation wing. Over the months the hospital had become far less strange and forbidding for all of us. In the beginning,

Peters had been totally immobilized, his back and neck held in rigid traction, but now he had finally worked his way into a wheelchair. Part of every visit included the girls wheeling him around the floor to call on some of the other patients. When they took off on their little jaunt, Amy Fitzgerald and I were left to chew the fat.

"You sure lit a fire under Ron this morning," Amy said with a fond laugh.

"What do you mean?"

"When I got here, all he could talk about was some boat that burned up out on Lake Union last week. I'm glad you let him help with your cases, Beau. It's good for him. It makes me feel like he's still making a contribution."

Of course, Logan Tyree and his burning boat weren't my cases at all, but I didn't tell Amy that. After all, why muddy the water with departmental nitpicking?

"He *is* making a contribution," I said. "Just because his legs don't work doesn't mean there's anything the matter with his brain."

Amy Fitzgerald laughed again, the sound of it bubbling to the surface like an irrepressible spring.

Peters and the girls came back from their trek around the floor with Tracie pushing the chair and Heather walking dejectedly alongside, her hand resting on her father's knee. She was weeping silently. Peters was doing his best to console her.

"Don't worry about it, Heather," he was saying. "It wasn't that big a deal."

"What's the matter?" I asked.

Heather looked up at me with two huge tears still glistening on her cheeks. "I didn't do it on purpose, Unca Beau," she lisped.

She was totally crushed, and my heart went out to her. "What happened?" I asked.

Peters chuckled in spite of himself as he answered. "Heather couldn't see where we were going. She ran my chair into a garbage can. It wasn't that serious, but one of the nurses climbed all over us."

Amy stood up quickly. "I'll bet I know which one, too," she said. Then she knelt down in front of Heather and wiped the tears from her face. "It's all right, hon," she said. "Let's go down to the car and get the dresses. Would you like that?"

Heather's broken heart was mended almost instantly. She nodded quickly and went racing off to call the elevator. Tracie, always the more reserved of the two, walked sedately down the hallway with her hand in Amy's.

Peters watched the three of them step into the elevator with a happy grin on his face. "They really like her," he said wonderingly.

That was obvious to even the most casual observer. "You lucked out, Peters," I said. "That's some girls' trio you have there."

I had watched from the sidelines as Peters' and Amy's romance blossomed. Amy Fitzgerald had never been married before, and she didn't have any children of her own. At first I had some serious misgivings about whether or not it would all work, but now, as the elevator door closed on a sudden gale of laughter, I could see it was going to be fine. Amy Fitzgerald was a born mother, and both girls seemed to accept her without question or reservation.

"They're okay," Peters agreed quietly. He turned back to me. "So did you finish the movie then? From what you said this morning, I thought you'd be busy all day."

"The movie's not finished, but I am," I said.

"So that's the way it is." Of all the people around me, Peters was the only one who really understood my frustration and boredom with the moviemaking assignment. Neither one of us was any good at enforced idleness although Peters was learning to deal with it better than I was.

I nodded. "For today anyway." I changed the subject. "Amy tells me you've been tracking after the boat fire."

"The explosion happened last Tuesday, just before midnight. A forty-two-foot fiberglass cruiser named *Boomer*. The missing man's name is Logan Tyree."

"I know."

"How do you know that?" Peters demanded.

"I stopped by Harbor Station before I came over here."

"Has anybody besides us made the connection yet?"

"Jim Harrison said Kramer and Davis are tracking after it. They had already been to the marina by the time I stopped there this morning."

"Oh," Peters said. He sounded disappointed. "I thought maybe we'd beat them on this one."

"We may have," I said. "I talked to Tyree's neighbor, an old codger named Red Corbett. He says Davis and Kramer are calling it an accident—faulty equipment. Corbett says that doesn't jibe with the Logan Tyree he knew."

"How's that?" Peters' curiosity was aroused the same as mine had been. I told him briefly everything Red Corbett had told me. He listened in silence. When I finished, he nodded slowly.

"It sounds like Kramer's up to his old tricks again."

"What do you mean?"

"Doesn't it seem a little odd to you that they've already decided it was an accident?"

"Corbett didn't tell them everything he told me."

"Because they didn't ask. Kramer's in the market for quick fixes, Beau. That's how he made such a name for himself in robbery, how he got on a fast track for promotion. He's left behind a trail of cases that got closed on paper, whether the close was for real or not."

"I thought maybe this was just a mistake."

"Mistake my ass!" Peters flared. "There's no mistake. Believe me, I've seen it before. You could wallpaper your house with his paper clears. They don't mean a god-damned thing but they look real good in the record books."

"But what about Manny?"

"You know Manny. He's easygoing. He'll take the line of least resistance, and that doesn't include standing up to Kramer's constant pushing."

"So what do you suggest we do?" I asked.

There was a long silence. Finally Peters looked over at me. "Would you consider checking this out on your own without anyone being the wiser?" he asked.

"I suppose so," I replied.

"Then do it," Peters said. "If there's anything to what that old man said and if Logan Tyree really was murdered, I'd love to see Paul Kramer take it in the shorts."

"Consider it done," I told him. "It'll be a pleasure."

Amy and the girls came back into the room just then. I was reluctantly drafted into the hem-pinning process. My job was to help the girls hold still while Amy measured the hem with a yardstick and stuck pins in the gauzy material.

"Did you know Amy made our dresses all by herself?" Heather asked.

"Yes, I did," I said, "and it doesn't surprise me. She's a pretty talented lady."

When we left the hospital, I took the girls to McDonald's for Big Macs. They promised they wouldn't tell their dad. Big Macs are not on his health-food list. Afterwards, Heather wanted to go down to Myrtle Edwards Park to feed the ducks. Myrtle Edwards is only about three blocks from Belltown Terrace. I knew from things the girls had said that they went there often with Maxine.

For me the problem with Myrtle Edwards Park was that I hadn't been back there since that unforgettable day when I had married Anne Corley in a simple sunrise wedding. I didn't want to think about it.

In the end, I caved in and went only because I didn't want to have to explain to Heather and Tracie why I couldn't go. I sat on a bench overlooking the water and tried not to think while the girls played tag and climbed up and down the rock sculpture.

When we got home to Belltown Terrace, it was time for dinner. I barbecued hot dogs outside on the recreation floor. I was standing over the grill, but my mind was still on Anne Corley. Heather came dashing up to me just in time to see me wiping my eyes on my sleeves.

"What's the matter, Unca Beau? Are you crying?"

She had me dead to rights, but I didn't admit it. "No," I told her. "It's nothing, just the smoke."

Satisfied with my answer, Heather went skipping off to the sport court where she and Tracie were playing badminton.

"Damn you, Anne Corley," I said aloud.

She broke my heart, goddamnit. In the process she made me a homeowner again and gave me back a barbecue grill.

Chapter 6

I DROPPED the girls off at their apartment downstairs and dragged myself home. My foot was killing me. I noticed it the moment I was alone in the elevator. A bone spur is one of those nagging, ever-present ailments that slips into the background when you're busy but comes throbbing to the surface the moment you're not fully occupied. I figured a Jacuzzi and an early out would do me a world of good. That was not to be, however, at least not as early as I would have liked.

The phone started ringing as soon as I put my key in the lock. It was Captain Powell, boiling mad and ready to chew ass, mine in particular.

"Just who the hell do you think you are, Beaumont?" he demanded. "Ten minutes ago I had a call here at home from the Chief who had just spoken to the mayor. It seems the Dawsons had dinner guests tonight—Mr. Goldfarb and his assistant as well as some other friends of the mayor. It was supposed to be a small reception to celebrate finishing the location shooting."

I had some idea of what was coming, but I decided to play dumb. "What does that have to do with me?"

"They're not done, goddamnit. According to Goldfarb, you're the one who held them up."

"Me?" I couldn't believe I had heard him right. "I held them up?"

"That's what Dawson said. That you screwed them around all afternoon on Saturday and then walked off the set today. They're going to have to pay a king's ransom to rent Lake Union Drydock for a half-day tomorrow."

My first instinct was to fight back, to tell the captain to cram it, but something told me that maybe Powell wasn't playing with a full deck. "Wait just a damn minute here, Larry. Did anyone happen to mention the body?"

"Body?" Larry echoed, sounding surprised. "What body?"

"Nobody told you about the corpse we fished out of the lake Saturday afternoon?"

Powell exhaled a deep breath. "No, they didn't. I've been out of town, haven't had a chance to glance at the paper. Maybe you'd better fill me in, Beau."

By the time I finished telling Powell about Logan Tyree making an unscheduled appearance on the set of *Death in Drydock,* the captain was already apologizing.

"Sorry about that, Beau. Either His Honor failed to mention it, or the Chief neglected to pass the word. I don't know which. Excuse the fireworks. Who did you say is handling the case—Davis and Kramer? I'd better get in touch with them and see if they can tell me anything more before I get back to the Chief. Thanks for letting me know."

He hung up the phone. I sat there looking at it, aware that I hadn't told Powell everything he ought to know. I hadn't mentioned my misgivings, that maybe Logan Tyree's accidental death wasn't. But then, aside from the vague ramblings of a talkative old man and my own gut-level hunch, I had nothing solid to tell him. Captain Powell has reamed me out more than once for what he calls my "off the wall" hunches.

I was still staring glumly at the phone when it rang again, making me jump. I picked it up. "Hello."

"Guess who?" There's a good deal of interference on the security phone in the lobby. I couldn't quite make out my male caller's voice.

"I give up," I said.

"It's me. Derrick. Guess who's with me?"

If I still owned a television set, I could have tuned to the building's closed-circuit channel and had a bird's-eye view of whoever was down in the lobby, but I didn't have one and I was far too tired to play games.

"I haven't the foggiest, Derrick. You tell me."

"Merrilee," he said. "Remember her? We're having a little party. BYOB. Can we come up?"

I could have said no. I didn't. When I opened the door it was clear neither one of them was feeling any pain. Out of uniform, Merrilee Jackson was more than moderately attractive. Her regulation shirt and trousers had concealed both her figure and her legs. The clingy knit dress she was wearing accentuated both.

Derrick made his way to the bar and poured three drinks, two from one bottle and one from another. "She offered to give me a little extra police protection," Derrick said with an exaggerated wink as he slopped an old-fashioned glass full of MacNaughton's in my direction. "Cutest little bodyguard I've ever had."

Merrilee had kicked off a pair of high heels at the door. Even without them, she was none too steady on her feet. She took the glass Derrick gave her and with a giggle the two of them toasted one another's health.

"How'd you two get here?" I asked dourly.

Merrilee grinned and toasted me as well. "A cab," she said. "I told him we're both too drunk to drive."

"You've got that right." It's hard to catch up when you come into a party that far behind the rest of the drinkers. I picked up the phone and dialed the doorman.

Pete Duvall is a full-time biology student at the University of Washington who works part-time as a doorman/limo driver for Belltown Terrace. It's a good job for a student. He can use the slack times to study.

Pete recognized my voice instantly. "Hello, Mr. Beaumont. What can I do for you?"

"What time do you get off, Pete?" I asked him.

"Eleven o'clock," he replied.

"How about making a limo run around ten-thirty. I've got some guests here who need to be hand-delivered."

"Sorry, Mr. Beaumont," he apologized cheerfully. "No can do. The Bentley threw a rod coming back from the airport tonight. We don't have a replacement vehicle until tomorrow afternoon at the earliest. Would you like me to call a cab?"

I turned around and looked at Derrick and Merrilee Jackson. They were sitting in my window seat, necking up a storm. I didn't much want to turn them loose in a cab in their current condition. Seattle still has enough of a small-town mentality to be scandalized by the comings and goings of movie people, stars especially. There had already been some unfortunate gossip about Derrick Parker's public antics, for which Cassie Young held me totally responsible. I had more faith in Pete's discretion than I did in some late-night cabbie's, but there wasn't much choice.

"You do that," I said. "Have the cab here just before you get off."

Parker was looking at me balefully over Merrilee's shoulder when I hung up the phone. "Some friend you turned out to be," he grumbled. "We just got here and already you're trying to throw us out."

"Look, Derrick, a few minutes ago I learned that I have to be back on the set at six tomorrow morning."

Parker poured himself another drink and offered one to Merrilee. She tossed down two fingers of Glenlivet as though she'd been weaned on it.

"Me, too," Parker sighed. "Isn't that a pisser! It was all scheduled to be over today. I mean, that's what the party's supposed to be for. Too bad." He dropped heavily back against the window. The drink in his hand sloshed precariously, but it didn't spill.

I glanced at the clock. It was only ten, but I picked up the phone and dialed Pete again. "Go ahead and call that cab right now, Pete," I told him. "The party's over."

Ignoring Derrick's noisy protest that it was his very last one, I relieved him of the remaining half-bottle of Glenlivet and then escorted the two of them downstairs. Merrilee was a happy drunk, and leaving was fine with her. Derrick turned morose.

"Spoilsport," he grumbled. "We were just starting to have fun. Besides, those makeup people can work miracles."

"You'll thank me tomorrow when Cassie Young doesn't string you up by your thumbs," I told him.

As the elevator door opened into the lobby, we were greeted by the sound of a raised voice.

"If I wanted a goddamned cab to pick my mother up at the airport, I wouldn't be living in a luxury high rise! I made that limo reservation over a week ago. The concierge assured me it would be no problem."

Pete Duvall was doing his best to be polite. The man who was berating him was someone I had never seen before.

"I'm sorry, Mr. Green," Pete said. "As I was trying to explain, the Bentley was out of order with a fuel-pump problem last week. We got it out of the shop day before yesterday, but tonight it threw a rod. We should be able to have a substitute here by early afternoon, a Caddy probably, but your mother's plane reservation is too early for that."

Mr. Green bristled. "You know, when they rented me this place, they told me that the Bentley was one of the amenities. It was in all the ads, remember? The property manager is going to hear about this. And so are the owners. Personally. I'll see to it."

Pete gave me a veiled look. "I'm sure they will," he said mildly.

In actual fact, I had already heard far more about the ancient Bentley than I wanted. It had been a pet project of one of the syndicate's five principals. The proposal had sounded fine when it was first suggested, but it had turned into a major headache once the Bentley actually arrived on the scene. The car spent far more time in the shop than it did on the road.

A cab pulled up out front and honked. Happy to be rescued from the irate Mr. Green, Pete hurried to the door. "Here's your cab, Mr. Beaumont."

He helped me shepherd Derrick and Merrilee into the cab. By the time we got back inside the lobby, Mr. Green had disappeared into the elevator. I watched the digits as the elevator monitor ticked off the floors of the building and stopped on seventeen.

"I take it Mr. Green is new to the building. I've never seen him before."

Pete nodded. "He's only been here a few weeks."

"He's not the one who works across the alley in the Labor Temple, is he?"

"I think so," Pete replied. "The concierge told me he's a big-time mucky-muck with one of the unions."

The elevator returned. With a good-night wave to Pete, I got inside. Once more I felt the aching throb in my foot. As soon as I was inside my apartment, I stripped off my clothes. Within minutes I was in my private Jacuzzi soaking away the day's problems. Not even early-bird Peters could be counted on to call at five A.M. I managed to fumble around and reset the alarm on my clock radio before I stretched out naked across my king-sized bed. I was asleep before my head hit the pillow.

When the alarm went off the next morning, the first thing I did was grope for the telephone and dial the Sheraton. I asked for Derrick Parker's room. The phone rang several times before anybody answered. Derrick sounded as though someone had pounded him into the ground.

"Up and at 'em," I told him, imitating Peters' brisk, early-morning manner.

"We . . . I just got to bed," Derrick croaked.

"Too bad," I said. "I'm picking you up in twenty minutes. You'd better roust your friend out of there. She's got to work today too, you know."

For an answer, Derrick slammed the phone down in my ear. Being the one making the wake-up calls for a change made me feel terribly self-righteous. I got to the Sheraton in time to see Derrick hustle Merrilee Jackson into a cab with a quick peck on the cheek. I wondered if she'd have time to get home and change into uniform before she had to report for duty.

Derrick was pretty hung over. He weaseled a couple of aspirin out of Wanda, the morning waitress at the Dog-house, and when the food came, he barely picked at it. He seemed unusually subdued.

"What's the matter?" I asked him finally.

He shook his head. "My conscience is bothering me. Groupies are one thing, but Merrilee's really a nice kid. I shouldn't have taken advantage of her that way."

I tried not to laugh aloud. The headlines on the *National Enquirer* never hint that movie stars might have attacks of conscience the morning after a romantic conquest, although AIDS has made old-fashioned one-night stands an endangered species.

"You don't strike me as the type for morning-after reservations," I said with a chuckle. "Besides, you're not that much older than she is. I'm sure Merrilee Jackson is perfectly capable of taking care of herself."

Parker brightened a little at that. He gave me a sardonic grin. "You know, you may be right. She was packing condoms in her purse."

I choked on a mouthful of coffee and spattered my clean tie. They don't seem to make women exactly the way they used to. For the most part, it's probably a good thing.

We got to Lake Union Drydock by a quarter to six. Unfortunately, someone hadn't negotiated an extension of the parking barricades for the last half-day of shooting.

Parking places are always at a premium in that Eastlake neighborhood. With both the weekday working people and the movie folks competing for space, it was almost impossible to park the car. We finally found a spot and walked back to the set at a respectable five after six.

The drydock was a whole lot more crowded than it had been on the weekend. The shipyard workers were all hanging around idle, swilling down free canteen coffee and doughnuts. I saw Woody Carroll just inside the gate with his own cup of coffee.

"What's going on?"

Woody shook his head in disbelief. "Nobody's working. Goldfarb's paying extra to keep the sandblaster turned off until they finish up. Too much noise, he says."

Captain Powell had been right about the king's ransom, then. If Goldfarb was paying wages to keep unionized drydock workers standing around on the job with their hands in their pockets, then it was indeed costing money. Lots of it.

Cassie Young was waiting in ambush with both hands on her hips. She didn't appear to be overjoyed to see us. "If it isn't the gold-dust twins," she remarked sarcastically. "Makeup's waiting for you, Derrick." He took off without a word. "So you decided to come back after all?" she said to me.

"I didn't have a choice."

She shrugged. "It's a good thing. Mr. Goldfarb wants to talk to you. He's out on the houseboat dock."

So Goldfarb was going to chew me out, too. Some days are like that. He was sitting up in the director's boom overlooking the houseboats when I got there. I waited until they lowered him to the ground.

"I understand you wanted to see me, Mr. Goldfarb?"

Instead of climbing my frame, he clapped one arm around my shoulder. "I'm glad to see you, Detective

Beaumont. You were absolutely right about that scene
with the little kid. I saw the rushes late last night. It just
didn't work. Too melodramatic. We're going to shoot it
again today, the whole scene. Now tell me, just exactly
how would you do it?''

Wonders will never cease. Sam "The Movie Man" Goldfarb's sudden change of heart left me completely bewildered,
but then I don't suffer from an overdose of artistic tem-
perament. In fact, there isn't an artistic bone in my body.

Artistic or not, we did it my way, the whole scene, from
beginning to end. Derrick Parker's gun stayed in its holster. When one stuntman finally tackled the other, it was a
full body blow that sent them both crashing onto the deck
of one of the houseboats. They rolled under the table
where the unsuspecting family was eating a picnic dinner,
but no one got hurt. The little kid didn't get shot and die.

Fight scenes are incredibly complicated and time-
consuming to map out. Choreographing, they call it, and I
can see why. It's very much like an elaborate dance.
Everything has to come together in total synchronization.
We worked on that scene all morning long, first one
segment and then another. For the first time, I had some
inkling of how the final product would look. Not only that,
I finally felt as though I was making a contribution, doing
what Captain Powell had asked me to do.

For a change, the cop didn't look stupid.

And I saved a little kid's life, even if it was only
make-believe.

Protecting the lives of innocent people is what I get paid
for, really. At least that's what it says in the manual.

Chapter 7

I LEFT the houseboat dock about noon. As far as I could
see, *Death in Drydock* was pretty much in the can, but I
had still not been officially dismissed. I headed for the
coffee station where I found Woody Carroll seated on a
folding chair leaning back against the building. He was

drinking coffee from a styrofoam cup and holding a newspaper in his lap. Several members of the Lake Union Drydock crew were gathered around and involved in a heated debate.

"I'd never let my wife work at a job like that. Never in a million years." The comment came from a long-haired type in grubby overalls.

Several of the group nodded in agreement while another hooted with laughter. "Come on, George, admit it. You couldn't stand it if your old lady made more money than you, that's all."

"It's not that," George insisted. "It's too damn dangerous for everyone else on the job. Women aren't strong enough. They got no business goin' where they're not wanted."

I edged my way over to where Woody was sitting. "What are they talking about?" I asked.

Wordlessly, he handed me the newspaper, opened to the front page. The picture that met my eyes was a real gut-wrencher. It was one of a construction worker tumbling head over heels past the face of an unfinished building. The headline across the page told it all: CONSTRUCTION WORKER PLUNGES 43 STORIES.

"It was a woman?" I asked.

Woody nodded. "Read it," he said.

I did.

"A 28-year-old Seattle-area construction worker fell to her death early yesterday during her fourth day on the job at Masters Plaza, a building under construction at Second and Union.

"Angie Dixon of Bothell, an apprentice ironworker, apparently became entangled in a welding lead and fell from the 43rd story of the new building, which is scheduled for completion late next year. Ms. Dixon was pronounced dead at the scene by King County's medical examiner, Dr. Howard Baker.

"One of the victim's fellow crew members, journeyman ironworker Harry Campbell, said he had sent Ms. Dixon to bring a welding lead. When she failed to return, he went looking for her in time to see her clinging to a welding hose outside the building. He was attempting to reach her when she fell.

"Mr. Raymond Dixon, the dead woman's father, said his daughter had only recently decided to break into the construction trade. He said she had previously worked in the union's bookkeeping department as a secretary and was frustrated by consistently low wages and boredom.

"Masters and Rogers, the Canadian developers of Masters Plaza, have been recording the emergence of the building with a series of time-lapse photographs. One of them, released exclusively to the *Seattle Times* today, happened to capture the woman's fatal plunge.

"Darren Gibson, local spokesperson for Masters and Rogers Developers, said a crew of ironworkers and operating engineers were working overtime both Saturday and Sunday in an effort to keep the building's completion deadline on schedule."

I didn't read any more. I threw the paper back in Woody Carroll's lap. "Those sorry bastards," I muttered. "They'll do anything to sell newspapers."

The debate was still swirling around me. "If she'da had more upper-body strength, she probably coulda hung onto that welding lead long enough for somebody to drag her back inside, know what I mean?" one man was saying.

"No way," the long-haired George responded. "He would have been killed, too."

Just then there was a sharp blast from the Lake Union Drydock whistle. To a man the workers got to their feet. "I guess that means we can get to work now," George said. He sauntered away, leading a group that headed in the direction of the drydocked minesweeper. There weren't any women in that particular crew. It didn't surprise me a bit.

Woody Carroll had pulled out a pencil and was making a series of calculations in the margin of the newspaper. "How tall do you suppose forty-three stories are?" he asked me.

I shrugged. "I don't know. In a commercial building each story is probably ten feet or so, give or take. And the lobby level is often taller than that, say fifteen feet, somewhere around there. Why? What are you doing?"

For a moment Woody didn't answer me, but concentrated on what he was doing, his brows knit in deep furrows. Finally he glanced up at me. "She must have been doing about a hundred fourteen miles an hour when she hit the ground."

"A hundred and fourteen?" I asked. "That's pretty damn fast. I've been a cop for a long time, and I've pulled my share of pulverized automobile victims from wrecked cars. At fifty-five it's bad enough. I'm glad I wasn't there to scrape her off the sidewalk."

Woody nodded. "Me, too," he said.

I poured myself another cup of coffee. Math has never been my strong suit. It took me a minute or two to realize that Woody Carroll, without benefit of so much as a pocket calculator, had just solved a fairly complicated mathematical problem.

"How'd you do that, by the way? You never struck me as a mathematician."

Woody grinned. "Snuck that one in on you, didn't I. It's simple. I thought I told you, I was a bombardier in the Pacific during World War II. I never got beyond geometry in high school, but the Air Force gave me a crash course after I enlisted. I cut my teeth on those Norden bomb sights. Did I ever tell you about that?"

"As a matter of fact, you didn't."

Woody was just getting ready to launch into one of his long-winded stories, when someone came looking for him. "Hey, Woody, they need you to help direct trucks in and out so they can load up and get out of our way."

Carroll got up and handed me the paper. "See you later," he said. "It's been a pleasure working with you, Detective Beaumont."

Left standing there alone, I didn't want to look at the newspaper in my hand, but I was drawn to it nevertheless. The picture repulsed me. The very idea repulsed me. I suspected that someone had made a nice piece of change, selling the developers' fortuitous snapshot of Angie Dixon's death to the newspapers. The editor who used it and the person who provided it were both scumbags in my book—but, inarguably, the picture would sell newspapers.

After all, look who was reading it. I was. Reluctantly.

Furtively. As though hoping I wouldn't be caught. I usually make it a point not to read newspapers, especially in public.

The article went on to discuss Seattle's poor showing in the construction industry's accident statistics, how the city was tenth in the nation for number of construction deaths per billion dollars' worth of new construction. There was even a quote, attributed to Martin Green, Executive Director of Ironworkers Local 165, saying that part of the problem was due to a lack of building inspections by the state.

Martin Green. The name leaped out at me. I wondered if it wasn't the same irate Mr. Green from the lobby of Belltown Terrace. Probably.

I sat down and read the entire article again, and then, out of boredom, I read the whole paper. On the back of the front page of the last section, just before the want ads, was a much smaller article, a brief obituary about Logan Tyree, the victim of a boating accident, whose body had been pulled from Lake Union on Saturday afternoon. That one told me nothing I didn't already know.

I was almost finished with the crossword puzzle when Cassie Young came looking for me.

"There you are, Detective Beaumont. I couldn't find you anywhere." My work on the set that morning had evidently redeemed me in her eyes and she had restored me to the rank of detective. "Are you coming to dinner tonight?"

"I don't know. This is the first I've heard anything about it. What is it, a command performance?"

"Something like that," she replied dryly, ignoring the derision in my response. "Mr. Goldfarb said for you to meet us at Gooey's, the bar at the Sheraton. Seven o'clock. We'll all go together from there."

Derrick Parker came up behind her just as she finished speaking. "Go where?" he asked. The miracle-working makeup had been removed. He had looked fine during the filming, but now he was a wreck.

"Dinner tonight. You're invited too, Derrick. Are you coming?"

"That depends," Derrick waffled. "Can I bring a date?"

"Suit yourself." Cassie turned and started away.

"Hey, wait a minute," I called after her. "Does that mean we're dismissed? School's out for the summer?" She didn't dignify my question with a reply. I watched her walk away. "For someone her age, she doesn't have much of a sense of humor," I remarked to Derrick Parker.

He was watching her as well. Her punk red hair looked like a rooster's comb in the glaring sunlight. "Nobody in the movie business can afford to have a sense of humor," Derrick told me, "least of all if they're assistant to someone like Goldfarb."

Without further discussion, he and I started toward my car. On the way I handed him the newspaper section with the page containing the article on Logan Tyree folded out. "Thought you might be interested. That's the guy we pulled out of the water the other day" I said.

"So you found out who he was?"

"Somebody did," I answered.

Derrick scanned the article as we walked. "You were right about him not being a jumper. It says here his boat burned. That's funny. He didn't look burned to me."

"It exploded first," I explained. "He was probably blown clear by the force of the blast. I've seen people come through things like that with hardly a scratch. He must have hit his head on the cabin roof on the way out, or maybe he struck something in the water."

"The article said he was thirty-seven," Derrick continued. "That's only two years older than I am."

Derrick Parker must have been feeling twinges of his own mortality. I notice symptoms of that occasionally myself, especially the morning after the night before, so I didn't have a whole lot of sympathy. "If you think that's bad, you should read what's on the front page," I told him. "She was only twenty-eight."

He read the construction accident article while we drove and, sure enough, he felt even worse. We went by my apartment so Derrick could retrieve his bottle of Glenlivet, then I took him back to the hotel. He said he was planning to take a nap. That seemed like a helluva good idea to me, too. As soon as I got home, I flopped across the bed fully clothed and fell asleep.

Peters called at six. "I gave you time enough to get home before I called," he said. "Did you see it?"

"Did I see what?"

"The article in the paper about the woman who fell off Masters Plaza yesterday morning."

"I saw it. What about her?"

"Don't you think it's a hell of a coincidence for two ironworkers to die in separate accidents in less than a week?"

Usually I'm the one who jumps to conclusions. I wondered briefly if Peters hadn't been in bed too long and his brain was going soft. "Wait a minute here," I cautioned. "Logan Tyree died in a boating accident. Angie Dixon fell off a building in front of God and everybody. How can the two be related?"

Peters didn't waste any time in throwing his best punch. "Tyree's ex-girlfriend left town."

"So what?"

Peters went right on, totally ignoring my question. "I was talking to Manny a little while ago, just passing the time of day. I asked how it was going. Manny said he and Kramer talked to Mrs. Tyree and then went to Bellevue looking for the girlfriend. She's split. Gone. Moved out along with her two kids. They talked to the girlfriend's mother."

"When did she leave?"

"This morning, I guess, not long before Manny and Kramer got there."

"Where are you going with all this?" I asked. "Did the mother act as though there was any problem?"

"No, she says Linda always pulls stunts like this, like taking off without telling anyone where she's going."

"So what's the point? The mother's not worried, but you are?"

"That's right."

"How come, Peters? What's eating you?"

"Think about it for a minute, Beau. Didn't you tell me that Corbett guy said Tyree had a jealous wife?"

"That's what he said."

"And that the girlfriend, Linda Decker, met him while she was attending an ironworking apprenticeship class?"

"That's right, too."

"And now this Angie Dixon. She's an apprentice, too. Maybe Logan Tyree made friends with more than one of his students."

It began to come together. I could see the pattern building in Peters' brain. It didn't take an overly active imagination. "You think maybe Linda Decker's scared that she's next? You think she's hiding out?"

"The thought crossed my mind."

"In that case, maybe somebody should check out Katherine Tyree."

Peters breathed a sigh of relief. "Bingo," he said. "You're not a fast study, Beau. I thought you'd never pick up on it."

"Is this a subtle hint?" I asked. "And is the somebody doing the checking going to be me?"

"It sure as hell can't be me," Peters responded bleakly. "In the meantime, those other assholes are absolutely determined that the incidents aren't related in any way."

"Did you mention your suspicions to Manny?"

There was a slight pause before Peters answered. "No," he said reluctantly. "Not exactly."

I laughed. I couldn't help it. "All right, all right. I'll do it. I can't today because in a few minutes I have to be down at the Sheraton, but I told Watty I'd be taking a few days off once we finished up on the movie. I'll have some time to check into it and no one will be the wiser. You're still gunning for Kramer, aren't you."

When he answered, Peters' voice was hushed. "You'd better believe it," he breathed. "You'd by God better believe it."

Chapter 8

JUST when I figure I can count on Peters to wake me up, he lets me down. The next morning he didn't call, and I slept until after nine. Fortunately, I didn't have to be at work early that day. In fact, I didn't have to go to work at all.

My head was pounding. I lay there in bed trying not to move for fear I would shatter into a thousand pieces. Try as I might to remember, the end of the evening was a total blank.

From seven o'clock on, it had been one long wild party all over the Sheraton. Booze flowed like water. Vaguely I could recall closing down Gooey's in the wee small hours. There's an old country-western song that talks about how even ugly girls look good at closing time. I must have been thoroughly smashed. My last coherent thought was that maybe Cassie Young wasn't that bad-looking after all.

I finally dared open one eye. Glaring sunlight exploded in my head. Then, cautiously, I peered over at the other side of the bed. Thankfully, it was empty. I was all right so far. Hung over as hell, but otherwise all right.

Dragging my protesting body into the bathroom, I stood for a good twenty minutes under a steaming torrent of water. I should have felt guilty. Profligate even. It had been such a long, dry summer that the City of Seattle had limited yard-watering and was asking for voluntary cutbacks on indoor water usage. But I couldn't help it. It was either take the shower or stay in bed.

I ordered breakfast sent up from the deli downstairs and was beginning to feel halfway human by the time I finished my third cup of coffee and a handful of aspirin. Mornings aren't good for me even under the best of circumstances. This was not the best of circumstances.

I was glad I had called in the day before to tell Sergeant Watkins we were done filming and to let him know I was on vacation until after Labor Day. Watty had suggested I go out and have fun, but the *Death in Drydock* party had been almost more fun than I could stand. By the fourth cup of coffee, I was ready to admit it was just as well my good drinking buddy Derrick Parker was on his way back home to Hollywood.

As the juices gradually began to flow I turned my mind over to the assignment Peters had given me the day before. After we had finished talking, there had been very little time to think about what he had said. On reflection, I could see that there was some merit in Peters' theory. Maybe Linda Decker was scared and hiding out. Despite what Red Corbett thought, it was possible Katherine Tyree had been jealous of more than just the boat.

Carrying Peters' conjecture one step further, I remembered something else Corbett had said, something about there being plenty more fish in the sea. If Logan Tyree had been mixed up with more than one woman in the apprenticeship program, nobody, including Katherine Tyree, had ever cornered the market on jealousy.

Both lines of reasoning were worth pursuing.

I already had Linda Decker's mother's name, address, and phone number jotted in my notebook. I didn't have a clue about Katherine Tyree. I turned to the detective's greatest alley—the telephone book. Logan Tyree wasn't listed there. K. A. Tyree was. The address given was on the Maple Valley Highway in Renton. That certainly squared with what Red Corbett had told me.

As I drove toward Renton, I wasn't looking forward to meeting Katherine Tyree. I'm not predisposed to like women who, deservedly or not, toss their husbands out of the house without much more than the clothes on their backs.

The house, a small, two-story bungalow, was on a wooded lot and set some distance back from the road. There were two cars parked out front, an older pickup and a late-model Honda. The man who answered the door was still buttoning his shirt. He told me his name was Fred McKinney, but he didn't say what he was doing there. When I showed him my badge, he invited me inside.

"Kate's upstairs taking a shower," he said. "She'll be down in a few minutes. The services are this afternoon, you know. Can I get you a cup of coffee?"

I followed Fred into the kitchen. He located two coffee mugs without having to look in more than one cupboard.

"Sugar? Cream?" he asked.

I shook my head. "Black."

He stirred several spoonfuls of sugar into his own cup and then offered me a place at the kitchen table. Fred, whoever he was, seemed to have an extensive working knowledge of Katherine Tyree's kitchen.

"Are you a relative?" I asked.

"Friend of the family," he said. "She's taking it pretty hard, you know," he added. "I mean the divorce wasn't final yet. It's like they weren't exactly married and they weren't exactly not. Know what I mean?''

"It's tough," I said, nodding. "It makes it difficult to know just how to act."

In another part of the house the sound of running water stopped. Katherine Tyree was evidently finished with her shower. Fred got up from the table. "I'll go tell her you're here."

I glanced around the kitchen. It was full of the kinds of decorative bric-a-brac popular with ceramic hobbyists— cutesy wall plaques complete with familiar Bible verses and age-old proverbs. To be honest, I suppose I had a preconceived notion of Katherine Tyree as some sort of femme fatale. Nothing would have been further from the truth.

The woman who followed Fred into the kitchen was a frumpy, overweight type wearing a frayed housecoat and floppy bedroom slippers. A damp bath towel was wrapped around her wet hair. She nodded silently in my direction when Fred introduced us, then went straight to the counter and poured herself a cup of coffee.

"Please accept my condolences, Mrs. Tyree," I said. She nodded again but then she turned away from me. Looking out the window over the sink, she quickly wiped her eyes. Fred had been right when he told me she was taking it hard. She seemed genuinely grief-stricken over Logan Tyree's death. It was a full minute before she turned back around and faced me.

"Fred tells me you're with the Seattle Police," she said, making a visible effort to control her emotions. "What can I do for you?"

She hadn't asked to see my identification, and I knew Fred hadn't examined my ID closely enough to remember my name. I decided to jump in with both feet. "I'm sorry to bring all this back up, especially since you've already been interviewed by a number of law-enforcement people, but I'd like to ask a few additional questions."

"What do you need to know?"

She came back over to the table and sat down between Fred and me. He reached over and patted the back of her hand. "Are you sure?" Fred asked solicitously.

"It's all right," she said wearily to Fred, and then to me, "Go ahead."

"A number of people seem to be operating under the assumption that your husband's death was an accident. I'm wondering if you have an opinion about that one way or another."

It was a back-handed way to start the conversation, but it struck a spark. The atmosphere in the room was suddenly charged with a surge of emotional electricity. Instantly Fred's hand closed shut around Katherine Tyree's fingers. His knuckles turned white. Fred's powerful grip must have hurt. Katherine Tyree winced but made no effort to pull away. The stricken look they exchanged told me I had unwittingly stumbled into volatile territory.

"You'd better tell him, Kate," Fred said grimly

Katherine Tyree shook her head stubbornly. "No. I don't want to, not today, not like this."

"If you don't, I will." His words were weighted with gloomy determination.

Katherine stole a glance at me then dropped her gaze to her lap. "I can't," she murmured, her voice a strangled whisper.

Fred sat up, squared his shoulders, and looked me straight in the eye. "What she means to say is, we're engaged," he announced defiantly. He paused, waiting for a reply. When there was none, he continued, his voice somewhat more subdued. "We had planned to be married just as soon as her divorce was final. We had no reason to kill him. Logan and I were friends once—asshole buddies."

The fact that Fred assumed I was accusing them of murder led me to believe there was a whole lot more to the story than anyone had let on so far. I kept quiet, leaving an empty pool of silence between us. Fred rushed in to fill it up.

"You see," he said, "what you don't understand is that *Boomer* was my boat originally."

"You say you *were* friends? I take it that means you weren't any longer?"

Katherine Tyree started to say something then stopped. "Nobody planned it this way. That's just how it worked out," Fred said. He shrugged. "Things sort of happened, got out of hand."

"Maybe you'd better tell me about it."

"Do you know what a boomer is?"

"Not really."

"In the trade it's a hand who knocks around the country, going from place to place, wherever there's work."

"What kind of work?"

"Construction. Working iron. That's how Logan and I met, on the raising gang down at Columbia Center. I came up here from California as a boomer and was living on the boat. Logan was interested in boats, had always wanted one. When he offered to buy mine, I took him up on it. I was tired of banging my head on the doorway every time I needed to take a leak.

"Logan and Kate here invited me out to dinner. Christmas, Thanksgiving, summer barbecues. That sort of thing. Kate and I just hit it off, didn't we."

Katherine Tyree gave a barely perceptible wordless nod.

"So that's how it started out, innocent like that. Once Logan had that boat, though, he wanted to spend every spare minute on it. He was gone a lot—on weekends, in the evening, after work. That's when things got out of hand with us, with Kate and me I mean. Like I said, we didn't intend for it to happen."

The last sentence lingered in the air for several seconds. I'm not exactly sure who Fred was trying to convince most—Katherine Tyree, me, or himself.

"Where were you two last Tuesday night?" I asked.

Fred didn't flinch or try to duck the question. "Right here," he declared resolutely. "Upstairs in the bedroom screwing our brains out."

"Fred!" Katherine Tyree wailed. "Don't!"

"Kate, honey, I've got to. Don't you see?" He let go of her hand and reached up and ran a finger tenderly along the full curve of her cheek. "We're better off telling him right up front, hon. It would be worse if he found out later. Lots worse. Besides, we had no reason to kill Logan. In another month the divorce would have been final and we could've been married, no questions asked. I'm sick and tired of sneaking around. With Logan gone, I don't care who knows about us. It's nobody's business but our own."

Fred's forthright narrative was pretty tough to counter. My gut reaction was that he was telling the truth, that his involvement with Katherine Tyree hadn't been planned or premeditated and that he was sincerely saddened by his former friend's death.

"Tell me about the boat," I said.

Fred shrugged. "There's not a lot to tell. It wasn't new. I bought it used for a song. Gasoline boats are a whole lot cheaper than diesel ones. I'd been living on it for a couple of years when I sold it to Logan."

"What did you think about it?" I asked, turning to Katherine. "About your husband's boat."

"I hated it," she said softly. "It was the last straw. I felt like he was using it to run away from me. It was a place for him to go, to hide out, instead of doing things around here."

"Was he hiding out?"

My question heaped salt on an open wound, but that's one way to get honest answers, to ask while people are still down for the count, before they have a chance to get up off their knees and reactivate their defenses.

"Yes," Katherine said softly.

"Why? What from?"

"I don't know. We were just too different, I guess. We sort of drifted apart. We got married way too young. Everybody said so—his family, my family. He wanted to have kids, I didn't. I wanted to travel, he didn't. When I met Fred, I could see how wrong it had been the whole time. We were only staying together because we didn't know what else to do."

"There are lots of marriages like that in this world," I observed. "Most of them end in divorce, not murder."

Fred leaped to his feet and slammed a fist onto the table in front of me so hard the three coffee cups went skittering in all directions. "Goddamnit! I already told you, we had nothing to do with it!"

I ignored him and once more directed my question to Katherine Tyree. "Does the name Linda Decker mean anything to you?"

There was a flicker of recognition in her eyes, but nothing else. No hurt, no animosity. "Yes," she answered quietly. "Linda was Logan's girlfriend."

"Did you ever meet her?"

Katherine shook her head. Satisfied that I was no longer on the attack, Fred sat back down.

"When they met, he was already living on the boat. I was glad for him when we heard about it," Katherine continued, "glad he had found somebody."

"But you don't know anything about her?"

Katherine shook her head. "I do," Fred offered. "I saw Linda down at the union hall a few times. When she and Logan started dating, word spread like wildfire. She's a little mite of a thing, but tougher 'an nails. Understand she's a bodybuilder. According to everybody I talked to, she was doing fine. Then, a week or so ago, she walked off the job, turned in her union book, and quit."

"She quit the apprentice program?"

Fred nodded.

"Any idea why?"

Fred shook his head. "I thought maybe she and Logan had gotten into some kind of fight."

I took a minute to go back over my notes, checking to see if there was anything I had forgotten to ask. I returned to the boat. "Tell me more about *Boomer*. You said this was Logan's first boat, is that true?"

Fred and Katherine nodded in unison.

"Would he have started the boat without checking to make sure the blower was running?"

"No way!" Fred's response was quick, involuntary. He answered without thinking of the possible consequences. "Logan was careful about everything he did. That's why they had him teaching that welding class. Safety first, that was his motto."

I turned to Katherine. "Would you agree with that?"

She nodded, tentatively this time. "That's what I thought when they first came here to tell me about the fire, that it didn't sound like Logan, but . . ." The sentence faded away.

"But what?" I persisted.

"I was afraid to mention it."

"Why, because you were afraid we'd come looking for you?"

"Yes."

I closed my notebook.

"Is that all?" Fred asked.

"For the time being," I answered, getting up. Everything they had told me had the ring of truth to it. Unless there was a lot more to it than I knew right now, there was no overwhelming reason for Fred and Katherine to knock off Logan Tyree, no motive to make risking a murder rap worthwhile.

Katherine Tyree stood up too. "I'll go get dressed," she said to Fred. "I don't know what I'm going to wear."

She disappeared upstairs and Fred showed me out. "I've gotta get dressed too," he said. "I'm going with her today, even if people talk. Moral support. She needs to have somebody there with her. Logan's relatives have written her off completely. As far as they're concerned, it's like she doesn't even exist."

"What time is the funeral?" I asked.

"Three o'clock. Out in Enumclaw. That's where Logan's folks are from. Are you going?"

I shook my head. "No," I said. "I'll let this one pass," not adding that since this wasn't officially my case, it would hardly be appropriate for me to show up.

When he got a glimpse of the 928, Fred followed me out to the gate. "Nice car you've got there. What are you, working undercover?"

I nodded.

"You don't think Logan was into something illegal, do you?"

"We're playing all the angles," I told him. My answer was vague enough that it would help keep me out of hot water as long as Manny Davis and Paul Kramer didn't tumble to the car. The red Porsche would be a dead giveaway.

Thoughtfully, I turned my key in the ignition. Old man Corbett had been right about some things and dead wrong about others. Katherine Tyree's screaming fits hadn't exactly been jealous rages—at least his interpretation of the boat being the root cause had been somewhat wide of the mark. And that little doubt made me begin to question his assessment of Linda Decker as well. I wanted to meet Linda Decker and decide for myself.

Ron Peters had already told me that Linda Decker had moved out of her mother's house, but that was the place to start if I wanted to learn anything about her. Of course, the sensible thing would have been to drop the whole program, to stay away, leave it alone.

But when have I ever done what's sensible? I pulled out of Katherine Tyree's driveway and headed for Interstate 405 and Linda Decker's former address in Bellevue.

I figured I could just as well be hung for a sheep as a lamb.

Chapter 9

BELLEVUE, a suburb which started out as a bedroom community due east of Seattle, has become a city in its own right. The transformation from sleepy suburb into a high-tech center has escaped the notice of confirmed cosmopolitan snobs who derisively refer to the entire east side of Lake Washington as the 'burbs.

To hear city dwellers tell it, Bellevue is a lily-white, bigoted, upper-middle-class sanctuary. From what I saw that day, the blush was off the rose. I wouldn't call some of the areas slums, but they certainly qualified as pockets of poverty.

To begin with, I had a tough time finding Leona Rising's address on S.E. 138th. It's always like that. Bellevue's incomprehensible street system is a cop's nightmare. While I drove around lost, wandering in ever-narrowing circles, I saw a duke's mixture of kids out skateboarding and biking their way through the last full week of summer vacation. It didn't look like a totally segregated bunch to me.

Then, when I finally did find the place, on a small dead-end street just off Newport Way, the address turned out to be in one of a series of battle-weary duplexes much older and much more worn than their single-family-dwelling neighbors.

On that particular block, a somewhat shoddy dead-end street, my red Porsche would have stuck out like a sore thumb. There was no point in advertising my presence. I drove back up Newport and parked a few blocks away in the lot of a nearby public library branch. I returned to the house on foot. The aspirin I had fed my hangover was also helping my foot. For a change, the initial stab of pain from the bone spur wasn't quite as acute as I expected.

Approaching the place, I noticed a young man sitting on the front porch. At least I thought he was young. He was dressed in a loud, orange plaid shirt. His Levis had been rolled up at the cuff to reveal a long length of white athletic sock. On the porch near his feet sat a large, old-fashioned black lunch pail as well as an expensive-looking stainless-steel thermos.

At first glance I thought maybe he was in his late teens or early twenties, but closer examination showed a slightly receding hairline with flecks of gray dotting the short brown hair. I revised my original estimate up to thirty-five or forty. He didn't look up as I neared the porch. Instead, he sat there unmoving, staring dejectedly at his feet. He was sucking his thumb.

"Hello," I said, stopping a few feet away. "Anybody home?"

Surprised by my unexpected intrusion, he started guilt-ily, pulling his hand from his mouth and shoving it under his other arm. He held it there, pressed tightly between his arm and his chest, as though by imprisoning it he could conceal it from himself as well as from me. He stared up at me for a long time before he shook his head in answer to my question.

"I'm looking for Leona Rising."

"She's . . . not here." He spoke slowly, haltingly, in a deliberate monotone.

"What about her daughter, Linda Decker?"

His lower lip trembled. He began rocking back and forth, the repetitive motion slow and hypnotic. For some reason my question had brought him dangerously close to tears. "She's . . . not here either," he answered. "It's her fault I missed . . . the bus. It's all . . . her fault."

With that, he did burst into tears. He bent over double and sobbed while the comforting thumb crept out from under his restraining arm and back into his mouth. I stood there feeling like someone who has just unavoidably run over a headlight-blinded rabbit on the open highway. Whoever this guy was, he was no mental giant. My question had unleashed a storm of emotion I was helpless to stop. There was nothing to do but wait it out. Eventually, he quit crying.

When the thumb was once more concealed under his arm, he stole a sly glance up at my face. "What's . . . your name?" he asked ingenuously.

I stuck out my hand. "My name's Beaumont," I said. "What's yours?"

He stared at my extended hand for a long time as if trying to decide what he was supposed to do with it. As if remembering, he wiped his hand on a clean pant leg and shyly held it out to me. His grip was limp and sweaty, but he grinned at me suddenly, his tearful outburst of the moment before totally forgotten. "Beaumont . . . that's a . . . funny name," he said. "My name is . . . Jimmy."

There were no nuances or shadings in his voice, and the long pauses between words made it clear that he spoke only at tremendous effort.

"Do you live here?" I asked, deliberately keeping my question as simple as possible.

He nodded and pointed to a curtained window to the right of the front door. "That's my . . . room over there. Lindy . . . used to live here. She . . . left."

"Lindy?" I asked. "Who's that? Do you mean Linda Decker?"

He nodded again, once more becoming serious. "She's my sister. My . . . baby sister. She's lots . . . smarter. She's not like me. Not . . . retarded."

He spoke the words as casually as someone else might have said they were right- or left-handed or that they'd been sick with a cold. All the while he looked directly into my eyes with a disconcerting, unblinking gaze. I felt myself squirming under it.

"Do you know where your sister is?" I asked.

He went on, giving no evidence that he had heard my question. "Lindy's good . . . to me. Always. I don't want her . . . to go away. I want her here. With me. I . . . need her."

Once more his lower lip began to tremble and he fell silent, rocking slowly back and forth.

"Did she say why she had to leave?" I asked gently.

He shook his head slowly from side to side. "She said she had to . . . go. That's all. And then . . . those men came. I didn't like them."

"What men?"

"Big men, like on . . . TV. Detectives. They were asking Mama about . . . Lindy. They even . . . had guns. Real ones. Not toys. I tried to tell them. They wouldn't . . . listen. And Mama told me to . . . go sit down. To get out . . . of the way and be . . . quiet. I didn't want to. I knew the answer. That's why I . . . missed my bus."

His ragged, halting delivery made it difficult to extricate meaning from what he was saying. The story was lacking several key ingredients. I struggled in vain to sort out the connections, to see through to the pieces that were missing.

"I'm afraid I don't quite understand," I said finally.

Jimmy looked up at me determinedly. "I'm not a k-kid, you know. I'm a grown-up. Just like . . . you. When I cry, sometimes people make fun of me. Kids at the . . . bus stop. They . . . call me a baby. It makes me . . . mad!" The last was said so vehemently that two small streams of spittle slipped unnoticed out the corners of his mouth.

The missing pieces fell into place. "So you were crying and that's why you missed your bus?"

He nodded, no longer looking me in the eye, but relieved that he didn't have to go on explaining. His chin dropped until it disappeared into the collar of his shirt. Once more his thumb edged toward his mouth. "I lost my . . . paper," he mumbled in little more than a whimper.

"Paper? What paper?"

"With the . . . numbers on it. Bus numbers. So I can . . . find the right . . . bus. I never missed . . . work before. I go there every day."

Uninvited, I sat down on the porch next to him. "What kind of work do you do, Jimmy?" I asked.

He straightened his shoulders proudly. "Micrographics," he said. Surprisingly enough, the syllables of the long word rolled unimpeded off his tongue. "I take pictures. Important stuff. I put it on . . . fiche." He paused. "You know about fiche?"

I nodded. "And where do you do this?"

"At the center."

"Is it far from here?"

"Too far to walk," he said glumly. He moved his foot slightly and bumped it against the lunch pail. He studied it for a long time as though he hadn't seen it before. "It isn't break," he said. "I'm hungry. Can I eat now?"

A golf-ball-sized lump bottled up my throat. Jimmy Rising was someone who was lost without his crib sheet to decode the bus system and without someone to tell him whether or not it was okay to eat his lunch. He needed permission from someone else. I swallowed hard before I could answer. "I'm sure it would be fine," I told him.

He quickly opened the lunch pail, pulled out a sandwich, unwrapped it, and ate it noisily with total self-absorption. When he finished the sandwich, he brought out an apple and poured some orange juice from the thermos. He bit off a huge hunk of apple. "Lindy gave me this," he said proudly, patting the top of the thermos. "It keeps hot . . . things hot and cold things cold. Did you know that?" he asked.

"Yes," I answered.

He reached over and touched the lunch pail, running a finger lovingly across the folded metal handle. "I bought this all by myself. With my own . . . money." He was speaking less hesitantly now. The nervousness of being with a stranger was gradually wearing off.

"Money you earned from work?" I asked.

He nodded smugly. "It cost . . . ten dollars and forty-seven cents. I bought it at K Mart. It's got some . . . scratches now. Lindy says that . . . happens to lunch pails. Everybody's lunch pails. They get scratched."

"You must love Lindy very much," I suggested quietly.

He looked past me and stared off into the vacant blue

sky. When he finally spoke, his voice was full of hurt. Again he was close to tears. "She was going . . . to take . . . me with her. She promised. But now she can't."

"Why not?"

"She lost her job. It was a . . . good job. Building great big buildings. She's got another one . . . now. Not as good."

"You told me you know where she is?"

He nodded, slyly, ducking his head.

"Would you tell me? I need to find her."

There was only the slightest pause before he began rummaging in his shirt pocket. Eventually he dragged out a rumpled wad of paper and handed it to me.

"Her . . . phone number's there," he said. "She told me I could call. Anytime I want to."

I unfolded the scrap of paper. It turned out to be two pieces, actually, one with a telephone number scrawled across it, and the other, neatly typed, saying "210 Downtown Seattle and 15 Ballard." Upset as he was, Jimmy had evidently crumpled his bus-schedule crib sheet in with his sister's telephone number.

I jotted the telephone number into my notebook then straightened the typed piece of paper on my knee and handed it back to him. "Is this the paper you lost?"

His eyes brightened when he saw it, then his shoulders slumped again. "That's it. But it's . . . too late to go now."

"I could give you a ride," I offered tentatively.

There was a sudden transformation on his face. Just as quickly, it was replaced with a kind of desperate wariness. "You're . . . making fun of me," he said accusingly. "I'm retarded. Not stupid. You don't . . . have a car. You can't give . . . me a ride. I'm too big to carry."

"My car's just up the street," I told him. "It's a red Porsche. We can walk up and get it and have you to work in half an hour."

Still he hesitated.

"What's wrong?" I asked.

"I'm not supposed to . . . ride with strangers. Lindy said."

Lindy had given him good advice, advice I wanted him

to disregard. "Am I still a stranger, Jimmy?" I asked.
"We've been talking a long time. And I really do have a
red Porsche."

"Like on TV?" Jimmy asked.

I nodded. He struggled through a moment's hesitation
before leaping off the porch like a gamboling puppy.
"Really? You . . . mean it? You'd take . . . me all the
way there?"

"I'd be happy to."

As quickly as it appeared, the animation went out of his
face. "But I don't know . . . the way," he said hope-
lessly. "Do you? Have you been there?"

The bus directions had given me a clue. Dimly I remembered back in the sixties how the U.S. Navy had surplussed
its Elliott Bay site, turning it over to a group of can-do
mothers who had transformed it into a model center for the
developmentally disabled.

I had gone to the center once on a mission to deliver a
batch of free tickets for the Bacon Bowl, a Seattle-area
police officer fund-raiser. It's an annual exhibition game
between Seattle P.D. personnel and a team made up of
police officers from Tacoma P.D. and the Pierce County
Sheriff's Department. It gives a bunch of frustrated ex-
jocks a once-a-year chance to get down on a football field
and strut their stuff. Looking at Jimmy Rising, I wondered
if he had been the recipient of one of those tickets, and if
he had, did he like football.

Quickly, Jimmy Rising began gathering his belongings,
his lunch pail and his thermos. "Can we go now?" he
asked. His eagerness was almost painful to see. I don't
think I've ever headed for work with that degree of unbri-
dled enthusiasm.

"Sure," I said. "Let's get going."

We set off walking at a pretty good clip, but I had
trouble keeping up. Jimmy kept bounding ahead, then he'd
rush back to hurry me along. Watching him, I had an
attack of guilty conscience, but I pushed it out of my
mind. He was such a guileless innocent—it had been all
too easy to con Linda Decker's phone number out of him.
Anybody could have gotten it from him, if they'd only
bothered to ask.

Of course, my guilty conscience wasn't so serious that I pulled the notation with Linda's phone number on it out of my notebook and threw it away. After all, as long as I had the information, I could just as well use it.

"Is Linda in . . . trouble?" he asked suddenly.

The question caught me off guard. I didn't know if he was asking me if she was pregnant or if he meant something else.

"What makes you say that?" I asked.

"Because those men were detectives. Just like on 'Miami Vice.' That's my favorite. What's yours?"

I don't watch television, but I didn't want to explain that to Jimmy Rising. "Mine, too," I answered.

"Who do you like the most?"

That was a stumper. He had me dead to rights. "I like 'em all," I waffled.

"Oh," he said, and we continued walking in silence.

When I unlocked the car door and let him into the Porsche, he was ecstatic. "I've . . . never been in a car this . . . nice," he said. "Are you sure you don't . . . mind?"

"I don't mind," I said.

"But doesn't it . . . cost a lot of money? Mama's always . . . saying that. Cars cost . . . money." Reverently he touched the smooth leather seat. "Is this brand-new?" he asked.

"No," I answered.

We headed back down toward I-90. Jimmy was fascinated by the buttons and knobs. He turned the radio on full blast, moved the seat back and forth, rolled his window up and down. He had a great time.

It was well after two when we turned off 15th onto Armory Way and stopped in the parking lot of the Northwest Center for the Retarded. A woman walked out of one building and headed down a shaded walkway toward another. Jimmy leaped out of the car and bounded after her. "Miss Carson, Miss Carson. I'm here," he shouted.

Miss Carson stopped in mid-stride, turned, and came back toward us. Even from a distance I could see she was a willowy blonde. I turned off the motor, telling myself that Jimmy Rising would probably need some help explaining why he was so late.

He came rushing headlong back to the car, dragging Miss Carson by one hand. "He's the one," he said, pointing at me. "He even knew how . . . to get here. I didn't have to . . . tell him."

Close up, Miss Carson was still blonde and still willowy. She had almond-shaped green eyes, a fair complexion, and a dazzling smile. She held out her hand. "Thank you so much for giving Jimmy a ride. That was very kind of you. He told me he missed the bus." She turned to Jimmy. "Did you tell him thank you?"

Suddenly shy, Jimmy Rising ducked his head and stepped back a step. "Thanks," he mumbled.

"I was glad to do it."

Miss Carson smiled at him. "You go on to work now, Jimmy. The others are just going on break. I want to talk to Mr. . . ."

"Beaumont," I supplied.

"To Mr. Beaumont," she added.

Jimmy hurried away without a backward glance, and Miss Carson turned to me. The smile had been replaced by a look of concern.

"I'm Sandy Carson," she said. "I run the micrographics department. Where did you find him? We called his mother, Leona, but she couldn't leave work to go look for him."

Briefly, I told Sandy Carson everything I knew about Jimmy Rising missing the bus, about his being upset because Linda Decker had left town without taking him with her.

"No wonder he got rattled," Miss Carson said when I finished. "His sister's really special to him. Are you a friend of the family? Do you happen to know his mother?"

I shook my head, not wanting to admit to Sandy that I was a total stranger who had wandered onto the Rising porch in the course of a police investigation.

"It's too bad Linda couldn't take him," Sandy said. "He'd be a lot better off with her. His mother's about at the end of her rope." She glanced down at her watch. "I'd better get going," she said. "They'll be tearing the place apart. Thanks again," she added. "Coming here is terribly important to people like Jimmy. It's more than just a job, you know. It's their whole life."

With that, she turned and walked away, still blonde and still willowy, disappearing behind the same door that had swallowed Jimmy Rising.

I couldn't help wondering if Jimmy Rising ever noticed that about her, or if to him she was simply Miss Carson from micrographics.

Either way, it was sad as hell for Jimmy Rising and not so sad for J. P. Beaumont.

Chapter 10

I'VE said it before and I'll say it again—the telephone is a homicide detective's most valuable tool. If we venture into areas where court orders are required, telephone-company people can be hard-nosed as hell. Outside those sticky areas, though, they are worth their weight in gold.

Using the telephone over the years, I've established working relationships with any number of people I never see, people I know by voice on a first-name basis but wouldn't recognize if I ran into them in the grocery store.

Gloria Hutchins is one of those people. I wouldn't know her from Adam if I met her on the street, but if I heard her speak, I'd know her anywhere. Gloria is the gravelly-voiced lady in the security department at Pacific Northwest Bell who handles requests for information from law-enforcement officers.

When I got back to Belltown Terrace late that afternoon, I took out my notebook, opened it to the page with Linda Decker's new phone number on it, and dialed Gloria Hutchins' number. I didn't have to look it up. That's one I know by heart.

"Hi, Gloria," I said casually. "Detective Beaumont here. How's it going?"

There was a warm greeting in her low voice when she

answered. "Why, hello there, Beau. Long time no see. Where've you been, on vacation?"

"No such luck," I responded. "I've been locked up on a special assignment."

"What can I do for you?"

"I've got a telephone number, but I need an address."

"Case number?" Gloria asked.

I just happened to have one. I had jotted down the boat-fire case number from Jim Harrison's file folder at Harbor Station. I gave Gloria the case number and Linda Decker's phone number.

"Things are really popping around here right now," Gloria said. "It's going to be awhile before I can get to this. What's your number?"

The problem was, I was calling her from home. I didn't much want to give her that number for a callback. That would look bad. Instead, I gave her my extension at work. "I'll be leaving here in a few minutes," I told her. "Just give the address to whoever answers. Tell them it's for me."

"Will do," Gloria said. "Anything else?"

"Nope. That's it for now. Thanks."

I hung up and turned to a stack of unopened mail that had accumulated on the table beside my chair. The first three envelopes were bills, but between the bills and the gaudy collection of junk mail addressed to "Resident" was a handwritten envelope with no return address. I slit it open and scanned down the scrawled page to the signature on the bottom—Martin Green.

Letting the letter drop back on the table, I went to pour myself a MacNaughton's. If I was going to be forced to endure a tirade about the Bentley, at least I could do it in comfort.

And tirade it was. Mr. Green informed that he was most unhappy with the lack of availability of the Bentley, especially since he had reserved it well in advance. He went on to say that the Bentley was one of the advertised amenities which had attracted him to the building in the first place. Since I was the only member of the real-estate syndicate who was readily available, he said he hoped we could get together to resolve the situation amicably. If not, he was prepared to take us to the Better Business Bureau.

I finished drinking the MacNaughton's and reading the letter at approximately the same time. I had wanted an excuse to talk to Martin Green. Now I had one, although it could hardly be called an engraved invitation. I retied my tie, grabbed my jacket off the dining-room chair, and retrieved my shoes from their place next to the front door. This felt like one of those situations where casual attire would be a distinct disadvantage. Somebody told me once that in winning by intimidation, you have to dress the part.

Secured-building etiquette requires that you call before you knock on someone's door. According to directory assistance, Martin Green had an unlisted telephone number. I went down to the garage and dialed his code on the security phone. A woman answered and I gave her my name. There was a good deal of background noise, and she evidently couldn't hear me very well.

"Who?" she demanded.

"My name is Beaumont," I repeated.

"There are too many people here. It's too noisy. Come on up. Apartment 1704."

The door to 1704 stood slightly ajar and the sound of voices told me a party of some kind was in progress. I'm not sure what I expected. For me the word "ironworker" conjures up a macho image of men in khaki work shirts and hard hats swilling beer and telling dirty jokes. Martin Green's party was nothing like that. The room was full of gray-suited bean-counter types and their female escorts who drank champagne from dainty crystal champagne flutes and nibbled bite-sized canapés.

A silver-haired lady in a pearl-gray dress met me at the door. "I'm Martin's mother." She beamed at me. "I'm playing hostess tonight. Won't you come in? What would you like to drink?"

"I just stopped by to see Martin for a few minutes," I told her. "Maybe it would be better if I came back another time."

She shook her head. "Oh, no. Don't do that. I'm sure he'd want to see you. He left just a moment ago to take some of his guests down to show them the recreation floor, you know, the pool and the Jacuzzi and all that. They'll be back in a few minutes if you don't mind waiting."

I allowed myself to be ushered inside. Almost instantly a glass of champagne appeared in my hand. The room was crowded and stuffy despite the fact that the heat-pump air-conditioning was going full blast. There were far too many people crammed in the relatively small living room. I made my way to the far side, hoping to escape the crush and also to gain a vantage point from which to watch the proceedings.

The 04 units in Belltown Terrace all have balconies which look out on the city. There was a lone man standing outside on the balcony peering out at the rank upon rank of downtown skyscrapers standing stiffly at attention against a pale blue August sky. Here and there hammerhead cranes served as lonely sentinels marking the emergence of yet more new buildings.

Another group of people came into the room, and those already inside pressed back. Feeling claustrophobic, I slid open the door and escaped onto the balcony. The lone man there glanced at me briefly, then continued to stare off into the distance. In his late thirties or early forties, he was reasonably well-built. The fabric of his jacket bunched tightly over muscular arms. He stood with one foot on the lower crossbar, his elbows resting on the upper railing. The drink in his hand wasn't champagne.

He said nothing, and I didn't either. Instead, I moved to the railing as well, and looked where he was looking— straight up Second Avenue toward the point where the raw skeleton of Masters Plaza climbed skyward. Swirling his drink, he gave me another sidelong glance as I stepped to the railing beside him, and then he drained his glass.

"It's bad luck to have a party like this the day after somebody went in the hole."

It was the first time I had ever heard that particular expression, but it wasn't hard to grasp the meaning. He was talking about Angie Dixon falling to her death. From the grim set of his mouth I could see it was gnawing at him. He assumed it was bothering me as well.

"Did you know her?" he asked.

"No," I said.

He shook his head balefully. "It always hurts to lose a

hand," he added. "No matter how long a guy stays in this business it never gets any easier."

His fingers tightened around his empty glass. For a moment, I thought he was going to crush it bare-handed. At last he opened his fist, letting the glass lay in his open palm. For the first time I noticed the callouses, the work-roughened texture of his skin. The rest of the men at Martin Green's party may have been bean-counting accountant types with Harvard MBAs, but the guy on the balcony seemed to be an ordinary Joe Blow, a regular working stiff. I wondered if, like me, he had wandered uninvited into the wrong party.

A waitress stepped out on the balcony carrying a tray of champagne glasses. I took one, but my companion ordered Scotch—neat. No rocks, no ice, no soda. As the waitress walked away, he reached up and yanked savagely on the knot of his tie, pulling it loose from the base of his Adam's apple.

"I hate these goddamned monkey suits," he complained, "'but we have to wear 'em whenever the visiting dignitaries come to call."

"What visiting dignitaries?" I asked.

He glanced at me wearily. "You're not one of them, then?" he asked, nodding toward the roomful of bean-counters.

I shook my head in answer. "I'm a neighbor from the building," I explained. "I stopped by to talk to Martin. I didn't mean to crash his party."

He frowned. "But you know about . . ." He jerked his head in the direction of Masters Plaza.

"I read the papers," I said. The young woman returned with his Scotch. He accepted it gratefully and took a swift gulp. I waited until the woman had gone back inside and slid the door shut behind her before I spoke again. "You were saying about the accident . . ."

He turned away from me, once more leaning over the balcony. "Me and my big mouth," he said. "I was talking out of turn."

"My name's Beaumont. I didn't catch yours."

"Kaplan," he answered, offering me his hand. "Don Kaplan."

"What do you do?"

He laughed bitterly. "Me? I'm just a broken-down rod-buster who went bad."

"Rod-buster?" I asked.

"An ironworker," he explained. "Rebar—reinforcing steel—as opposed to structural. If my back hadn't given out on me, I'd probably still be tying rods on the I-90 bridge. As it is, they kicked me upstairs. I'm a business agent now."

A burst of laughter inside the room behind us. "And what's this all about?" I asked.

Lifting his glass to his lips, Don Kaplan paused before he took a drink. "VIP's from International out pressing the flesh." There was an unmistakable trace of sarcasm in his voice.

Before he could say anything more, the door slid open behind us. "There you are, Don. I've been looking all over for you." Martin Green stepped onto the balcony behind us, leading a trio made up of two men and an accompanying sweet young thing. All three were laughing uproariously.

"Here's Don. You three will be riding with him. You know how to get into the parking garage at Columbia Center, don't you, Don?"

Don Kaplan nodded shortly, as though he didn't much relish the ride.

"And then if you'll drop them back off at the Sorrento after dinner."

"No problem," Don mumbled.

Green turned to me with a puzzled expression on his face. "I don't believe we've been introduced," he said, extending his hand.

"My name's Beaumont." I reached into my breast pocket and extracted the envelope. "I didn't mean to crash your party. I came by to talk to you about this. The lady at the door mistook me for one of your guests."

Martin Green laughed. "That's my mother all right, but this really isn't a very good time for me. We have a dinner reservation downtown in a little while. Could we make an appointment for tomorrow or the next day?"

The charming smile never left Green's face as he took

me by the elbow and guided me unerringly through his guests to the front door where his mother was still holding court. It was one of the smoothest bum's rushes I've ever experienced. Smooth as glass and absolutely effective.

"What time tomorrow?" I asked.

"Nine? Nine-thirty? Whatever's good for you."

"Nine-thirty," I said. "Where?"

"Do you know where my office is next door in the Labor Temple?" he asked.

"I'm sure I can find it."

"Good," he said. "I'll see you then." With that he closed the door and left me standing in the hallway. Here's your hat; what's your hurry.

I had no more than gotten back to my apartment when the phone rang. The last person I expected to hear from was Marilyn Sykes, the Mercer Island Chief of Police. She and I had met several months earlier and had become friends. She was single and so was I. On occasion things came up where one of us needed to have an escort and we had called on each other to pinch-hit. We had good times when we were out together, with no pressure for our relationship to be either more or less than it was. We had only one hard-and-fast rule between us—no talking shop.

"How about a hot date?" she asked.

I laughed. "With you?" Our rare dates were fun but hardly hot.

"I know this is late notice. I was supposed to be out of town today and now I'm not. The Mercer Island Chamber of Commerce is doing its big benefit dinner tonight. Would you consider coming along and bailing me out of hot water? I really should put in an appearance."

"Sure," I said. "What time?"

"It's supposed to have started at six, but if we're a little late, it won't matter."

Had the Bentley been working, I would have had Pete drive me over to Mercer Island to pick her up—just to make a splash. As it was, I took the Porsche.

The first time I ever saw Marilyn Sykes she was a take-charge lady wearing a gray pin-striped suit and directing a SWAT team. When I picked her up at home that night, she had on a low-cut cream-colored evening gown.

She's tall for a woman, five eleven or so, with hazel-colored eyes and naturally curly brown hair. I liked the dress a whole lot more than the suit.

I drove while she gave directions. It was a circuitous route that took us to the backside of the island and down a long hill to a magnificent house on the water. A parking attendant met us in the circular driveway to take care of the car while I went around to open the door for Marilyn.

"By the way, Beau," she said, taking my hand and letting me help her to her feet. "There's one thing I forgot to mention."

"What's that?"

"I told you it's a benefit dinner, but I didn't tell you what kind."

"Don't worry about it," I said. "As long as it's not my own cooking, I'll eat anything."

She smiled. "It's a murder mystery dinner."

I stopped in my tracks. "A what?"

"You know, one of those dinners where they hire actors to do a fake murder and the guests try to figure out who did it. I was afraid if I told you, you might not want to come."

"You're right about that," I said. "But we're here now. We could just as well go on in."

The host and hostess met us at the door. Mercifully, when she introduced us, Marilyn kept quiet about my profession. When they ushered us inside, I could see we were more than a little late. The huge living room was already full of people. I guess it was a nice enough place, but I didn't have a whole lot of opportunity to check it out.

We had barely gotten inside the door when an elegant blonde made a move on me and started bending my ear about buying some real estate, something about the house next door. What did I think? Would it be a good investment or not? Totally without an opinion on the subject, I glanced around looking for Marilyn, hoping she'd rescue me. Instead, she made a beeline for the food and left me to handle the blonde on my own. I had about convinced myself the lady was a mental case when a man came striding up to us carrying two drinks, one of which he shoved in the woman's direction.

"You just can't do it, can you," he commented snidely to the woman. "You can't be trusted alone long enough for me to go order a drink."

"Wait a minute," I began, "we were just . . ."

"You stay out of this," he snarled at me. "This is between us. After all, she *is* my wife."

The blonde began twisting her wedding ring nervously. "Come on, Carl. It wasn't anything like that. I was only telling him about buying the house next door."

"Like hell you were! I saw the way you looked at him when he walked in the room. He's your type, isn't he. Tall—" He paused long enough to look at me. "Tall, gray, and handsome."

"Please, Carl, don't do this. Not here in front of all these people."

Carl shook his head. "I'd stay away from her if I were you. She collects men the way some people collect bowling trophies. They don't mean much afterwards, do they, my dear."

A deep flush began creeping up the back of my neck. Everyone in the room was staring at us, overhearing every word. On the far edge of the crowd, there was Marilyn holding a plate of hors d'oeuvres. She wasn't going to be any help at all.

Carl turned to me and gave me a companionable whack on one shoulder. "No hard feelings, of course, old boy!" he said. With that, he walked away.

At a loss for words, I turned back to the blonde just as she took a tentative sip of her drink. "I'm so sorry," she apologized. "He's been like that more and more lately, and the doctors can't tell me what's wrong."

"Try a shrink," I suggested. "I think he's off his rocker."

Suddenly, the blonde's eyes got big. She sputtered and choked.

"What's the matter?" I asked.

She looked at me helplessly, shook her head, and clutched at her throat. Staggering away from me, she fell facedown on the carpet and lay there without moving.

Carl raced to her side and turned her over. He placed his ear against her breast.

"Get an ambulance," someone shouted.

Carl sat up, gravely shaking his head. "It's too late for an ambulance," he said. "She's dead."

I glanced over at the spot where I had last seen Marilyn. She was almost doubled over with laughter. That's when I finally realized what was going on, that these were the actors and they had suckered me into their script as a reluctant leading man.

When I finally pushed my way through the crowd to Marilyn, she was still laughing.

"What's so funny? Did you know they were going to do that?" I demanded.

She shook her head. "I had no idea, but you were perfect. I didn't know you could act."

"I can't," I answered grimly.

Marilyn handed me a plate of food—smoked salmon, fruit and vegetables with dip. "Try this," she said. "After all that hard work, you should at least get something to eat."

Much as I hate to admit it, the evening turned out to be fun. The rest of the party was occupied with trying to figure out who had murdered the blonde. Some even suspected me which I found hilarious. Most suspected Carl. When all was said and done, though, the killer turned out to be Carl's gay lover.

It was late when I finally took Marilyn home, but she invited me up to her apartment for a nightcap. We sat there for some time, laughing and comparing notes on the evening. I was about to get up and leave when she put her hand on my leg.

"You wouldn't be interested in spending the night, would you?" she asked casually.

I slid my hand over hers. "I could probably be persuaded," I replied.

And so she set about persuading me.

Chapter 11

MARILYN SYKES fixed breakfast for us the next morning. It was the kind of breakfast that made me think I'd died and gone to heaven—crisp bacon, over-easy eggs, toasted English muffins, black coffee, fresh orange juice. When she stopped beside me long enough to pour a second cup of coffee, I gave her a playful pat on the rump.

"You're my kind of woman," I said. "Your breakfast ranks right up there with the Doghouse."

She laughed. "Just don't let anybody around my department hear you say that. After all, I have a certain professional image to maintain, you know."

"You mean the chief's not supposed to cook great over-easy eggs."

She smiled. "Among other things."

"Don't worry. Your secret's safe with me."

When it was time to leave, Marilyn walked me to the door. By then she had put on her dress-for-success costume as well as her sensible shoes. The transformation seemed complete, but at the door she took hold of the two loose ends of my tie, pulled me close to her, and tied it for me. A perfect four-in-hand.

It was an awkward moment. I didn't know what to say, so I leaned over and kissed her. "I had a wonderful time," I said. "Thanks."

"Me too," she murmured. "We'll have to do it again sometime."

Marilyn's condominium complex has a guard shack with twenty-four-hour coverage. A young security guard had noted down my license number the night before when I brought Marilyn home, and now another beardless youth waved and checked off something on a clipboard as I drove past. I admit to feeling a little guilty, which was silly since Marilyn Sykes and I are both well past the age of consent. Nevertheless, it's one thing to do a sleep-over.

93

It's something else to have a security guard taking down your vehicle license number while you do it.

I was soon too immersed in traffic to worry about the security guard. Living downtown, I seldom had occasion to drive from Mercer Island back into the city during morning rush-hour traffic. I hope I never have to again. It was a mess. Despite years of work, that section of I-90 still wasn't complete, and I soon discovered what Mercer Island commuters have been saying all along, that there aren't nearly enough on-ramps to allow island residents adequate access to the roadway.

I inched forward, one car length at a time. It wasn't as though there was a tangible reason for the problem on the bridge, not even so much as a flat tire or a fender-bender. I guess rush-hour traffic moves like that every day of the week. It would drive me crazy. It makes me glad I can walk to work.

Back home in Belltown Terrace finally, I had just time enough to change clothes before my scheduled interview with Martin Green. To reach his office, all I had to do was go downstairs and cut through the garage entrance on Clay. That's my idea of commuting. It was evidently Martin Green's as well.

The Labor Temple has been at First and Broad for as long as I can remember. It's a low-rise, two-story building that occupies the entire half-block. My only previous visits had been on election day when I went there to vote. The building directory told me Ironworkers Local 165 was located on the second floor.

There were a few men lingering in the gray marble hallway outside the ironworkers' office, burly men in plaid flannel shirts and work boots with telltale faded circles of tobacco cans marking their hip pockets. On the door was a typed notice announcing that the office would be closed the next day from 1 to 4 P.M. so office staff members could attend the funeral of deceased member Angie Dixon.

I stepped inside and announced myself to a female clerk who was seated behind a counter. She glanced uneasily over her shoulder in the direction of a closed door. "Is Mr. Green expecting you?" she asked.

"Yes," I said. "My name's Beaumont. I have an appointment at nine-thirty."

She looked slightly hesitant. "He has someone with him just now, if you don't mind waiting."

I sat down on a surly, swaybacked vinyl couch that squatted against the outside wall. Next to it sat a scarred end table with a few dog-eared magazines and a smelly, overflowing ashtray. If ironworkers had heard anything about the Surgeon General's warning on cigarettes, they weren't paying attention.

At the far end of the room, a second woman finished running an exceptionally noisy copy machine and returned to her desk. In the newly silent office, I became aware of the sound of raised voices coming from behind the closed door I assumed led to Martin Green's private office. I was looking at it when the door flew open and a man stormed out.

"I quit, goddamnit! If all I'm fit for is to sit in a tool shack and make up bolts, that's what I'll do, but I'll be goddamned if I'll do this son of a bitch of a job one more minute."

Saying that, he slammed the door to Green's office with such force that the frosted glass window shattered and slipped to the floor. As he rushed past, I realized it was Don Kaplan, the man I'd met on Martin Green's balcony the night before. He strode by me without any sign of recognition. I don't think he noticed anyone was there.

The two women working in the outer office exchanged guarded looks, then one of them rose and stepped gingerly toward the broken door. Instead of speaking to Martin Green through the jagged hole in the glass, she carefully opened the door.

"There's a Mr. Beaumont here to see you," she said. Green must have said something in return because she motioned to me. "You can come in now, Mr. Beaumont."

Martin Green came to the door to greet me. "You'll have to forgive the mess," he apologized. "We've had a little problem here this morning."

"I noticed."

He ushered me into the room. "We've got a hell of a union here, Mr. Beaumont, almost perfect. But it's like anything else. There are always people who don't like the way things are going.''

"People who want it to be more perfect?" I asked.

Green nodded. "You could say that," he said with a laugh. "A more perfect union."

He directed me to one of the two chairs facing his desk. Perfect or not, Martin Green's union work space was a far cry from his private living quarters in Belltown Terrace. His apartment was definitely upscale, first-class cabin all the way and spare no expense. In contrast, Ironworkers Local 165 had him in lowbrow digs. The chair he offered me was one of the gray-metal/green-plastic variety. I recognized it instantly as a littermate of chairs we still use down at the department. You don't often see relics like that anywhere outside the confines of municipal police departments and old county courthouses.

Martin Green seated himself in a creaking chair behind a battered wooden desk and smiled cordially. "Now what can I do for you, Mr. Beaumont?" Under his outward show of easy congeniality, I sensed that he was still deeply disturbed by whatever had gone on between him and Don Kaplan.

"The Bentley, remember?" I reminded him.

"Oh, yes, that's right. In all the hubbub it slipped my mind. Is it going to be fixed soon?"

"Within a matter of days, we hope. In the meantime, we have the Cadillac. I know it's not quite in the same class . . ."

"Oh, the Cadillac's fine," he interrupted, waving aside my explanation. "As long as there's something available. Forgive me. I never should have gone ahead and mailed that letter to you. I was just so irritated. My mother would have been thrilled to be picked up at the airport in something as exotic as a Bentley. You know how mothers are.''

I was a little taken aback by Green's total about-face, but I wasn't going to argue the point. If he was happy, I was happy.

"Does that mean you won't be taking us to the Better Business Bureau?"

"Of course not. There's no call to do that, none at all.

As I said, I was upset at the time, but I'm not an unreasonable man, Mr. Beaumont. Surely you can see that.''

"Indeed I can.'' I hadn't anticipated that the interview would go quite so smoothly. Martin Green was already getting ready to show me out of his office and I hadn't had time to mention my other reason for coming. "By the way, I noticed on the front door that one of your members passed away. That wasn't the woman who died in the accident at Masters Plaza on Monday, was it?''

He rose and came around the desk, stopping in front of me with his arms crossed, nodding his head sadly. "I'm afraid it was. Angie Dixon was one of our newer apprentices. A most unfortunate circumstance, but then nobody ever said working iron wasn't dangerous.''

Green motioned toward the broken window. "Actually, the guy who was in here just a few minutes ago, Don Kaplan, I think maybe you met him last night. He's the one who's in charge of our apprenticeship program. He's taking Angie's death real hard. Personally, I guess you could say.''

Martin Green moved away from the desk and led me to the door. "Watch your step,'' he cautioned as I started across the jagged shards of glass. "I wouldn't want you to slip and fall. Kim, is someone going to clean this mess up?''

The woman who had let me into his office nodded. "I've called maintenance, Mr. Green,'' she answered. "A janitor is on the way.'' Something about the speed of her response, her quick retreat to the safety of her typewriter made me suspect Martin Green wasn't an altogether easy man to work for.

I stopped beside the counter and turned back to where he was still standing in the layer of broken glass.. "By the way,'' I said. "Thanks for the champagne last night. I didn't mean to crash your party.''

He waved. "Think nothing of it,'' he replied absently. With that, he turned and disappeared back into his office, closing the shattered door behind him while the two secretaries exchanged discreet looks of undisguised relief.

I left the Labor Temple with the feeling that my mission had been totally successful from a property management

point of view. I had gotten Martin Green off the backs of
the Belltown Terrace management group and made sure
the Bentley wouldn't cause us any more adverse publicity.
Green was willing to let bygones be bygones, and so were
we.

In addition, I had discovered that Don Kaplan, someone
I knew, if only slightly, was a person I could talk to in
order to learn more about the ironworker apprenticeship
program. How I'd go about it and under what pretext were
details I hadn't quite handled yet, but at least I knew who
to ask.

When I got back home there was a message on the
answering machine from Margie, my clerk down at the
department. The message said to give her a call.

"What are you doing, working on your vacation?"
Margie asked.

"What makes you think that?"

She laughed. "Easy. I've got a message here for you
from Gloria over at the phone company. She says the
address you need is 24 Pe Ell Star Route. Where's that?"

"Beats me. Down around Raymond somewhere, I think."

"That's a little outside the city limits, isn't it?" Margie
asked.

She was teasing me, and I knew what she was thinking.
Cops do it all the time, use official channels to get the
address or phone number of someone they've met and
want to see again. It isn't legal, but it does happen.

"Leave me alone," I said. "Anything else?"

"As a matter of fact, there is one more message. It's
from Big Al. He wants to know when you're going to stop
farting around and come back to work."

"Tell him Tuesday, and not a minute before."

"Will do," she answered with a barely suppressed giggle. "He misses you."

Once I was off the phone, I dragged my worn *Rand
McNally Road Atlas* off the bookshelf. It was several years
out of date, but I suspected the only real difference would
be in a few freeway interchanges. The rural roads, especially ones running through little burgs like Pe Ell, would
be essentially unchanged.

The town was right where I thought it would be, about

twenty-five miles off Interstate 5 between Chehalis and Raymond on Highway 6. I had never been there, had never wanted to go there, but I was going nevertheless.

By noon, I was on the freeway, headed south. Traffic was fairly heavy as out-of-state recreational vehicles lumbered home toward Oregon, California, and points south and east. There weren't any log trucks, though. The lack of rain had turned Washington's lush forests tinder-dry and shut down the woods to logging and camping both.

As I drove, I tried tuning in the radio. I heard a snippet of news reporting a fatal fire somewhere on the east side of Lake Washington. I switched the dial. I wanted music, not news. I was on vacation, out of town. Whatever was on the news wasn't my problem.

Highway 6 turned off at Chehalis and meandered west through wooded hills. Sometimes it ran under trees so thick they formed an impenetrable green canopy over the roadway. Other times it moved along near the bed of the shallow headwaters of the Chehalis River. I stopped at a wide spot in the road, a hamlet called Doty, to buy a soda and ask directions.

"Where does Pe Ell Star Route start?" I asked the woman clerk as she gave me my change.

"Just the other side of town," she answered, eyeing me suspiciously. "How come you wanna know? Lookin' for somebody in partic'lar?"

"A friend of mine from Seattle," I said. "She just moved down here."

"You must mean that crazy lady with the two little kids. Yeah, she's up the road here apiece—five, six miles or so. It's a blue house on the left. You can't miss it. Looks more like a jail than the real one does over in Chehalis."

I puzzled over that remark, but only until I saw the house. It was easy to find. The house, just across the road from the river, was nestled back against the bottom of a steep, timber-covered bluff. It was small, as two-story houses go. All the windows and doors on the lower floor had been covered with ornamental iron bars. It did indeed look like a jail.

A beat-up Datsun station wagon was parked near the house. On one side, two children were playing under a towering apple tree. A little girl sat in a swing with her hair flying behind her, while a boy, somewhat older, pushed her high enough to run underneath the swing when it reached its highest point.

I drove all the way past the house once, then made a U-turn and came back from the other direction. As I pulled into the driveway behind the Datsun, the little boy grabbed the rope and stopped the swing so abruptly the little girl almost pitched out on her face. He grabbed her by one arm to keep her from falling and pulled her down from the swing.

Stepping out of the car, I called across to them. "Hello there. Is your mother home?"

The little girl opened her mouth as if to answer, but the boy yanked on her arm and dragged her toward the house.

"Wait a minute," I said. "I just need to ask you a couple of questions."

Without a backward glance, the two of them scurried away from me like a pair of frightened wild animals, with the boy urgently tugging the girl along beside him. I paused long enough to look toward the house. An upstairs curtain fluttered as though someone behind it had been watching us.

I closed the car door and started after the children. When I rounded the end of the house, I expected to see them there, but they weren't. The back porch was empty. I stepped up onto the porch and tugged at the iron grillwork over the door. It was still securely fastened from the inside. That puzzled me. I didn't think the children would have had enough time to get inside the house and relock the door.

Just then I heard what sounded like a door slamming shut on the backside of the house, the side closest to the steep bluff behind it. I walked around the corner and looked, expecting to find an additional outside entrance. Instead, the only thing I could see was a rectangular box built next to the foundation of the house. The top of the box was a full-sized wooden door. The door itself was slightly ajar, resting on an empty metal padlock hasp that had been closed inside.

Was this the door I had heard slam, or was there another

one, farther around toward the front of the house? I walked around to the front door. It too was protected by a formidable grillwork cover, the kind that give fire fighters nightmares. I tested the bars. They had been carefully welded and solidly set by someone who knew what he was doing.

There was a doorbell next to the door, so I rang it. I heard a multi-note chime ring in the bowels of the house, but no one came to the door—not the kids, and not whoever had been watching from the upstairs window, either.

I rang again, and again nothing happened. Linda Decker must have given her children absolute orders about not speaking to strangers. That's not such a crazy idea. I believe in that myself, but I was sure there was someone else in the house, some adult. That's the person I wanted to talk to. I needed some answers.

I rang the bell a third time.

"What do you want?" A woman's voice wafted down to me from an upstairs window. I stepped back far enough to see. Above the front door a window stood open, but the curtain was drawn. No one was visible.

"Are you Linda Decker?" I asked.

Instead of answering my question, she asked another of her own. "How did you find me?"

"Your brother," I said.

"What did you do, promise him a ride in that fancy car of yours if he'd tell you?" There was a hard, biting edge to her words. There was also a hint that the information wasn't news to her.

"It wasn't like that," I said. "He was upset. He had missed his bus. I gave him a ride to the center, that's all. I'm a police officer," I added.

"Right, and I'm the Tooth Fairy," she responded.

"Look," I said. "I've got my ID right here. Come to the window. I'll toss it up to you."

"Go ahead," she said.

I felt like an absolute idiot, standing out front of the little house, throwing my ID packet toward an open window. It took several tries, but finally I made it. My ID dropped inside the windowsill and fell between the window and the curtain. There was a slight movement behind the curtain as someone stepped forward to retrieve the wallet.

"See there?" I called. "That's me. That's my picture. Can I come in now?"

"Why are you here?"

"I'm investigating the death of Logan Tyree. I want to ask you a few questions."

"Just a minute," she said.

She was gone a long time, not one minute but several. I still couldn't see her, but eventually she returned to the window and tossed my ID back down to me. "You can come in now," she said, "but you'll have to use the kids' door."

"Where's that?"

"Out back along the side of the house."

"The side!" I echoed. "But there isn't any door there."

"The coal chute."

"That's how they get in and out?" She didn't answer. I was right then—the kids had gotten into the house some other way besides the back door. I couldn't help wondering what kind of mother would make her children come in and out of the house through a coal chute. Not your standard, garden variety, cookies-and-milk type mother, that's for damn sure.

"I'll meet you in the basement," Linda Decker called down to me. "I'll go switch on the light."

With a sigh I turned away from the front door of the house. The woman at the store in Doty was probably right. Linda Decker was crazy as a bedbug.

Regretting that I was wearing good clothes, I walked back to the coal chute and lifted the door. It was heavy but not so heavy that kids wouldn't be able to open and close it themselves. There was no squawk of protest from the hinges. Although there was still some rust showing, they had recently been thoroughly oiled.

I paused long enough to run my hand over the padlock hasp on the outside of the door. I wondered if sometimes Linda locked her children inside the house when she was away. If she did, she wouldn't be the first mother who made that sometimes fatal mistake in houses with barred doors and windows. They lock the doors to protect their children, and the children die of smoke inhalation or worse. The idea made me shudder.

I peered down into the coal chute. The top of a ladder was visible, coming up out of the darkened depths of the basement. It leaned against the inside of the box close enough that the top rung was within easy reach. A light switched on in the basement below me. I heard Linda Decker's voice again.

"Just step over the edge of the box and climb down the ladder."

Beneath me, the ladder seemed to be set firmly enough on a bare concrete floor. I put one hand on it and tested it for stability. It didn't wobble at all. If Linda Decker trusted the ladder enough to let her children climb up and down it, I supposed it was good enough for me. Not only that, the coal chute itself looked as though every trace of coal dust had been carefully scrubbed away. That must have taken some doing.

Swinging one leg up and over the side of the box, I found the top rung of the ladder with one foot and stepped onto it. Before starting down the ladder, I took one last look around outside. I was half afraid some neighbor would see me and think I was breaking into Linda Decker's house. There was no one in sight.

The ladder was solid and steady beneath my feet. I started down, one rung at a time. As my shoulders and head descended into the basement, I could see that the room was nearly empty, except for a scatter of boxes and a few odd pieces of discarded furniture. The room was lit by the glaring glow of one bare bulb dangling from an ancient cord in the middle of the raw plywood ceiling.

One foot was on the floor and the other was still on the bottom rung of the ladder when suddenly the heavy door to the coal chute slammed shut over my head. At the same instant the light went out, plunging me into total darkness.

Above me, I heard somebody struggling with the hasp. The padlock! Someone was trying to fasten the padlock!

Scrambling hand over hand, I raced back up the ladder only to crash head-first into the door just as the lock clicked home.

"We got him, Mommie," a child's voice crowed in triumph. "We got him."

They sure as hell had.

Chapter 12

REELING from the self-inflicted blow to my head and afraid of falling, I clung desperately to the ladder as tiny pinpricks of light exploded around me. Unfortunately, the stars flashing before my eyes did nothing to lighten the inky blackness of Linda Decker's basement.

My legs shook uncontrollably. Fighting vertigo, I made my way back down to the floor. I counted the rungs on the ladder. Seven in all from the point where I'd banged my head.

I stood on the floor holding the side of the ladder for several minutes trying to get my bearings, waiting for the shaking and dizziness to stop, hoping that somehow my eyes would adjust to the darkness. Eventually the trembling diminished, but I still couldn't see my hand in front of my face when I tackled the ladder again. I didn't know what was going on, but one thing was clear: I had to try to get out.

Careful not to damage my head further, I counted the rungs as I climbed, inching my way up the ladder far enough to brace my back and shoulders against the door. I grunted with exertion, pushing against the resistant wood as hard as I could, but the pressure wasn't enough. The hasp, the hinges, and the wood all held firm.

Giving up, I stood for a moment hunched under the door, listening for any sound of voice or movement outside or inside. There was nothing—no footsteps in the room above me, no whispered deliberations outside—only the dull interior thud of my own pounding heartbeat.

I was over being surprised and scared. Now I was angry. Pissed. I was certain the childish cry of victory had come from the little boy as he slammed shut the coal chute door. What the hell were they up to? I could picture the three of them, Linda Decker and her two children, standing somewhere just out of earshot, gloating over my having fallen into their little trap.

They'd trapped me all right, but we'd see who had the last laugh on that score. Assaulting a police officer is no joke. Kidnapping one isn't either. Linda Decker hadn't figured that out yet, but I fully intended to show her, just as soon as I got the hell out of her goddamned basement.

Cautiously counting the rungs, I made my way back down to the floor. In the instant before the light had gone out, I could remember glimpsing a stairway on the other side of the basement. Now, with my eyes finally accustomed to the dark, I could see a faint glow that had to be daylight leaking into the basement through a crack under a door at the top of the stairs.

I attempted walking toward it, only to stumble over an invisible box on the floor and crash, nose-first, into a solid upright timber. A quick spurt of blood told me I'd done something to my nose—something bad, something that would add another lump to it and give my face more character. Just what I·needed.

Maybe I'm not too bright at times, but at least I learn from my mistakes. I dropped to my hands and knees and began crawling toward that tiny sliver of light at the top of the stairs. The concrete floor was cold and damp beneath me as I groped my way across it, creeping along like an overgrown baby. The basement was musty and reeked with the smell of long-resident mice. The house had probably stood vacant for some time before Linda Decker and her children moved into it.

I made slow progress. The actual distance across the basement couldn't have been more than twenty feet or so, but in the dark it was one hell of an obstacle course. What had seemed like a relatively empty room with the light on was actually a jumble of wood and boxes, furniture and tools.

Along the way I jammed my knee down on something sharp, a piece of broken glass or a loose nail that my scouting hands had missed. There was a sudden telltale wetness on my knee and leg, unmistakably warm and slick. The texture of rough concrete on lacerated skin told me I'd torn the hell out of both my knee and my pants. The knee would heal; the pants wouldn't. And this was one pair I wouldn't be able to voucher. I'd never get

Seattle P.D. to agree that tearing my pants in Linda Decker's treacherous basement ought to qualify as a line of duty mishap.

Had the lights been on, I'm sure I would have made quite a sight. The bloodied nose and the torn knee created a symmetry of sorts, the top and bottom halves of a matched set. An ugly matched set.

At last my fingers touched the far wall. I inched my way along it until I located the bottom of the stairs. They were made of rough-hewn cobweb-covered planks open at the back end. My hands searched in vain for a handrail on the outside. There wasn't any. Running my hands up and down the wall I located a two-inch pipe that had been bolted to the wall as a make-do banister. Clutching it gratefully, I eased my body up the stairs, feeling my way one step at a time, clinging to the pipe with one hand while sharp wooden splinters from the steps bit into the palm of my other hand.

Being blind must be hell, but real blind people have canes and seeing-eye dogs. I only knew things were in my way after I ran into them. That's a little late.

On step number twelve I barked a knuckle against something metal—something round and metal and cool. It was another grill, more of the ornamental iron bars I had seen on the outside of the house. Beyond the bars was the smooth finished surface of a wooden door.

Suddenly, I heard swift footsteps coming toward me. The light came on and the wooden door fell open beneath my hand. When the door gave way, it took me by surprise and I lost my balance. I had to grab hold of the metal bars to keep from pitching ass over teakettle back down the stairs.

When I righted myself and looked up, I found myself staring into the barrel of the biggest pistol I'd ever seen. From where I was, it looked a hell of a lot more like a cannon than a handgun. I was only dimly aware of the woman behind it, but her words came through loud and clear.

"Let go of the bars. Now!"

I let go and retreated down the stairs a step or two.

Her voice was steady even though the gun wasn't.

"Mister, if you've got a gun on you, you'd better shove it under this rail right now before I blast you into a million pieces!"

There was no doubt in my mind that Linda Decker meant what she said. Even if she didn't, I couldn't afford to call her bluff, not with a gun pointed right between my eyes from some three feet away. A shaking gun at that.

"Okay, okay," I said. "Take it easy."

Cautiously I eased the Smith and Wesson out of my shoulder holster. I didn't want to do anything to alarm my captor. She was nervous enough already. Her finger was still poised on the trigger while the barrel of the gun trembled violently. It scared the holy crap out of me.

I slipped my gun, handle first, through a flat, clear space at the bottom of the metal bars. With a quick, deft movement she kicked it behind her, sending it spinning away across the linoleum floor until it came to rest against the bottom of a kitchen cupboard.

"Now take off your jacket and push it through here, too," she ordered.

"Look," I began. "You're making a terrible mistake."

"Shut up and take off the jacket."

I did. "What's going on? You already saw my ID. You know I'm a cop." I finished poking the jacket under the bars and glanced up at the gun. It was still pointing at me, still shaking.

"I don't know anything of the kind," Linda Decker answered. Without ever taking her eyes off me, she kicked my jacket away as well.

"Call my partner, Detective Lindstrom at Seattle P.D. He'll vouch for me."

"Cop or no cop, you're still working for them," she retorted.

I took a deep breath, summoned my most conciliatory tone, and tried again. After all, I'm supposed to be trained to talk my way out of tough situations. "Linda, I already told you, I'm investigating the death of Logan Tyree. I thought you'd want to help."

She winced when I mentioned his name, but she didn't back off. "Cut the bullshit. You tried that line already. I called Seattle P.D. just a few minutes ago. You're not assigned to Logan's case, so what the hell are you doing here?''

There was no point in trying to explain that I was on vacation and looking into Logan Tyree's death on my own because I felt like it, because I didn't like the way the official investigation was going. She wouldn't have believed that in a million years. Actually, I hardly believed it myself.

''I just wanted to talk to you, to ask you some questions.''

''You went to a hell of a lot of trouble. I figured you'd show up today. I warned the kids to watch out for you, told them to come inside the minute they saw a strange red car.''

She must have noticed the puzzled expression on my face. She answered my question without my ever asking it. ''I talked to Jimmy last night. He told me all about you, about how you'd been so nice to him and given him a ride to the center. He told me you had asked about me, but he couldn't remember whether or not he'd given you my phone number. I guess we don't have to wonder about that anymore, do we. If you were on the up and up, you would have picked up a telephone and called.''

She jerked the gun in my direction and my heart went to my throat. ''Empty your pants pockets,'' she added. ''Turn them inside out.''

''Wait a minute . . .''

''Do it!'' she commanded. ''Now!''

I did. My car keys, change, and pocketknife ended up in a pitiful pile which I shoved under the grill.

The little girl appeared at her mother's side and clung to one leg, whining. ''I'm scared, Mommie. What are we going to do with him? What's going to happen?''

''I don't know yet, Allison. Go on outside and play with Jason. I'll be out in a few minutes.''

Allison backed away from the door, watching me warily through the bars as she did so.

''Now the ladder,'' Linda Decker ordered.

''The ladder!''

''Go get it, bring it over here, and shove it under the bars. It'll fit.''

Linda Decker had evidently thought this whole scene

through in some detail. She was leaving no stone unturned. I wouldn't get out of there until she was damned good and ready and not a moment before.

When the ladder had been shoved under the bars and moved safely out of reach across the kitchen, she sighed with relief.

"Now what?" I demanded. "I suppose the next thing you'll want me to take off my pants."

No matter how old I get, I'll never learn to keep my big mouth shut. I doubt she would have thought of it on her own if I hadn't been such a smart-ass and made the suggestion.

"That's a good idea."

And so the belt and pants came off, and my socks, and finally my dress shirt. I sat there in nothing but my shorts, feeling as naked as a plucked chicken. A trickle of blood was still running down my leg from the gash in my knee, but at least by then my nose had stopped bleeding.

"Now put your hands behind your head and keep them there."

I did as I was told, but I tried once more to talk some sense into her head. "Will you please listen to reason?" I asked. It's tough to sound reasonable when you're down to nothing but your skivvies, when you're talking to a total stranger who's packing a pistol.

I took a deep breath, searching for some scrap of dignity. "I'm a sworn police officer, Linda. Are you aware you can go to jail for this?"

She waved the gun impatiently. She wasn't listening to me, hadn't heard a word I was saying. "Who sent you here?" she demanded.

"Nobody sent me."

"You tell me who sent you and then I'll figure out whether I should call the cops or plug you full of holes myself."

"I already told you, I came on my own," I insisted.

"You still expect me to believe that? Just how stupid do you think I am?"

When I didn't answer, she shrugged and turned away from me. She walked over to the counter long enough to pour herself a cup of coffee. Taking both the coffee and the gun with her, she sat down on a tall kitchen stool. She placed the gun on the counter beside her then sat there sipping coffee while she gazed at me speculatively. We had reached an impasse. Neither one of us said anything for some time.

Having the gun out of her hand made me feel a little better. Not a whole lot better, but a little. A loaded gun in the hands of a frightened person can be a deadly combination. There are plenty of dead cops out there to prove it's true. I didn't want to join them.

"Please listen to me. I'm a cop. A detective. I work for the Seattle P.D."

She laughed, but the sound was harsh and humorless. "Sure you are," she responded. "Can't you come up with something a little more original? We've been through that already and I'm not buying, remember?"

I didn't give up. "I came because I don't think Logan Tyree's death was an accident."

"Think?" she asked bitterly. "You *think* it wasn't an accident, or you *know*. Which is it?"

"You think I killed him?"

"Didn't you?" The countering question was quick and accompanied by a look of sheer hatred. "It doesn't matter," she added. "They're not here, either. You won't find them. They're in a safe place."

"What's not here?"

"After what happened to Logan, do you think I'm dumb enough to have those tapes with me?"

"What tapes?" I asked.

"And if anything happens to me . . ."

She was interrupted by a frantic pounding on the outside door leading into the kitchen. "Mommie, Mommie. Open the door quick. Somebody's coming."

Linda Decker leaped to her feet. She was wearing a loose-fitting sweatshirt and Levis. She stuffed the gun under her shirt and raced to the kitchen door, frantically unlocking a series of dead bolts and pushing open the grill to let the breathless children inside just as the doorbell rang at the front of the house.

"Who is it, Jason?" she hissed as she closed both the grill and the door and fastened all the locks.

"It's a policeman," Jason answered, his voice a high-pitched squeak. "With blue lights on top of the car and everything."

My first reaction was one of relief. A policeman. An ally. Someone who would make Linda Decker listen to me, someone who would help me out of my predicament.

The doorbell rang again, insistently. Wavering, Linda Decker glanced over her shoulder in the direction of the front door and then down at her two frightened children. Last of all she turned to me. Her face hardened. She reached under her shirt and tentatively touched the gun. For a moment I was afraid she was going to give it to Jason, but she evidently changed her mind. Quickly she retrieved my Smith and Wesson and shoved it under her shirt as well.

Then she came over to the barred basement door, close enough for me to hear her harsh whisper, but far enough away to remain safely out of reach.

"If you so much as make a sound, so help me God I'll kill you!"

With that, she slammed the door shut. The light went out. I was once more left in darkness, sitting almost naked on the wooden steps in Linda Decker's damp basement, smelling the mouse crap and feeling like a load of shit.

I didn't doubt for one minute that she'd do exactly what she said. I couldn't afford to doubt it. I was convinced she had balls enough and then some.

She also had the gun.

I waited. For a long time. I heard the sound of voices, and then the creak of footsteps as someone walked across a room, then the murmur of someone's voice, only one voice this time—Linda talking, but no one answering. She must have been on the phone. Again there was the creak of footsteps followed by voices again and then a whole flurry of footsteps, but no one came near the kitchen. No one opened the door to the basement for probably ten minutes or maybe longer. I'm not sure.

When the door did finally open, it was Linda Decker herself who flung it wide and hard, banging the doorknob into something metal, probably a stove.

She was different, totally different. Something had happened. Something had changed, and not for the better.

Before that, despite the trembling gun, she had been relatively calm, calculating, working a plan that she had laid out and rehearsed well in advance. Now as she stood staring at me through the barred door there was an icy fury behind her dangerously pale face. Her lips were pulled tight over clenched teeth.

Thankfully, she wasn't holding the gun. If she had been, I think she would have shot me on sight.

"You son of a bitch!" She barely whispered the words, her voice shaking with rage while ragged tremors raced through her whole body. "You goddamned son of a bitch!"

Jason hurried into the room, dragging the whimpering Allison with him. He stopped near his mother and looked up at her. What he saw must have frightened him. "Are you all right, Mommie?" he asked. The grave concern written on his face was far older than his years.

She tore her eyes from me and glanced down at her son. For a brief moment, her face softened. Her throat worked furiously as she tried three times to choke out an answer. Finally she nodded.

"I'm all right, Jason. Take Allison out to the car and fasten her seat belt. I'll be out in a minute."

"But the door is locked," he said.

Without a word, she walked to the door and unlocked the series of locks. I watched her hands. They were shaking so badly it was all she could do to control them. What had happened? What had made the difference? And where was the cop Jason had said was there?

When the outside door closed behind the children, she swung around to face me again. For a moment, she leaned heavily against the door as though every bit of strength had been drained from her body, as though she needed the door to hold her up.

"I'm sorry . . ." she began, then stopped as another violent tremor shook her body. By force of will she drew herself away from the door and started toward me.

She had begun with the words "I'm sorry," but there was no hint of apology in her body language. The gun was out of sight, but at that point she didn't need a gun. She was a menacing cat ready to spring at my face and claw me apart. For the first time, I was grateful for the bars that separated us.

"I'm sorry I didn't shoot you when I had a chance," she finished. She stopped only inches from the iron grill. Maybe I could have grabbed her through the bars, but I didn't try it. I don't believe in tackling wildcats with bare hands.

"It's up to them now," she added, "but if they don't take care of you, I will. That's a promise!"

With that she stepped back and slammed the wooden door shut. Once more Linda Decker's basement was plunged into total darkness. I didn't know I had been holding my breath until I let it out.

I felt a sudden rush of gratitude. I was the lucky man who is aware of seeing a rattlesnake only after he's already pulled his foot out of harm's way.

Linda Decker was gone, but in those last seconds before she turned away and slammed the door I looked into her eyes and knew what was different.

Before she left the kitchen to answer the doorbell, she had been undecided about what to do with me. Now she wasn't. Her mind was made up. And when I looked into her eyes, they were empty of everything but cold hatred. Hatred and a naked desire to kill me. I've seen it before. I know the danger.

In that moment, my life had hung in the balance, and yet, inexplicably, she had closed the door and walked away. Someone or something had stayed her hand, had kept her from killing me. I had been reprieved.

Almost sick with relief, I took a deep breath and settled down to wait.

I suppose my mother would have been proud of me. At least I was wearing clean shorts.

Chapter 13

I HAVE no idea how long I waited. A half hour? Longer? It seemed forever, sitting there in the dark. There was no sound in the house. I knew Linda Decker had driven away. I had heard the door slam and the engine of a car turn over. What about the cop? Had he left along with them?

If I was really alone, I knew I should crawl back down the stairs and try to find some kind of tool that might help me break out of my prison, but I was understandably reluctant to search around in the dark. My knee still hurt. So did my nose.

I had started picking my way down the steps when I heard the distant wail of a siren. It was coming closer.

Cops don't believe in coincidences. They can't afford to. If there was a siren outside the house, it was because of me, because I was locked up in Linda Decker's basement.

The siren came almost to the house and then wound down to silence as I listened. Several car doors slammed shut and I heard a series of shouted commands. I should have felt relief. Here were the reinforcements I had wanted riding to the rescue, but now that they were outside, I didn't feel better. And I didn't call out to them. Some instinctive warning system told me that although they were cops and I was a cop, this time we weren't on the same side.

Heavy footsteps mounted the outside steps and entered the kitchen, accompanied by a series of barked commands. "She's got him locked up in the basement," someone said. "That's his car out there in the driveway. The red Porsche."

Whoever had come to the door hadn't left when Linda did, but he was cautious. He had called for a backup and then waited outside until they showed.

"Stay clear of that door," another voice ordered. It was a much deeper voice than the first one, that of an older man, someone in authority. "Is he armed?"

The first voice answered. "I don't think so. She said she took his gun away. It's right here."

Linda must have given him my Smith and Wesson. I listened as heavy footsteps creaked across the kitchen floor. There was a short silence, then the second voice, the older one, said:

"Beaumont?" The way he said it made my name sound ominous, threatening. "We've got this place surrounded. You can't get out."

"Surrounded?" I yelped the word. "Of course I can't get out. She locked the door. Who the hell do you think I am? I'm not armed. She took my gun."

"We *know* who you are, Beaumont. On the count of three, we're opening this door. I want to see you with both hands up behind your head or we'll shoot first and ask questions later. One. Two. Three."

Hands behind my head? What was going on? I sat down as the door flew open. There was no one there, only a doorway full of brilliant daylight from the kitchen window shining down the stairs, hurting my eyes, and casting long shadows of bars down the stairway. Then a lone man stepped into the light. He was a big sucker. His burly silhouette filled the entire doorway.

"Where the hell's the light switch?" he demanded. "I can't see a damn thing."

There was a quick shuffling of feet as someone searched for and found the switch to the basement light. It came on, leaving me exposed in all my bloody, nearly naked glory. The silence was so thick you could have cut it with a knife.

The heavyset man shook his head as though he couldn't quite believe his eyes. "I'll be damned," he said. "I been to three barn dances, a county fair, and a goat ropin', and I ain't never seen nothin' like this before. This what off-duty Seattle cops are wearing these days? On your feet, Beaumont. Come on up the stairs. Easy-like. No sudden moves."

I got to my feet and padded barefoot up the stairs with my hands behind my head.

"Stop right there," the man said, when I was almost at

the top of the stairs. "Who has the key to this damn thing? Louis, did she give it to you?"

"Yessir."

A much younger, shorter man came into view and handed something over. A key. The big man fumbled with it briefly before inserting it into the lock and shoving the gate open. I had to dodge backward to keep from being pushed back down the stairs.

"Watch it, Beaumont. I said no sudden moves." He wasn't holding a weapon, but he spoke with the unquestioned authority of someone who doesn't think he needs one.

"What am I supposed to do, stand here while you knock me down the steps?"

I was close enough to see the badge on his khaki uniform, but there was no name tag.

"I'd keep a civil tongue in my mouth if I were you," he replied. Beyond him someone else in a uniform was sifting through my pile of belongings. He came up holding my car keys.

"Got 'em," he said. "They're right here. Want me to go search the car?"

"Right. Know what to look for?"

The younger man nodded.

"Hey, wait a minute. You can't search my car. You've gotta have a warrant."

"We've got one," the older man said, patting his breast pocket. He opened his jacket and drew out a long, slim envelope. "We've got ourselves one of those little hummers right here. It's all in order. Come on up here now. All the way into the kitchen. Keep your hands on your head."

I walked through the kitchen doorway into a crowded room. All told, there probably weren't that many people in the room—not more than six, me included—but it seemed like more. They were all cops, much younger ones except for the old guy who was in charge, all wearing versions of the same khaki uniform, all of them packing guns. If I'd made a break for it right then, they probably would have blown each other away, but I was in no mood for running.

And they were in no mood for laughing, either. Despite

my lack of clothing, nobody cracked a smile. This was serious stuff. Dead serious.

Everyone waited on the older guy for direction. As soon as he spat out orders, they jumped to carry them out.

"What the hell is this all about?" I demanded. The older man didn't answer me. Instead, he turned to one of the younger ones.

"Cuff him, Jamie. Make sure there isn't a weapon concealed in his shorts. Shut up, Beaumont. You'll have plenty of time to talk later."

Jamie was a little shit with lifts in his shoes and a pencil-thin moustache. His search was enthusiastically thorough. "He's clean, Sheriff Harding," he reported.

I wanted to punch Jamie's lights out, but I didn't. He had given me one important bit of information, told me I was dealing with W. Reed Harding, Sheriff of Lewis County. Reed Harding wasn't a totally unknown quantity.

Like so many small-town sheriffs, he had cut his law-enforcement teeth in the big city, in this case Tacoma, and then moved into small-town police work when he tired of the rat race. I had never met Harding personally, but I knew officers who had worked with him and for him. Word of mouth said he was both tough and fair. I could have done a hell of a lot worse.

"Do you mind if I put my pants on?" I asked.

He shrugged. "Those them over there?" He pointed toward my pile of belongings still on the kitchen floor.

I nodded.

"Check 'em out, Jamie. If they're clean, let him put his pants back on. Then we'll find out what he's doing half-naked in this nice lady's basement in the middle of the afternoon."

Nice lady my ass! Linda Decker wasn't a nice lady in my book, but I didn't contradict him. Harding had gone to the door of the kitchen with his deputies, and the whole group was conferring with someone outside when Jamie brought my pants.

With my hands cuffed behind my back, there was no way I could manage them myself. Jamie held them out for me to step in. I knew the little bastard was suckering me, but I wanted clothes on so badly that I fell for it. As I raised my leg to step in, he brought the pants up and caught my foot, knocking me off balance.

I toppled over backwards. I knew what the metal hand-cuffs would do to my body if I rammed them into the small of my back. Twisting to one side in midair, I managed to land on one shoulder with a heavy, bone-jarring thud that knocked the wind out of my lungs. I almost blacked out.

Harding whirled and came back into the room, angrily looming over me. "What the hell happened?" he de-manded of Jamie who was still standing there innocently holding my pants.

"I was helping him get these on. He tried to kick me," Jamie complained.

"Is that right!" Harding said. "Leave the son of a bitch naked, then." He glared down at me. "You try anything funny again, Beaumont, and you'll be wearing a strait-jacket next, understand?"

I still hadn't gotten my breath back. "I understand," I croaked.

When Harding turned away, I caught Jamie's narrow-lipped smile of amusement. The asshole. He was probably five-six and a hundred and thirty pounds soaking wet—a little guy with a big chip on his shoulder. Sneaky, weasely, true to type. He wouldn't have lasted ten minutes at Seattle P.D., wouldn't have made it past the first physical, so he had to content himself with throwing his weight around in Lewis County.

I filed his face away in my memory banks. I'm no good with names, but I *do* remember faces. Maybe someday little Jamie would end up in Seattle and our paths would manage to cross. He'd best be looking over his shoulder if that ever happens.

Reed Harding returned to the outside door. "Come on, Jamie. Hustle on out there. They say the car's clean. He probably stashed the stuff somewhere nearby. Davis is organizing a search. You go help with that. I can handle this character. He won't give me any trouble."

"Yes, sir."

Jamie hotfooted it out of the house and Harding came back over to me. "Okay, Beaumont. On your feet."

He grabbed me under my arms and lifted me like I was a ten-pound-bag of potatoes. W. Reed Harding was strong as an ox. He dumped me unceremoniously on the kitchen stool where Linda Decker had sat earlier to drink her coffee. I didn't object. There wasn't an ounce of fight left in me.

"Is anybody ever going to tell me what the hell is going on?" I asked wearily.

"You bet, Beaumont," Harding answered. "I'll be glad to tell you. We're going to find where you stowed the stuff and then we're going to take you off the streets for awhile, lock you up, and throw away the key. I don't like it when cops take walks on the wrong side of the law. It gives all of us a bad name."

"Wrong side of the law? What are you talking about? What stuff?"

Harding bent down, holding his face only inches from mine. "The stuff you were going to use to burn down this house."

I was so dumbfounded I almost fell off the chair. "Burn the house down? You've got to be kidding. What makes you think that, for Christ's sake?"

"Because you already did it once."

"Did what?"

"Burned down a house," he answered grimly.

"Whose house?" I asked.

W. Reed Harding didn't answer me right away. His unblinking eyes bored into mine. I know how to do that too. It's a look calculated to make creeps squirm in their seats, to get them to spill their guts.

"Whose house?" I repeated.

"Linda Decker's mother's house," he said slowly. "Her mother's dead, and her brother isn't expected to make it."

His words hit me with the weight of a sledgehammer blow. Linda Decker's mother and her brother? Jimmy Rising? The enthusiastic little guy with his stainless-steel thermos and K Mart lunch pail?

"No," I said.

Harding nodded. "And Bellevue P.D.'s got witnesses who say they saw you prowling around the house yesterday afternoon. Would you care to tell me where you were at midnight last night, Detective Beaumont? And you'd better make sure it's something that will hold up in a court of law, because you're going to need it.''

Suddenly the snippet of news I had heard on the car radio, the one about the fatal eastside fire, resurfaced in my brain. Leona and Jimmy Rising. A cold chill passed over me. It had nothing whatever to do with the weather or my lack of clothes.

Somewhere outside myself I heard the words to the Miranda warning. Reed Harding was reading me my rights, as if I didn't know them already.

"So?" he asked when he finished. "Where were you?"

And that's when I remembered Marilyn Sykes. At midnight the night before, she and I had been getting it on in her Mercer Island bedroom. Dragging her into this for the sake of an alibi was out of the question.

"I want to talk to my attorney," I said. "His name's Ralph Ames. He lives in Phoenix."

Reed Harding looked at me gravely and shook his head. He seemed disappointed. "So that's the way you're going to play it?"

"Believe me," I answered, "I don't have any other choice."

Chapter 14

THAT gossipy store clerk in Doty had been right. Linda Decker's house with its barred windows and doors looked a whole lot more like a jail than the new one did in Chehalis. Except for the discreet lockup and secured-entry system at one corner, the building we entered didn't remotely resemble a county courthouse.

Before they stuffed me in a patrol car somebody other than Jamie had finally helped me into my pants and put my shirt over my shoulders. Once inside the courthouse, Sheriff Harding told a deputy to take me into an unoccupied office to make my one phone call. That and removing my handcuffs were his only grudging concessions to professional courtesy. If I hadn't been a cop, I'd have been stuck out in the lobby using a pay phone along with all the rest of the scum. My escort removed the handcuffs but made sure I understood that an armed guard would be posted outside the door.

The advantage of having a high-priced attorney like Ralph Ames on retainer is that he cuts through both bull-shit and red tape with equal dispatch. As soon as I got him on the phone and told him what was going on, he let me have it with both barrels.

"Wake up, Beau. Get out from under your rock. That kind of chivalry went out with the Middle Ages. You tell that sheriff, Harwin . . ."

"Harding," I corrected.

"Whatever his name is, you tell him to get on the horn to Marilyn Sykes and straighten this mess out before it goes any further. Is there anyone else besides her who can say for certain you were there all night?"

Sheepishly I remembered the security guard and his all-knowing clipboard. "There was somebody else," I admitted reluctantly.

"Who for Chrissakes?" Ames demanded. He wanted this fixed, and he wanted it fixed now. He wasn't about to let me hide out under a blanket of genteel niceties.

"A security guard at her condominium complex. They keep track of all cars coming and going."

"Great. Have the sheriff talk to the guard as well. In the meantime, I'll catch the next plane out of Sky Harbor and be in Seattle sometime tonight. You take the cake, Beau. If it isn't one thing, it's three others. Try to get word to Peters if you still need me to come down to Chehalis. Otherwise, I'll meet you at your apartment."

"Do you think you need to come up?"

"Of course I'm coming up. If I leave right now I can catch the six-fifty. It's a direct flight."

There may be take-two-aspirin-get-plenty-of-rest type attorneys in this world, but Ralph Ames isn't one of them.

"How come they picked you up, anyway?" he asked. "Didn't you tell them you're a cop?"

"I told them," I said, "but this woman was so totally

convinced I was there to kill her, that she made the Lewis
County Sheriff's Department believe it too.''

''If she could convince them of that, she ought to be in
sales,'' Ames suggested dryly. ''Time-share rowboats
maybe, right here in Phoenix.'' With that, he hung up.

For several minutes, I sat alone in the office thinking
about Linda Decker. I had been thinking about her all the
while I was locked in the back of Reed Harding's patrol
car with my hands cuffed firmly behind me. There hadn't
been anything else to do *but* think.

I was sure now that I wasn't alone in thinking Logan
Tyree's death was no accident. Linda Decker thought so
too. Not only that, she was so sure she was the next target
that she had barricaded her home and gone to some fairly
dangerous lengths to entrap whoever might come looking
for her.

Linda Decker was gutsy, I had to give her that, but she
was also stupid. Her plan had worked, but only because I
had come alone. If there had been anyone with me . . .

My old pal Jamie peered through the glass in the door
and saw that I was off the phone. He entered without
knocking. ''Get going,'' he ordered curtly.

''I want to talk to Harding,'' I said.

''You already had your chance with Harding. You blew
it.''

''Look, you little jerk, my lawyer told me to confess,
and I'm ready. Go get Harding and let's get this over
with.''

As soon as I saw the look on his face, I knew I had him
by the short hairs. Jamie wanted to be a hero every bit as
much as I had wanted my pants on earlier. He swallowed
the bait whole. ''I'll be right back,'' he said.

He took off at a dead run and was back in three minutes
with Sheriff W. Reed Harding rumbling along behind him.

''Jamie here tells me you're ready to confess,'' Harding
said to me. ''Is that true?''

I grinned at Jamie. ''I told him I wanted to talk to you,
but he's blowing smoke about the rest of it. I don't know
where he got the idea that I wanted to confess.'' My
mother taught me not to lie. It's taken me a lifetime to
overcome that training, but I'm learning.

Jamie flushed. I had gotten a little of my own back. Not enough, but it was a start. Harding bristled and turned away. "In that case, I'm going home to dinner. Lock this creep up."

Jamie started forward, but my next words caught Harding just as his hand closed on the doorknob. "Does the name Marilyn Sykes mean anything to you?"

Harding stopped and so did Jamie. The sheriff swung back around to face me. "I know Marilyn," he replied deliberately. "She's vice president of our state association. She's good people. Why? What about her?"

"Call her," I said. "Ask her what she was doing last night between midnight and one o'clock."

The sheriff's eyes narrowed. "Is this some kind of joke?"

"Believe me, it's no joke. I'm only following my attorney's orders."

"It's too late to call her," he objected. "She wouldn't still be at the office, and I doubt she'd have a listed number."

"I have the number," I said. "It's in my wallet. You've got that, don't you?"

Harding stood for a moment, looking at me, pondering, then he nodded to Jamie. "Go out and get me the envelope with his stuff in it. And don't open it." Once Jamie was outside, Harding closed the door, walked slowly back to the desk, and eased his heavy frame down into the chair behind it. "What's this all about, Beaumont? What are you up to?"

"Just call Marilyn and ask her what she was doing last night between midnight and one o'clock," I said again.

Jamie returned and handed over the envelope. While Harding fumbled with the flap, I was aware of Jamie's cold eyes drilling into me. Talking to Ames had buoyed my confidence. Now, for the first time, I wondered what would happen if Marilyn Sykes weren't home, or if for some reason she couldn't or wouldn't corroborate my alibi. After this latest set-to with Jamie, if Harding left me alone again with that squirrelly little shit, I was in big, big trouble.

Marilyn, Marilyn, answer the phone.

Harding was still searching for the number. "It's on the back of one of her cards," I said helpfully. "Behind the money."

Harding located the card, turned it over, picked up the phone, and dialed. She must have answered on the first or second ring. I felt myself breathe a huge sigh of relief.

"Howdy there, Marilyn," He drawled. "This is Reed Harding, down in Chehalis. Oh sure, I'm fine. How's it going with you?"

I wondered if Reed Harding had always talked that way, or if he had affected the backwoods, good-old-boy style as a vote-getting technique. The accent wouldn't have played worth a damn in Tacoma or Seattle either one, but it sounded perfectly at home in Chehalis.

There was a short exchange of pleasantries, while Jamie and I stared at each other. I was gloating. There wasn't a goddamned thing he could do to me now, but suddenly I wanted him out of that room in the very worst way. Whatever Marilyn Sykes told Reed Harding was fine, but I'll be damned if I wanted Jamie to be privy to it.

"Well," Harding was explaining to Marilyn, "it's like this. We've got ourselves a sticky little situation down here. I hate to put you on the spot, Marilyn, but I need to know exactly what you were doing last night around midnight or so."

Jamie was bright enough to know that the tables had somehow turned, but he still hadn't figured out what to do about it. I stood up and stretched. Harding was so deeply embroiled in his conversation with Marilyn that he didn't pay the least bit of attention to me. With an armed deputy in the room and another stationed just outside the door, he didn't really need to worry.

I ambled over to the door where Jamie was still standing. "You'd better get out of here, you cocksucking little son of a bitch," I whispered, "before I crush your balls with a nutcracker and use 'em for chicken feed."

Jamie stiffened, paled, and left without a word. No guts. I turned back to Harding. He was still on the phone and shaking his head.

"So there was no way he could have gotten away between say midnight and one o'clock this morning without your noticing." There was a pause, and Harding chuck-led. "No, I suppose not."

Chivalry be damned, Marilyn Sykes was coming through like a champ.

"And you say the security guard there keeps track of all vehicles after ten P.M.? Could you give me that number?" He jotted something on a sheet of paper. "Well thanks, Marilyn. You've been a big help. You want to talk to him? Sure. Hang on."

Shaking his head, he looked over at me and held out the phone. "She wants to speak to you," he said.

I can't say that I wanted to speak to her right then, but I took the phone anyway.

"I thought you told me you weren't the type to kiss and tell," Marilyn Sykes said accusingly.

"Marilyn, I'm sorry. It's just that . . ."

She laughed. "Don't apologize and don't give me any excuses, Beau. From what Reed tells me, it's a damn good thing we were at my place instead of yours. Your doorman goes off duty at midnight. You need to live in a class-act place, Detective Beaumont, one with twenty-four-hour security."

Marilyn was sticking it to me and to Belltown Terrace as well, but I was in no position to object. I kept quiet.

"Anything else I can do to help?" she asked brightly.

"Not at the moment." I didn't want to say more, not with Reed Harding sitting there in the room. Marilyn was perceptive enough to figure it out.

"Call me when you get back home and let me know what's going on. It must be serious."

"It is that," I said. "I'll be in touch." I handed the phone back to Harding. He took it from me and sat there unmoving for several seconds with the receiver cupped in his hands. Finally, he tapped the phone on the desk a time or two.

"You'll bear with me while I go by the book and check out one more thing, won't you?"

I shrugged. "Be my guest."

He looked down at the notes he had taken during his call with Marilyn and punched a number into the phone. "Who am I speaking to?" he asked when somebody answered.

"My name's Harding, Sheriff W. Reed Harding down here in Chehalis. We've had a tip that one of our stolen vehicles was sighted in your complex last night. I understand that you keep track of license numbers of all vehicles entering and leaving the property, is that true?"

There was a pause. "I see, but you don't have last night's list there with you? Do you know where we could locate it? Yes, it is important. Fine, I'll hold."

Harding held his hand over the mouthpiece. "He's transferring me to the security company's main office in Seattle," he said. "What's the license number on that Porsche of yours? I've got it in the file in my office, but I need it now."

I gave it to him. Harding went back to the phone. "Sure, just read me the whole list. That'll be fine." It took several minutes. Finally the list was completed. "Okay," Harding said. "Thanks for all your help. What's your name again?" He scribbled a name and number on the sheet of paper. "Sounds to me like we must have been mistaken."

He put down the phone and looked over at me. "In more ways than one, Beaumont," he added. "Just like you said. The number's there. In at eleven and out again this morning. I owe you an apology."

"It happens," I said. "We all make mistakes." I could afford to be magnanimous with Harding. He wasn't the one who had knocked me on my ass.

"But what the hell were you doing out there in Pe Ell anyway? And what's Linda Decker so scared of? It's a miracle she didn't shoot you on sight. She said you claimed to be working on her boyfriend's case, on his homicide, but that when she called to check, Seattle P.D. said no."

In less than a minute, Harding and I had gone from adversaries to allies. The shift was so sudden, it almost made me dizzy.

"There are two other detectives who are actually assigned to the case," I told him. "I've been working it anyway. I felt like it."

"Oh," Harding replied with a nod. "I got that much from Watkins."

"Watkins?" I asked.

"You know, Watkins, your sergeant up there in Seattle. I talked to him just a little while ago while we were still trying to check you out."

If Harding had talked to Sergeant Watkins, then my tail was already in a gate but good.

"Wonderful," I said. Watty would be ripped, ready to chew me to pieces. So would Detective Paul Kramer.

I changed the subject. "Is that when she called you for help, then, after they told her I wasn't assigned to the case?"

"She never called."

"She didn't? But what about the deputy who showed up at the house? How'd he get there?"

"We sent him out to notify her about what had happened to her mother and her brother. Someone from the brother's job had called us and asked us to let her know. As soon as she found out, she told the deputy about you. He radioed here for help while she loaded up her kids and headed for Seattle."

"To the hospital?" I asked.

Harding nodded. "Harborview. The burn unit." He cocked his head to one side and studied me. "I wonder what she would have done to you if my deputy hadn't turned up right then."

It was a sobering thought. "I don't want to think about it," I said. There was a pause. "Did she mention any tapes to you?"

Harding sat up straight, alert, interested. "Tapes? What kind of tapes?"

I shrugged. "Beats me. Videotapes. Cassettes maybe. She let something slip about tapes, something about them being hidden in a safe place where no one would be able to find them."

"So she thought you were after her or the tapes."

"Or maybe both. Somebody must want those tapes real bad."

Harding pulled a small notebook from his pocket and jotted something into it. "I'll call Watkins and have him put a guard on her."

"Good idea. On her brother, too," I added.

"Tell me more about the tapes."

I shrugged. "I don't know anything else, except if they were in her mother's house, they're gone now."

"Burned up?"

"That's right. I understand it's a total loss. Not so much as a toothpick left standing."

I didn't want to think about the house or Leona and Jimmy Rising, especially not Jimmy, but Harding had given me an opening.

"How'd the fire start?"

"Gas hot-water heater exploded. I guess initially the fire investigators thought it was an accident, but it didn't take long for them to figure out otherwise. Not Linda, though. She knew right off."

"Knew what?"

"That it wasn't an accident. As soon as the deputy told her, she said 'They did it again.' And she was right. By then the arson guys in Bellevue had discovered that someone had messed around with the water-heater controls."

"And since I had been seen in the neighborhood the day before . . ."

Harding nodded. "You got it. Everybody jumped to the wrong conclusion, including Linda Decker who figured you were after her even *before* she heard about the fire."

"If I'd been in her shoes, I probably would have thought the same thing," I said.

We were quiet for several moments and then Harding stood up. Slowly. Leaning against the desk for support like a man whose back hurts if he straightens up too fast.

"Come on," he said. "We'll go back over to my office and get your stuff. I had your car towed into a garage here in town. No charge, of course, but we'll have to bail it out of there before you'll be able to head home."

By eleven o'clock, I was back on I-5 heading north. It had taken time to get my car out of the impound lot and then hours more at the St. Helen's Hospital emergency room. They said my nose was broken but my shoulder wasn't. I could have told them that myself, but Harding insisted on doing it right.

As I drove, there was a dull ache in my shoulder where I'd fallen on the floor thanks to my friend Jamie. If it hurt this much already, by the next day it would be giving me fits. I was almost sorry I hadn't accepted the doc's offer of a painkiller, but I figured that and driving home to Seattle were contraindicated.

It was less than twelve hours from the time I had turned off the freeway onto Highway 6 going to Pe Ell. Twelve hours and a lifetime ago.

Those are the kind of hours that make a man old before his time. Driving home that night I was feeling downright ancient.

When the elevator door slipped open on the twenty-fifth floor of Belltown Terrace, an ocean of garlic washed over me. The garlic was thick enough that I could smell it despite my broken nose. Without opening the door I knew Ralph Ames was inside my apartment, cooking up a storm. My interior designer created a kitchen that unleashes Ames' culinary genius.

As I walked in the door, Ames glanced up from ladling a pot full of fettucini Alfredo into one of my best bowls. "How about a midnight snack," he grinned. "I'll bet you're starved."

Two places were set in the dining room. The middle of the table held a large wooden bowl of tossed salad as well as an uncorked bottle of wine.

I had kicked off my shoes and was shrugging out of my jacket when Ames came into the dining room and put the bowl of fettucini on the table. He gave me an appraising look.

"Other than a pair of shiners and a hole in your knee, how are you, Beau?"

I knew about the hole in my knee, but shiners? "You're shitting me."

Ames shook his head. "Go look for yourself," he said.

I did, he was right. I looked like hell.

"What did you do, walk into a door?"

"An eight-by-ten timber," I answered.

"Same difference. Are you hungry?"

"You bet." It had been some time since that long-ago breakfast Marilyn Sykes had fed me. I may not be the type to cook fettucini, but I certainly don't object to eating it. I dished up a mountain of salad and started on that while Ames poured two glasses of wine.

"By the way," he said. "Marilyn Sykes called here looking for you a couple of times. I told her you'd give her a call as soon as we finished eating. Hope you don't mind, but I filled her in on some of the details."

"Things would be a hell of a lot different if I had been home alone in my own little beddy-bye," I said. "Marilyn's alibi was what did the trick."

One of the things I appreciate most about Ames is that he's not above saying he told me so, but he doesn't usually rub my nose in it. He simply nodded. "I figured as much," he said.

"There are a few other messages as well," he added. "Two calls from Sergeant Watkins, and one from someone named Kramer. He sounded real upset. What's this all about?"

And so, during the course of our late-night dinner, I explained to Ralph Ames what I could about what was going on. I told him about finding Logan Tyree's body and about what I regarded as the erroneous determination of accidental death. I told him about Logan Tyree's womenfolk, his moderately grief-stricken widow and his grieving ex-fiancée. I told him about my meeting with Jimmy Rising and the subsequent fire. Sometime later, over wine, I even remembered to tell him about Angie Dixon and the news photo that had captured her fatal plunge from Masters Plaza.

Ralph Ames listened to it all, nodding from time to time, asking questions periodically. "There does seem to be a pattern," he observed when I finished. "Certainly with Logan Tyree the killer or killers went to some length to make his death look like an accident. And the woman falling off the building sounds like an accident, too. Is there any connection between them?"

"Between Logan and Angie Dixon?" I shook my head. "Other than the fact that they were in the same union, there's no connection that I know of. Logan Tyree taught a certified welding class for apprentices. Presumably Angie Dixon was in Logan's class."

"The same one, you think?"

I shrugged. "Maybe, or maybe a later one."

"But you think they all knew each other?"

"Probably."

"What are you going to do about it?" Ames asked.

"Nothing. Not a goddamned thing. From now on, it's hands off as far as I'm concerned."

Ames smiled. "I'm glad you're being sensible for a change, Beau. From what he said on the phone, I'm afraid Sergeant Watkins will insist on it."

That turned out to be something of an understatement.

Chapter 15

I DIDN'T go to the department the next day. I didn't have to. The mountain came to Mohammed. Sergeant Watkins turned up on the security phone downstairs at ten after eight. Once Watty was inside my apartment, Ralph Ames stayed around only long enough to say a polite hello and then made himself scarce while the sergeant and I retreated into the den.

"Coffee?" I asked.

Watty shook his head. "It's not a social visit. Just what the hell do you think you're pulling, Beau? Since when do homicide detectives go out and investigate any damn case they please? Since when did I stop making the assignments?"

"I didn't do it on purpose. It just happened. You know how that Tyree case started. He floated up right under my nose while I was working on the movie set. I know I wasn't assigned, but I was involved. I couldn't help it."

"That's bullshit, Beau, and you know it. 'I couldn't help it' is an excuse a little kid uses on his mother after he wets his pants. You didn't *try* to help it. You got a wild hair up your ass that Kramer and Manny had it all wrong, and you set out hell-bent for leather to prove it."

"Maybe," I said.

"Maybe nothing! What's going on between you and Kramer anyway? He's been in my office twice this week complaining that you were messing around in his case. Bird-dogging him. I told him he was full of it, that you were working on the movie and later that you were on vacation. Obviously I was wrong. The shit is really going to hit the fan when he finds out about what happened yesterday.''

"I think he already has. He called here last night before I got home.''

"But you didn't talk to him?''

I shook my head. "Not yet.''

"If I were you, Beau, I'd do some pretty serious thinking before I called him. He's pissed as hell, and he has every right to be. So's Manny. The homicide squad's based on teamwork, remember? We're supposed to work together, all of us. I don't need some loose cannon rolling around on deck screwing up the works for everybody.''

There wasn't a damn thing I could say, because I knew Watty was right, and he was only warming up.

"We've worked together for a long time, Beau, been through the wars together, but you left me with my ass hanging out on this one. I spent all day yesterday dodging bullets in every direction. Calls from upstairs, calls from the press, and yes, goddamnit, calls from some of my own squad. All of 'em asking the same thing. All of 'em wanting to know what the hell was going on and how the hell you ended up in that woman's basement without any clothes on.''

"Shorts,'' I put in lamely. "I still had my shorts on.''

"Big fucking deal. Tell me about it. What happened?''

I took a deep breath. "I was convinced that Logan Tyree's death wasn't an accident.''

"That's no answer,'' Watty interrupted. "Harbor Patrol disagrees with you. So does the Coast Guard. And the same goes for Manny Davis and Paul Kramer. Logan Tyree's their baby, and don't you forget it.''

"But you asked me how it happened and I'm telling you. I was interested, so I talked to people—his friends, his ex-wife, people he worked with. They all said the same thing, that Tyree was careful, exceptionally careful, that he wouldn't have been out in a boat without the fume sensors and the blower working properly.''

"That's it?'' Watty demanded. "That's all you had?''

"Then there was the fight with his girlfriend. One of the

neighbors said they had a serious quarrel and that they broke up a week or so before it happened.''

"Breaking up with his girlfriend days before he died doesn't tell me Logan Tyree was murdered.''

"There was something else as well. Tyree told his neighbor that he had to take some kind of action. I forget the words exactly, but something about a man doing what a man has to do.''

"And this neighbor . . .''

"His name's Corbett, Red Corbett.''

"What else did he tell you?''

"He gave me Linda Decker's name. Told me how to get in touch with her.''

"How come, Beau? Why'd this Red Corbett character spill his guts to you and not to Manny and Paul? I've got their reports. I remember seeing Corbett's name. He told them some of this, but not all.''

"Can I help it if Paul Kramer's an asshole?''

"Leave personalities out of this, Beau.''

I went on. "Corbett offered to give Manny and Kramer Linda's name, but they said they didn't need it. That since the death was an accident, the ex-wife's name was enough.''

Watty was shaking his head before I finished. "So they made a mistake. Kramer's new to homicide. He's entitled to some mistakes, but by the time they decided they did need to talk to her, Linda Decker was already gone. Not even her mother knew where she was. How'd you manage to find her when they couldn't?''

"I talked to her brother.''

"The retard? The one who's in the hospital?''

"Is that what Kramer told you about Jimmy Rising, that he's a retard?''

"Developmentally disabled. You like that better?''

"Look, Watty, whatever's wrong with him, Jimmy Rising is one hell of a nice guy. He would have told Kramer and Manny just what he told me if they had bothered to listen. They ran right over him, ignored him, treated him like shit.''

"And you didn't?''

"That's right.''

Watty leaned back on the couch and looked at me, his

arms folded over his chest. I had worked with Sergeant
Watkins for a long time, but I had never seen him so
thoroughly steamed.

"You're out to lunch on this one, Beau. This case,
accident or not, is none of your goddamned business."

"So I'll leave it alone," I said.

"You'd by God better!"

"What about the woman who fell off the building?"

"What about her?"

"Is that classified as an accident, too?"

"Are you saying the two deaths are related?"

"Can you prove they're not?"

After this exchange we sat there for several long moments with neither one of us speaking. Finally, abruptly,
Watty stood up to go.

"I came over here to tell you to mind your own business, Beau. It's not an official warning. Kramer hasn't
filed a grievance yet. If he does, then it will have to be
official, go across desks, through channels, and end up in
your file. But just because it isn't official yet, don't get the
idea that you're home free. You're not.

"I've known you for years, Beau. This isn't like you. I
know you're a good cop. I can't believe you'd pull such a
dumb-ass trick. With you down there by yourself, if that
crazy broad in Pe Ell had blown you away, it wouldn't
have done anybody a damn bit of good.

"I don't usually pay much attention to departmental
gossip. Neither do you, but I think it's time you did. This
is a hell of a nice place you have here. That 928 you drive
is a sweet little piece of machinery. I happen to know
where all of it came from, but you're getting a whole lot of
notoriety both inside and outside the department. People
are starting to talk about the playboy cop. When you go
around pulling fool stunts like this, it sure as hell adds fuel
to the fire."

I must have winced when he said it. The words "playboy cop" had hurt badly enough when I heard them from
Paul Kramer. Coming from Watty, from someone I've
worked with for years, someone I respect, they cut clear to
the bone.

He didn't miss my reaction. "So you have heard it then," Watty said.

I nodded.

"Being a cop isn't something you do when you feel like it. It isn't something you do now and then just to keep your hand in. It's not a goddamned part-time job. It's something you do because you have to, because it's in your blood. But you do it by the rules. If you're tired of those rules, if you're tired of taking orders and being on the team, then quit. Get the hell out.

"Your net worth doesn't mean a damn thing to me, Beaumont. It doesn't make you sergeant. I'm still calling the shots. I assign the cases, and my people answer to me. I don't need any goddamned Lone Ranger on my squad. I won't tolerate it, and if you've got a problem with that, then maybe you'd better make this vacation permanent or put in for a transfer. You got that?"

"I've got it," I said.

I followed Watty to the door. He opened it and stepped into the hallway, then he turned back. "If I were you, I'd have someone take a look at that nose. It looks broken to me."

I watched him go. Watty had just climbed all over my frame, but he still worried about my goddamned broken nose. That hurt almost as much as the ass-chewing.

Ralph Ames came out of the guest room with an empty coffee cup in one hand and a fistful of papers in the other. He had told me that as long as he was in Seattle he could just as well do some work for the Belltown Terrace real-estate syndicate and save himself another trip later.

"How was it?" he asked, refilling his cup.

"Pretty rough," I said. "Watty told me to shape up or ship out. Either get back on the team or get the hell off it altogether. From the sound of it, he doesn't much care which way it goes."

"I see," Ames said and let it go at that. He took the fresh cup of coffee and disappeared into the guest room, leaving me to stew in my own juices.

There was plenty of stewing to do. Over the years, I've been in varying degrees of hot water on occasion, but that's not unusual among detectives. As a breed we're the ones who ask the questions, who ferret out information people often don't want us to have. It's a world that attracts pragmatists—self-starters with strong streaks of independence.

I had been reprimanded before, called on the carpet and brought back to heel, but never anything like this. Watty's words had gutted me, hit all my professional cop buttons, and left me empty, with nothing to say in my own defense because I knew damn good and well he was right. I had been out of line, off the charts.

Pouring myself a cup of coffee, I took it out on the balcony and stood looking down at the street far below, hoping the sound of morning commuter traffic hurrying down Second Avenue would help lessen the sting of Watty's departing words, but it didn't. Nothing could. Because for everything Watty had said, I could add three more burning indictments of my own.

Of course I should have gone to Manny Davis and Paul Kramer and told them what I had found out, what I suspected. Of course I shouldn't have driven to Pe Ell to question Linda Decker alone. Going without a backup was stupid. Inexcusable.

The personality conflict between Kramer and me was like a couple of little boys duking it out on a playground, fighting over who ruled a small square of gravel turf or who got the biggest swing. But I had let that little-boy game overshadow my professional judgment.

Professional? Who the hell was I to call myself a professional?

The phone rang, interrupting the self-flagellation. I was sure it was Kramer, and I started rehearsing my apology as I went to pick up the receiver. Instead it was Peters, calling from the hospital.

"So you made it back all right after all." He sounded relieved.

"Yeah," I said. "I should have called you last night, but it was too late. Sorry."

"Don't worry about that. How are things?"

"Watty was just here and reamed me out good. I deserved it."

"One thing to be thankful for, though. At least the

papers didn't name names this morning. They called you an 'unidentified off-duty Seattle Police officer.' "

"So it's in the paper today?"

"Front and center."

"Great. Did the article say anything about Linda Decker's brother?"

"The one who got burned? Only that he's in the burn unit down here at Harborview. Critical condition. Intensive care. You know what that's like."

"One step away from the Spanish Inquisition."

Peters laughed ruefully. "Something like that," he said. "I assume Watty told you hands off?"

"In a manner of speaking," I allowed.

Peters knew me well enough to sense that what I said was only the tip of the iceberg, but he didn't press the issue. Instead, he went on to something else. "Has Maxine gotten hold of you to arrange a schedule for Bumbershoot?" he asked.

I had forgotten all about the outing I had promised Peters' girls. "No," I said guiltily. "She hasn't caught up with me. I've been a moving target."

"Maxine called here yesterday and said that she heard that kids get in free on Friday. She wondered if it would be possible for you to take them then. She's got a doctor's appointment in the early afternoon. Otherwise, she'll have to locate another sitter."

"Tell her that'll be fine. By tomorrow afternoon, I'm sure time will be hanging heavy on my hands. Tell her to send them up here about eleven. We'll eat lunch over at Seattle Center."

"Okay," he said, "I'll let her know." He paused. "Don't kick yourself too much, Beau. You never would have done it if I hadn't been egging you on from the sidelines, remember?"

"Sure," I said, and we hung up.

I know Peters was trying to make me feel better, but it didn't work. When you've been flat on your back in bed for six months, you're allowed some lapses in judgment. When you're still supposedly dealing with a full deck, when you're still walking around upright, carrying a badge and packing a loaded .38, it's a whole different ball game.

Ames came out of the bedroom again. He was dressed in a suit and tie, briefcase in hand. He found me sitting in the chair by the telephone, staring off into space. He set the case down on the table for a moment and stood there looking at me.

"You could always quit, you know," he said.

"Quit?"

"The force. You don't need to work if you don't want to."

The realization that Watty might fire me had shaken me to my very core, but the idea of quitting had never crossed my mind.

"It's what I've always done," I said.

Ames shrugged. "Maybe that's reason enough to make a change. Lots of men your age do, you know," he added quietly. He picked up the briefcase again and started toward the door. "What are you going to do today?"

"I don't know yet," I said. "I'm going to have to think about it."

After Ames left, the silence in the room was oppressive. I felt restless, ill at ease. Unbidden, Jimmy Rising came to mind. I remembered how much he had wanted to go to work the day he missed the bus, how proud he had been of the thermos and the lunch pail. Well, he wasn't going to work now. The micrographics department at the Northwest Center would have to do without him for awhile. Maybe forever. The burn unit at Harborview is good, but they can't always work miracles.

I wasn't conscious of making the decision. Like an old war-horse that doesn't have sense enough to quit, I got up, put on my holster and my jacket. With my hand on the doorknob I paused. Would going to the hospital to see Jimmy Rising be considered meddling in Paul Kramer's case?

No, goddamnit. Sergeant Watkins could fire my ass if he wanted to, but I was going to go to the hospital and pay my respects to Jimmy Rising come hell or high water.

Chapter 16

WHEN I got on the elevator at Harborview, force of habit made me push the button to floor four where Peters is instead of nine for the burn unit ICU. A couple of uniformed nurses who were also in the elevator were openly contemptuous when I got off, looked around in confusion, and then got back on before the elevator continued up.

I've been in the burn unit before. I know the routine. Because recovering burn patients are so susceptible to infection, visitors are required to don sterile clothing before entering patients' rooms. The problem was, whenever I'd gone there before, it was always as a police officer on official business which gave me the secret password for admittance.

This time, I had no such magic wand. It was easy to tell which was Jimmy Rising's room. A uniformed officer, crossed arms resting on his chest, was seated on a folding chair outside a closed door just up from the nurses' station. When I asked about Jimmy Rising, the ward clerk, a scrawny man with an equally scrawny beard, eyeballed me thoroughly up and down. "Are you a member of the family?" he asked.

"No, just a friend."

"Mr. Rising is in no condition to have visitors," the ward clerk announced firmly. "Family members are allowed in for a few minutes each hour, but that's all."

I stood there flat-footed with no possible argument or comeback. The guard glanced in my direction, and I gave him a halfhearted wave. What the threat of losing my job had failed to accomplish, hospital bureaucracy did without a moment's hesitation.

I must have looked crestfallen enough that the ward clerk took pity on me. "If you'd care to leave something for him, I'll be sure it reaches him," he offered.

Nodding my thanks, I made my way back down the short hallway to the main corridor. Leave Jimmy Rising something? What? A note, a card, flowers? Before I knew it, I was standing in front of a gray-haired clerk in the gift shop on the main floor, and I still hadn't made up my mind.

"May I help you, sir?" she asked.

"Some flowers, I guess," I answered stupidly.

She pointed toward a refrigerated display. "What we have available is right there. Is this for an adult? A child?"

I looked at the display. It was an uninspiring batch of tired flowers in equally tired receptacles—the milk-white, lumpy-glass kind so popular in hospitals, with one or two ceramic teddy bears thrown in for good measure.

"An adult," I said.

"Man or woman? Does this person have any particular preferences?"

She was trying hard to be helpful. The problem was, I didn't know anything at all about Jimmy Rising's preference in flowers. All I knew about him was what I had learned during that brief afternoon interview on his porch and the equally short ride to the Northwest Center in Seattle. I could still see him sitting there on the top step, carefully pouring orange juice into the cup from his thermos.

And all at once it hit me. I knew exactly what Jimmy Rising needed. It had nothing at all to do with flowers.

"Never mind," I told the startled lady behind the counter. "I don't think he likes flowers."

With that, I beat it out the door and headed for the car. Smiling to myself, I made my way down to Jackson Street.

Welch Fuel and Hardware has been doing business on Jackson for as long as I can remember. I first saw the store years ago when I was a rookie. Back then it was a hole in the wall next to a Safeway store. Gradually the neighborhood changed, transforming into Seattle's less than malignant version of inner-city squalor. The grocery store had pulled out altogether, but not the hardware store. It had quietly expanded to include both buildings. While the neighborhood around it had slowly deteriorated, the store itself had unobtrusively prospered.

The displays seemed crowded and jumbled. Just because some item was no longer manufactured didn't mean it wasn't still available in some hidden nook or cranny of the store. The clerks, all of them old hands, knew what they had and where to find it. When asked, one of them pointed me to an aisle halfway down the long room. "The lunch pails are over there," he said. "You'll find the thermos there, too."

I found what I wanted without any trouble on a crammed shelf bulging with housewares. There was a huge shiny black lunch pail for $10.88 and a stainless-steel thermos for three times that. I took them both off the shelf and went up to the cash register.

"You do gift-wrapping here?" I asked.

The clerk gave me an odd look. I don't know if it was because requests for gift-wrapping are that unusual or because my two black eyes, not black so much as deep purple, made me look like death warmed over.

"Not here, we don't," he said at last.

With no further comment, he rang up my two purchases and put them in a plain brown paper bag. They were still in the bag a few minutes later when I carried them up to the nurses' station in the burn unit at Harborview. The same ward clerk was still on duty.

"I see you found something," he said.

"Yes," I answered. I took the thermos and lunch pail out of the sack and put them on the counter in front of him. He seemed dismayed by my choice. He was expecting flowers. I didn't bother to explain. "Could I use a paper and pen to write a note?"

"Sure," he answered.

I was just signing my name to a brief note when a woman's voice interrupted me. "What are you doing here?"

The voice was all too familiar. I had heard it before. I looked up quickly and almost dropped the pen. Linda Decker was standing right beside me, loosening a surgical mask that covered the lower half of her face. Without the gun she was much smaller than I remembered, but every bit as scary.

"I brought him something," I said evenly, unsure how she would react to my presence, much less to what I had brought. I folded the note and stuck it under the latch on the lunch pail. Warily I glanced over at Linda Decker. She wasn't looking at me. She was staring at the lunch pail, tears welling up in her eyes.

Without a word, she reached out and stroked the shiny metal handle. It was almost a mirror image of what Jimmy Rising had done that day on the porch. "He may not live to see them," she managed.

"It's that bad?" I asked.

She nodded. "Less than fifty-fifty." She started crying in dead earnest then.

Quickly the ward clerk came around the counter and put a protective arm around her shoulder. "Come on, Mrs. Decker," he said quietly. "Let's get you in where you can sit down and rest for a few minutes. You've had a long day of it."

Worried about who I was and what I was up to, the guard hurried over as well, but Linda waved him away and allowed the ward clerk to lead her down the hall. As he did so, he glared at me over his shoulder as though he believed I was somehow personally responsible. He didn't order me to leave, however, and I followed them into a small waiting room around the corner. The room was windowless and crowded with furniture, the air thick with the smoke of a thousand despairing cigarettes. Still sobbing, Linda Decker sank onto one of the couches.

The clerk stepped away from her and saw me at the door. "I think maybe you'd better go," he said to me. "She needs to sit here and rest. She's had a rough night."

With a shrug, I started to leave. There was no sense in arguing. "No, it's all right," Linda Decker mumbled through her tears, as she groped for a tissue. "Let him stay."

I don't know who was more surprised, the ward clerk or J. P. Beaumont. The clerk shook his head dubiously. "All right. If you say so. What about the thermos and lunch pail?"

"Put them in Jimmy's room," Linda Decker said. "Put them somewhere so he'll be able to see them if he ever gets a chance."

The ward clerk gave me one last disparaging look and left. I stood there awkwardly, not knowing what to say or do, while Linda searched for another tissue and blew her nose. There was a coffee pot and a stack of styrofoam cups sitting on a table across the room. The light was on and the coffee smelled as though it had been there for hours.

"Would you like a cup of coffee?" I offered.

She nodded. "Please."

"Black?"

She nodded again. I poured two cups and brought them back to where she was sitting on the couch. Her hand shook as she took the cup from me. "Thank you," she said. The room was stuffy and hot, but she sat there shivering for several moments with both hands wrapped around the cup as though hoping to draw warmth out of the coffee and into her hands. She stared unseeing through a wavering column of steam.

"I'm sorry about what happened," she said, her voice almost a whisper. "Someone named Powell was here a little while ago. He said that you're a good cop, that you wouldn't be mixed up in anything crooked."

Under any other circumstance, a vote of confidence from Captain Larry Powell would have been welcome, but in this instance I was sorry to hear that he too had been dragged into the melee.

"It's all right," I answered. "You don't need to apologize. If I'd been in your shoes, I probably would have done the same thing."

She looked up at me, her face pained. "No, it's not all right. That was my fault, and so is this. Jimmy went back to get Patches." She broke off and put one hand over her mouth to stifle an involuntary sob.

"Patches?" I asked.

"A dog. A stupid stuffed dog that I gave him years ago. The firemen got him out of the house all right, but he broke away and went back after the dog. He was right in the doorway when the roof came down. He was completely engulfed in flames."

"Just because you gave him the dog doesn't make you responsible."

"You don't understand, do you." It was an accusation.

"I guess not."

"I used Jimmy as bait!" The last word was a cry of anguish torn from her body, one that left her doubled over and weeping. Unnoticed, the coffee spilled onto the floor beside her. I found a roll of paper towels and began to soak up the mess.

"Bait?" I asked, when she finally quieted. "What do you mean, bait?"

"Jimmy can't lie," she answered. "I knew if I told him where I was and if anyone asked him, he would tell them. After Logan and Angie, I figured I was next on the killer's list. And I was ready for him, ready and waiting. But you came instead."

I nodded. She closed her eyes and put one hand over them, shaking her head as if to deny the reality of what had happened. "I didn't think he'd hurt Jimmy and Mom. It never occurred to me."

My ears pricked up at the word "he." Not some name-less, faceless, sexless entity. Not some vague numberless they. But he. One person—a single, identifiable, male, he.

"Do you know who that person is?" I asked the question gently. I never considered not asking it. I'm a cop. They pay me to ask questions, but I was finally learning that for me asking questions is more than just a job. It's as necessary as breathing, a cornerstone of existence, and this time I was asking for free.

Slowly Linda Decker raised her head. Her eyes met mine and she nodded.

"Who?" I asked.

"Martin Green."

I tried to contain my reaction. Martin Green. The iron-worker union executive director who was busy creating a "more perfect union." The same man who lived in my building and who had thrown a temper tantrum because his mother didn't get to ride home from the airport in the Bentley.

"Are you sure? Do you have any proof?"

"The night he was killed, Logan had an appointment with Green to tell him about the tapes. He called and told me so. I begged him not to go. I told him it was too dangerous, that they wouldn't tolerate someone messing up their little racket."

There were the tapes again, the tapes she had mentioned before.

"What tapes?"

"The accounting tapes. The ones Angie stole."

"Wait a minute. Angie Dixon? The woman who fell off Masters Plaza?" Linda Decker nodded. It was all coming together too fast. So there was a connection between Logan Tyree and Angie Dixon.

"Angie didn't fall," Linda said grimly. "I can't prove it, but I know she was pushed."

"One thing at a time. Tell me about the tapes."

"Angie used to work for a guy named Wayne Martinson. He kept the books for the local."

"More than one set?" I asked speculatively.

Linda looked at me quickly. "How did you know that?" she asked.

"It fits," I answered.

"Angie wanted to make more money. Martinson had her working part-time at minimum wage. Guys working iron make good money. Eventually, through her job, Angie figured out there was a lot of hanky-panky going on— people buying and selling union books, people bypassing the apprenticeship program, boomers paying to get put on the A-list. She started stealing the tapes. Not the journal entries, just the tapes. She took them at night as she left work."

"And then she blackmailed somebody to let her into the union?"

Linda shook her head. "That was what was funny. It ended up she didn't have to. They let her in anyway."

"But I thought you said . . ."

"Nobody knew anything about it, until this party thing came up. I think she was too scared to tell."

"What party thing?"

"International sent out an inspection team. Probably because of what happened to Wayne."

"Wayne?"

"Martinson, the bookkeeper."

"What did happen to him?"

"He went salmon fishing in Alaska last month and never came back. He's officially listed as missing. They haven't found his body."

"Another ironworker accident? How come nobody made the connection?"

"Wayne didn't just work for the ironworkers," she said. "He worked for several different unions."

"You mentioned something about a party."

"According to Don Kaplan, Martin Green expected some of us to show up and improve the scenery at his little get-together. A command performance. I figured he wanted to create enough of a smoke screen so no one would figure out what had really been going on. He's big on public relations."

Remembering the attractive young women scattered here and there around Martin Green's apartment the night I crashed his party, I suddenly saw that party in a far different and more ominous light. So that's what had been going on.

"And you were supposed to be part of the scenery?"

"Show up or else. That was the way Don Kaplan put it. We'd have drinks and dinner and guess who was supposed to be dessert."

"Angie Dixon too?"

Linda nodded. "That's when she went crying to Logan about the tapes."

"And what did you do?"

"I called Green on it. Told him I'd see him in hell before I'd do that. I turned in my union book and told him he could shove it up his ass."

"So you quit, but you said Angie went crying to Logan?"

Linda bit her lip and nodded.

"Logan didn't know about the tapes before?"

"Nobody did except Angie. He thought he could put a stop to it. I told him he was crazy, that he should mind his own business, but he was determined."

"Is that what you two broke up over, about his going after Green?"

She hesitated. "No," she said quietly.

"What then?"

"Angie. Logan was too naive, too big-hearted and honest to see that she was making a play for him. He asked me to copy the tapes. When I found out we had copied them for her, that was the last straw."

We were back to the tapes again. "But you did copy them."

"I didn't. Jimmy did."

"Jimmy!"

"I guess Sandy Carson over at the center is the one who actually did the copying. Logan had met her several times when we took Jimmy over to the center or went by to pick him up."

"Sandy Carson, the one who runs the micrographics department?"

"That's the one. And that's where the tapes still are, in a file in her office. Not the originals. I'm sure Logan had those with him on the boat. But the copies are there, on microfiche. After Logan died, I told Sandy that if anything happened to me, she should turn them over to the police. Angie knew about the copies, not where they were, but that they existed. I tried to warn her that she was in danger, but she didn't want to listen any more than Logan did. They both thought as long as the copies were safe, so were they."

"But she wasn't," I added. "And neither was Logan. Why didn't you come forward with this earlier, Linda? Why did you keep it quiet?"

"The cops insisted from the beginning that Logan's death was an accident. Martin Green has lots of money, lots of pull. I figured there was a payoff somewhere along the line."

Linda Decker stopped speaking. For several moments I couldn't think of anything else to ask. I didn't like her all too easy assumption that homicide cops were on the take. "Stupidity, maybe," I said finally. "Bullheadedness maybe, but not payoffs."

Linda Decker nodded. I wasn't sure whether or not she was convinced until she spoke. "I really was wrong about you, wasn't I," she said quietly.

"Yes."

"I'm sorry," she said again. "I know after what happened yesterday, I've got no right to ask, but you came here this morning because of . . ." She stopped and swallowed. "Because of Jimmy. You must care, or you wouldn't . . ." She paused again. "Will you help me, Detective Beaumont? I don't know where else to turn."

For the first time, in all the while we had been talking, Watty's words reverberated in my head. Keep your goddamned nose out of it. Mind your own business. And here I was, back in it up to my neck.

Linda Decker was looking at me, pleading, waiting for my answer.

"I don't know what I can do," I told her at last, "but I'll do what I can."

It wasn't much, but what the hell. I've always been a soft touch.

Chapter 17

As I went down in the elevator, I got off at four to see Peters. His bed was empty, and his roommate told me he was down the hall lifting weights in the gym.

"What's the matter with you?" Peters asked as soon as he saw my face. "Aside from the fact that you look like somebody beat you to a bloody pulp."

"It's a long story," I replied.

In a quiet corner of the small gym, Peters sat in his wheelchair and listened while I told him what Linda Decker had said.

When I finished, he nodded his head. "You don't have much of a choice, do you. Like it or not, you're going to have to talk to Manny and Kramer."

"That's the way it looks."

"Linda Decker doesn't have any solid proof?"

I shook my head. "Only the tapes."

"That's not much to go on. Purely circumstantial."

"Purely," I agreed. "The problem is, if somebody doesn't start looking in the right places pretty damn soon, there's never going to be anything *but* circumstantial evidence."

Peters looked thoughtful. "What about this Martinson guy, the one who disappeared in Alaska? Is anyone down at the department following up on that case?"

"I don't know. Missing Persons, maybe. Without a body, it wouldn't have come to homicide."

"Did she say where in Alaska?"

"No."

"It's a big place. Maybe I can do some checking on that from here."

I got up.

"Where are you going?" Peters asked.

"To find Kramer and see if there's any way to eat crow and still keep my self-respect."

Peters looked at me, his eyes serious and steady. "Sounds to me like you'll have to find a way to do both," he said.

I nodded and started to leave, giving him an affectionate whack on the shoulder on my way past. "Thanks for the fatherly advice," I said.

He grinned. "Anytime. Advice is freely and cheerfully given."

Outside the hospital, the sky was a clear, unremitting blue. I was tired of summer, tired of blue skies, and tired of the sideways glances people gave me when they caught sight of my face. I needed to go somewhere to think. In the end I sought out the shady serenity of the Japanese garden in the Arboretum. There, beside a small, quiet pool, I sat for a full hour, trying to marshal my thoughts into some sort of reasonable order.

According to Linda Decker, we were dealing with union fraud perpetrated by thugs who didn't hesitate at murder. There were four victims dead already, if you counted Wayne Martinson, the guy missing in Alaska. Four and a half, if you counted Jimmy Rising in the burn unit at Harborview.

Martin Green and whoever else might be involved had to be stopped, one way or the other, and I sure as hell wanted to be part of the process, part of the solution. There was a major barrier to my doing just that—my bullheaded, bullnecked nemesis, Paul Kramer.

And I couldn't very well go to Kramer with nothing in hand but a lame apology and some farfetched suppositions, wild-sounding accusations from Linda Decker, a lady who had lost big. Someone who has suffered that many losses is going to have a vested interest in seeing the situation resolved, in pinning the crimes on someone regardless of how remote.

I had to have something more solid than Linda Decker's unsubstantiated allegations. I had to come up with something powerful enough to jar Detective Kramer out of our juvenile rivalry and make him pay attention, take action, preferably some action other than going straight to Sergeant Watkins and having my wings clipped.

That brought me back to the question of what was actually solid. The tapes. The microfiche copy of the tapes. And what else? In my mind, I went back over everything Linda Decker had said. What was it about the union? What all had she claimed they were doing? Selling union books, taking payoffs to let people bypass the apprenticeship program.

But those kinds of bribes only worked if the applicant had plenty of money available. For women, especially poor ones like Angie Dixon and Linda Decker, maybe the rats running the scam had been willing to take it out in trade, in services rendered, services that never made it onto Wayne Martinson's accounting tapes. Like being dessert at Martin Green's party for instance.

And what about Martinson's books, the journals themselves? Where were they? Despite what Angie and Linda had believed, the tapes themselves weren't that damning, not without the journal entries to go with them. But who had them? Had Martinson taken them with him on his ill-fated fishing trip, or were they still in his office somewhere? Or—and this was far more likely—had they been removed by person or persons unknown shortly after his disappearance?

I went back once more to what Linda had said about the union. Something was bothering me—something I couldn't quite put a finger on kept nagging at me, scratching at the door to my subconscious, demanding admittance. The union books, the apprenticeship program, and something else, a third item. At last it came to me. Boomers. That was it.

Boomers from out of town paying to get put on the A-list, that top work list of members who got called out first. Every union on earth has those kinds of lists, and every union comes equipped with a whole catalog of by-laws to say what you have to do to get on that list.

Well, I just happened to know a boomer—Fred McKinney, Katherine Tyree's fiancé. He had dropped into the Seattle union hall and landed on the ironworker's A-list close enough to the top that he had worked on Columbia Center, Seattle's newest showcase high rise. Reason told me that work on that particular building would have been the private preserve of local hands no matter what trade union was involved.

Maybe, if Fred had paid bribe money, and maybe if he knew the same people had been involved in Logan Tyree's death, he would be willing to come forward and name names. Often, just knowing that we're nosing around in the right direction is enough to spook crooks into doing something stupid.

And there was Don Kaplan, the guy on the balcony at Martin Green's party. Unless I missed my guess, Angie Dixon's death had gotten him where he lived. He had seemed nice enough. If I tracked him down, it might be that he could shed some light on the subject.

About that time a busload of camera-carrying tourists came wandering through the Arboretum and interrupted my reverie. I turned toward the water, keeping my face and black eyes averted from the clicking cameras. I heard some whispered gritching to the effect that I should have sense enough to move on so people could get a better shot of the pool. I refused to take the hint.

By the time they left, I found myself thinking about Angie Dixon. Linda Decker's comments were the first real link between Logan Tyree and Angie Dixon. I had theorized that there might be a connection, but now I knew for sure it existed. Logan and Angie had indeed known each other. Enough to make Linda jealous. Enough that Angie had confided in Logan about the tapes. Why did she find it necessary?

And if Linda was right, if Angie had been pushed, who had pushed her? Suddenly, the haunting picture from the paper came back to me as clearly as if I were holding it in my hand. In my mind's eye, I once more saw Angie Dixon plunging to her death. A comic-book light bulb clicked on over my head as I realized the picture might hold the key to the puzzle.

Adrenaline coursed through my body—adrenaline and

questions. How many pictures were on that roll? How often were the pictures taken? And was there a chance, even a remote one, that another shot, taken earlier or later, might provide a clue as to what had gone on in the minutes before and after Angie's fatal plunge?

Getting a look at that film, prying it loose from whoever owned it was something only officialdom could accomplish, and officialdom would go to work on it only if I filled Manny Davis and Paul Kramer in on what was happening. It was time to straighten up and fly right, no matter how much I didn't want to do it.

I left the Arboretum and drove back downtown, conscious as I drove that it was after lunch and I had eaten nothing since Ralph Ames' midnight fettucini. The 928 headed for the Doghouse on automatic pilot.

The Doghouse is disreputable enough that no one raised an eyebrow at my purple bruises. It's the kind of place that says "Breakfast Anytime'" and means it. That's what I had—bacon, eggs, toast, and coffee. Plenty of coffee. I didn't try calling the department until after I had finished eating. I believe it's called avoidance behavior. When I finally couldn't think of another plausible excuse to put it off any longer, I used the pay phone near the pinball machines.

I asked for Manny Davis. He wasn't in. I asked for Paul Kramer. He was. Too bad.

"Detective Kramer speaking."

"Hello, Paul. This is Beaumont."

Behind me some guy was racking up a huge score on the Doghouse's primo pinball machine. A group of enthusiastic buddies was cheering him on.

"Who?" Kramer demanded. "I can't hear you. There's too much noise in the background."

"Beaumont," I repeated, raising the volume. "I need to talk to you."

He paused. A long pause. "So talk. I'm listening."

At least he didn't hang up on me. I took a deep breath. "Not on the phone. I want to talk in person. To both you and Manny."

"Manny's busy. He's in court this afternoon."

"Well, to you then."

Behind me the pinball crowd cheered again.

"What's that? I can't hear you."

"To you then. Can you meet me?"

"Where?"

"Do you know where the Doghouse is at Seventh and Bell?"

"I know it," he answered. "What are you doing, out slumming, Beaumont?"

So that's how it was. He hadn't hung up on me, but we hadn't exactly kissed and made up, either. I didn't say anything.

"When?" Kramer demanded.

"As soon as you can get here."

He hung up and I went back to my table. My plate and dirty silverware had been cleared away. Left were a freshly poured cup of coffee and a newspaper with the unworked crossword puzzle folded out. The waitresses at the Doghouse take good care of me. That's one of the reasons I go there. It's got nothing to do with gourmet cuisine.

The crossword puzzle contained only three unfinished words by the time Detective Paul Kramer strode up to the table twenty minutes later.

"You wanted to see me?" he asked, easing his sizable frame into the booth across from me.

I set the nearly finished puzzle aside. "Wanting is probably overstating the case," I said. Kramer made as if to rise. "Sit," I ordered. He sat.

Jenny, the waitress, came to the table just then and offered him coffee which he accepted with a grudging nod. We sat without speaking until she finished pouring it and walked away, leaving us alone.

"What do you want? This ain't no pleasure trip for me, Beaumont, and I'm damned if I'm going to sit here while you dish out insults."

For some strange reason, the situation reminded me of the time years before when, at Karen's insistence, I had taken Scott to a local diner to administer the obligatory birds and bees talk. My son had been full of teenage resentment, angry and embarrassed both. In the end, the talk could in no way be called an unqualified success. We both went home frustrated and neither of us mentioned it again.

Now, with Detective Paul Kramer sitting across the table from me, I felt the air charged with the same kind of irritation and arrogance, the same counterproductive determination to miscommunicate. But that was where the similarity ended. With Scott and the birds and the bees, adult complacency had been on my side. I had known I was right and that time would bear me out. With Kramer I had no such delusions. He was right and I was wrong, and he didn't waste any time beating around the bush before he let me know it.

"Who the hell do you think you are that you can go messing around in my case?"

"I'm sorry," I said.

It wasn't what he expected. My two-word apology didn't derail him altogether, but it threw a real monkey wrench in his attack.

"Logan Tyree's our case," he went on. "Manny's and mine. You've got no business screwing with it."

"I know."

Kramer stopped and sat with his head cocked to one side, like someone who's afraid he's been suckered too far into enemy territory. "What did you want to see me for then?" he demanded.

Biding my time, I took a careful sip of my coffee. "Why'd you become a cop, Kramer?" I asked evenly.

"What is this, an occupational aptitude test?"

"Just tell me."

He shrugged. "It's something I have to do, that's all."

"You want to make the world a better place to live in?" I suggested.

"Something like that." He frowned. "What kind of deal is this, Beaumont? I'm here because I'm pissed as hell, and you sit there making fun of me."

"I'm not making fun of anybody, Kramer. I've never been more serious in my life."

Reluctantly, Kramer settled back in the booth, holding his cup while he studied me warily. He said nothing.

"And how long do you plan to be in homicide?" I asked.

"Me? As long as it takes."

"As long as it takes for what?"

"To be promoted out." At least we had cut through the bullshit. He was being honest.

"So you see homicide as a stepping-stone to bigger and better things?"

"There's nothing wrong with that," Kramer said defensively.

"I never said there was. What were you doing seventeen years ago?"

"Seventeen years ago?" He laughed. "I was thirteen and in the eighth grade down in Tumwater. What does that have to do with the price of peanuts?"

"Because seventeen years ago, I was just starting out in homicide. Fresh up from robbery, same as you are now."

"So?"

"It's my life's work, Kramer. I've never wanted to do anything else. I never saw homicide as a springboard. I do the job. I like it. I'm good at it.

"A few days ago, you called me a playboy cop. It hurt me real good, but I've been doing some thinking. It's true. I've got more money right now than I'll ever know what to do with. I could quit the force tomorrow and never have to work another day in my life, but you know what? I don't know what the hell I'd do with myself if I quit. There isn't anything else I'd rather do except maybe drink too much and die young."

Kramer shifted in his seat. "Why are you telling me all this? What's the point?"

"The point is, we're on the same team, Kramer. Different motivations maybe, but we work the same side of the street. Logan Tyree's death is important, far more so than anyone's figured out. Solve it, and you'll be a hero. Screw it up, and your time in homicide gets that much longer."

"Does that mean you know something we don't know?"

"Maybe," I said.

"You can't do this, Beaumont," he protested. "You can't withhold information and you know it."

"I'm not withholding anything. That's why I called you here, to tell you what I know. But I want in on it."

Kramer looked astonished. "You're going to ask Watty to put you on the case?"

I shook my head. "No, Kramer. You are."

"Why would I? And why do you want on the case?"

"Because I give a shit about Jimmy Rising and Linda Decker and Logan Tyree and Angie Dixon. Because I want to see the creeps who did this off the streets."

When I mentioned Angie Dixon's name, a spark of excitement came to life in Kramer's eyes. "The woman who fell. Did she have something to do with the others?"

I could see he needed to know the answer. As far as that was concerned, he was just like me, but I deliberately left him hanging without directly answering his question.

"I want in because I'm a good cop, Kramer. Because I've discovered things you need to know. I want this case solved. I want it every bit as much as you want to be Chief of Police."

I finished what I had to say and shut up. The cards were all on the table now. The question was, would he pick them up or not? There was a long silence. I was determined to wait him out. Selling Fuller Brush taught me that much. After you've made your pitch, keep quiet. The first one to open his mouth loses. I waited. The silence stretched out interminably.

"You want it that bad, do you?" Kramer said at last.

I nodded. "That bad."

"Then you'd better tell me what you know."

Eating crow was as simple as that.

Chapter 18

WHEN we left the Doghouse an hour and a half later, we had hammered out rough guidelines for an uneasy alliance. Kramer had called Watty, and Detective J. P. Beaumont was now officially part of the investigation into Logan Tyree's death. It was a big improvement over the other alternative of being flat-out fired.

We took Kramer's car and drove to the Northwest Center on Armory Way. The receptionist summoned Sandy Carson from the micrographics department. When she arrived, she was still blonde and still willowy, but she looked like hell. Her eyes were red. I'm sure she had been crying.

"I didn't want any visitors out in the shop today," she explained. "Everyone's still too upset about Jimmy. But Linda called and told me you'd be coming by. She said for me to give you this." She handed me a large brown interdepartmental envelope with its string fastener firmly tied.

"Who actually took the pictures?" I asked.

"Jimmy did. I supervised, of course."

"And do you have any idea what became of the originals?"

She shook her head. "I gave them to Logan when he came by and picked Jimmy up one day. He asked me to keep the copies here. He said he thought that would be safer."

"Do you remember when that was?"

"Several days before he died."

"And did you go to the police with it?"

"There wasn't any point. Everyone said it was an accident."

I glanced at Kramer, but I didn't say anything. There was no sense rubbing his nose in it.

"Any idea where we should go to take a look at these?" I asked.

Kramer nodded. "I know a place."

He drove us to the *Seattle Times* building on Fairview and pulled into the parking lot. "I know people here," he said. "They'll let us use their fiche reader. Not only that, maybe I can get a line on that Masters Plaza film."

One of my objections to the new breed of law enforcement officers is their total preoccupation with the media. These cops want to solve crimes, all right, but they also want the publicity. They want to be sure their names are spelled right in the papers, pronounced right on the eleven o'clock news. Old war-horses like Big Al Lindstrom and me don't give a damn what the media have to say one way or the other.

In this case, however, Detective Paul Kramer's cozy friendship with the Third Estate paid off. Kramer's buddy in the news department hooked us up with someone from photography. He said the picture of Angie Dixon had come to the paper through a local free-lance film editor. The guy at the *Times* wasn't sure exactly how that had transpired, and the person who had handled the transaction wasn't in, but he was able to tell us that the company actually doing the filming was a small outfit called Camera Craft in the Denny Regrade.

Kramer's buddy also let us use a microfiche reader. It didn't do us any good. The fiche showed nothing but accountant's tapes, some with barely legible notations on them. Without the accompanying journals, they were worthless.

Kramer leaned away from the viewer long enough to let me take a look. "None of this makes sense," he said. "These aren't something worth killing for. Are you sure this is what Linda Decker thought they were after?"

"Positive."

"So what now? Go down to Camera Craft?"

"Seems like."

We were told that the owner of Camera Craft was grabbing a late lunch at the Rendezvous, a small restaurant just up the block. We followed him there. Like other places in the Regrade, the Rendezvous has a checkered past. In the old days it was a private screening house where local movie distributors could get a sneak preview of Hollywood's latest offerings. For years now, it has been a blue-collar hangout. The private dining area still boasts a minuscule stage and a battered projection screen, hold-overs from days gone by. Occasionally some shoestring drama company will stage a production there.

The owner of Camera Craft, Jim Hadley, wasn't in the Rendezvous' old screening room. He was hunched over a hamburger and fries at a small table in the back of the dimly lit main dining room. He was evidently a regular. When we asked, the cashier had no difficulty pointing him out to us.

Kramer approached Hadley's table, flashed his ID, and introduced us both. Busy chewing, Hadley nodded us into chairs and swallowed a mouthful of hamburger. "What's this all about?" he asked.

"The picture in the paper."

"Oh," he said. "That one. It was a fluke, an absolute fluke. The odds of the camera going off just as she fell . . . It's like that guy taking pictures of Mount Saint Helens just as it exploded."

"I understand your company is in charge of doing the filming for the Masters Plaza folks?"

"That's right. We unload and load the cameras every morning, refocus, and reset the timers. After that they run all day and all night on their own. We've got a free-lance editor who supervises the film-to-tape transfer and then edits out all the night scenes and rough stuff."

"What kind of transfer?"

"You know, from film to videotape. That's where we do all the fine-tuning."

"You said cameras. Does that mean there's more than one?"

He nodded and swallowed another bite of his hamburger. "Two actually. Each of them is set to take one picture every four minutes—not at the same time, of course. One is set up right across the street in the Arcade building. The other's a block or so away. Now that they're up to the forty-second floor, the Arcade building isn't tall enough to show the whole building. The developer wants it for a corporate dog and pony production, a video to show what a hell of a good job they do."

"Which camera took the picture that was in the newspaper?" I asked.

"The one on the Arcade building. We keep that one focused on the raising gang. Putting up those beams is a lot more spectacular than most of the rest of it. It's certainly the most visual."

"And the most dangerous," I added.

Hadley shrugged. "That too, although it all looks pretty damn dangerous if you ask me."

Kramer shifted impatiently in his seat. "So how did the picture end up in the newspaper?"

"Our editor pulled a workprint that night. She's the one who noticed. She said she had some friends down at the *Times*, and she wondered if Darren Gibson would mind if she passed that one picture along. Of course he didn't mind. Publicity's publicity, especially if it's free."

"Who's Darren Gibson?"

"The local project manager for Masters Plaza. He said fine. Do it. Kath was way ahead of him."

"Kath?"

"Kath Naguchi. The editor I told you about. She figured he'd say yes. She was all set to pass it along to the *Times* as soon as he gave her the go-ahead. She was on her way down there within minutes. It was in the paper the next day."

"What about the rest of the film?"

Hadley shrugged. "Beats me. I suppose it's back at the shop where it belongs, along with the rest of the project."

"Could we see it?" I asked.

He shook his head. "Not without permission. The Masters and Rogers folks are paying us real good money to do this job. I'm not going to screw it up by showing you something I'm not supposed to."

"Has anyone else asked to see it?"

"No. Why would they?"

"So, the editor made a print of that one picture?"

Hadley shook his head. "She provided the film. I think the guys down at the paper did the actual blowup."

"Did anyone make prints of any of the other frames, either before or after the one in the paper?"

Hadley shook his head. "No. Not so far as I know. Like I said, she saw that one when she was doing the dailies."

"Dailies?" Kramer asked.

"It's a one-light print," I explained. "It tells what's on the previous day's shoot."

Kramer glowered at me. "Movie talk?" he asked disgustedly.

"You asked," I replied.

He turned back to Hadley. "We're helping the Department of Labor and Industries on this case. How do we get a look at that film?"

"I already told you. You've got to get permission from Masters and Rogers. They're the guys who write my checks. I wouldn't step on their toes on a bet."

"And Darren Gibson is the person we'd need to talk to?"

"Yes, but right now he's out of town. He was supposed

to be in Toronto today. Back tomorrow most likely. I don't know if you'll be able to get hold of him or not."

"Do you have a phone number?"

Hadley leaned back in his chair and wiped his mouth with a paper napkin. "Back in the office," he answered.

He paid for his lunch. We followed him out the door of the Rendezvous and back down Second Avenue to his shop where he thumbed through a gigantic Rolodex on his receptionist's desk and read off two telephone numbers—one local and the other in Toronto.

Leaving Camera Craft we drove to the department. In our cubicle I found Big Al Lindstrom sitting in my chair with his feet on my desk. He was eating an apple and reading a newspaper.

"I didn't expect you in today," he said, scrambling out of my chair.

"That's obvious," I growled, sweeping stray bits of apple off the chair before I sat down.

"I thought you were on vacation until Tuesday." Big Al quieted suddenly when Paul Kramer appeared over my shoulder.

"I'll try reaching Gibson," Kramer announced, barely pausing on the way to his and Manny's cubicle. "You check with Missing Persons."

Big Al eyed me quizzically. "You taking orders from Kramer now? What's going on?"

"I *am* on vacation," I replied, dialing the number for Missing Persons. "Doesn't it look like it? I'm taking a busman's holiday."

Big Al shook his head in disbelief. "To work with Kramer? No way."

"Hide and watch," I said.

"What happened to your face?"

"Walked into a post," I told him.

Big Al shook his head. He was unconvinced. "Like hell you did," he said. With that he picked up his cup and went in search of coffee.

That's the wonderful thing about telling the truth. People believe what they want to believe. It's a hell of a lot simpler than lying. There isn't the ever-present danger of getting caught.

It felt good to sit down at my desk again, to pick up my phone and dial a familiar number. It felt like I had been away from work, real work, for a long, long time. Naturally, Missing Persons put me on hold. While I waited, Margie popped her head in the door.

"I just wanted you to know that I never breathed a word about Gloria and the phone number."

"Thanks," I told her. "I owe you."

If Watty had heard about my tracking down Linda Decker's phone number under false pretenses, he would have fired my ass before I knew what hit me.

"What's this about a phone number?" Big Al asked, coming back with a cup of coffee.

"Never mind," I said.

The clerk in Missing Persons finally came back on the line. "This is Beaumont in homicide," I explained. "Do you have anything going on a guy by the name of Wayne Martinson?"

"Let me check." She put me on hold a second time, giving Big Al another crack at me.

"So what's it like to be in the movie business?" he demanded. "Are you ready to get yourself an agent and take the plunge?"

"Get off my back. The movie business sucks."

The clerk in Missing Persons returned once more, and I spent the next few minutes explaining that I hadn't said what she thought I said and that I certainly hadn't said it to her. Once her ruffled feathers were smoothed, she connected me with Detective Janie Jacobs who had Wayne Martinson's file in hand when she picked up the phone.

"Are you actively working the case?" I asked.

"Not so as you'd notice," Janie answered. "We took the report. His wife called it in, but since Martinson disappeared from a fishing resort in Alaska, it's outside our jurisdiction. The detectives there tell me they've got nothing to indicate foul play. He went fishing by himself in the morning and didn't come back. Most of his clothing was left in his room."

"Most?"

"That's right. Most but not all. Some of them weren't there. That's what makes the detectives at the scene think maybe he took a walk, a powder. He and his wife were evidently having problems. They think he decided to take off rather than hold still for a divorce.''

"Sometimes running away has a whole lot of appeal," I said.

"It makes my life a hell of a lot tougher," Janie responded, adding with a half laugh, "but then, a job's a job I guess. Anything else, Detective Beaumont? You want the wife's name and number? Let me give it to you. It's unlisted." I wrote down Gail Martinson's phone number.

"Thanks."

"So why's homicide interested in Wayne Martinson?" Janie asked.

"There may be a connection to a case we're working."

"Let me know if you put anything together. It would be nice if there were a connection for a change. Most of the time I feel like I'm working in a vacuum."

I hung up. "Who's Martinson?" Big Al asked.

"An accountant. The former bookkeeper for the ironworkers' local here in town."

"He's missing and you think there's some connection between him and that ironworker who got blown up down on Lake Union?"

"It's beginning to look that way."

"And that's why you're here working with Paul Kramer instead of taking vacation?" Big Al was incredulous. "You don't need a vacation, Beau. You should be on medical leave to have your head examined."

Big Al Lindstrom always says exactly what he's thinking. "You're not the first one to tell me that," I said just as Paul Kramer came back to the door of our cubicle.

"Tell you what?" Kramer asked, pausing there.

"That I'm a couple of bubbles out of plumb," I answered.

Kramer let it drop. "Gibson already left company headquarters in Toronto. He's catching the red-eye back to Vancouver tonight. We'll have to try to locate him in the morning if we want a look at that film. What did you find out from Missing Persons?"

I told him briefly what I had learned from Detective Jacobs. Paul Kramer shook his massive head. "It still doesn't make sense. If Martinson ran off, I'd lay odds it's got more to do with the ironworkers and those goddamned tapes than it does with his wife.''

It hurt like hell to admit Kramer might be right, but his supposition certainly tallied with mine.

''Whoever the lady was on the phone in Toronto,'' Kramer continued, ''she said Gibson is due back at work here in Seattle tomorrow morning by seven. Either at the job site or in their temporary headquarters in the Arcade Building. Want to meet there about seven-fifteen?''

''In the office?''

Kramer shook his head. ''Let's meet outside first. By the fountain at Second and Union.''

''All right, but I'll have to be back home by ten-thirty. I've got a date for lunch.''

I'm not sure why I said it that way instead of coming right out and telling him that taking Tracie and Heather to Bumbershoot was a prior commitment. By then we had been working together for several hours with no recurrence of our ongoing feud.

A look of barely concealed contempt washed over Kramer's face. ''By all means, don't let this case screw up your social life.'' With that, he turned on his heel and stalked away.

Good riddance, I thought. If he's still looking for playboy cop symptoms, I'll give him one every now and then. Just for drill.

Chapter 19

RALPH AMES has been on an Italian food kick for as long as I've known him. By the time I got home that night, he had invited Heather and Tracie to dinner and had enlisted their help in making a gigantic batch of spaghetti. The three of them were already eating when I put my key in the lock.

My kitchen was a shambles. Some charred remains, vaguely recognizable as slices of French bread, sat on the counter giving mute testimony to at least one failed batch of garlic toast. A thin dusting of Parmesan cheese covered the floor. More dirty cooking pots than I could possibly own were scattered throughout. Whoever was volunteering for KP duty was in deep trouble.

I poured myself a MacNaughton's and water and carried it with me to the table. Heather beamed as Ames put a plate stacked high with spaghetti in front of me.

"We got to help, Unca Beau. He let us," she lisped happily. Her triumphant grin was missing two front teeth. "I got to stir, and Tracie fixed the bread."

With a slight warning shake of his head, Ralph Ames passed me a basket full of garlic bread which was only somewhat less charred than the discarded batch still in the kitchen.

I took a bite and nodded appreciatively at Tracie. "Delicious," I said.

She ducked her head and wrinkled her nose. "It's a little burned. I forgot to set the timer."

"It's fine," I told her.

The kids were excited and overflowing with news, babbling to Ames and me about their father's upcoming wedding, their new dresses, the foibles of poor Mrs. Edwards, and our planned outing to Bumbershoot the next day. I tried to stay with the flow of conversation, but my mind kept wandering back to Logan Tyree and Jimmy Rising and Angie Dixon. At least one of those three cases was now officially mine.

I must have been on my third or fourth MacNaughton's by the time the kitchen was mucked out and the girls had gone back downstairs. Finally, mercifully, the apartment was quiet. I leaned back in my ancient recliner, resting my head, closing my eyes. But as soon as I did, it all came back to me—Logan Tyree, Jimmy Rising, and Angie Dixon. Names with questions and no answers.

Sitting up, I wrestled the Seattle telephone book out of the drawer in the table next to my chair. I checked the K's and found there was only one Don Kaplan, a Donald B. Kaplan on N.E. 128th. I dialed the number. It rang and rang, and nobody answered.

Ralph Ames came into the living room from the kitchen

just as I put the phone back in its cradle. He looked at me quizzically.

Instead of answering his unasked question, I got up and poured myself another drink, offering him one in the process. Ames shook his head.

"I was calling someone from Martin Green's party," I explained. "Remember me telling you about the man on the balcony, a guy named Don Kaplan? He's not home right now, but if he shows up there before it gets too late, I'll stop by and see him tonight."

I sat back down in my recliner. A little too hard. Some of the MacNaughton's slopped into my lap. I wiped it off.

"It's already too late, Beau," Ames said.

"What do you mean? It's just barely ten."

"It's too late for driving. Look at yourself. You're in no condition to drive, much less question a potential witness."

It wasn't the first nudge Ames had given me on the subject of drinking, not just counting drinks that night in particular, but drinking in general. He had mentioned my alcohol consumption on several earlier occasions, and I always resented it. I resented it now. Just because I had a drink or two or three in the evening after work didn't make me an alcoholic in my book. I thought he was overreacting and told him so.

"So what are you, my mother?"

"I'm your attorney, Beau. I'm concerned about you."

"Get off it, Ralph. If I want to drink too much, I'm not hurting anyone but myself."

Ames shrugged and dropped it for the moment. "What's bugging you tonight? All evening long when the girls tried to talk to you, it was like there was nobody home. You barely paid attention."

"This is beginning to sound a whole lot like a lecture," I countered. "I've been thinking about the case, that's all."

"The case," he echoed. "What case? And why do you want to talk to Don Kaplan? When I left this morning, I understood you were on vacation until Tuesday morning. Whatever happened to that?"

"I got Watty to put me on it after all," I said.

"The case he gave you strict orders to leave alone on pain of being fired."

I nodded. "That's the one."

Ames shook his head in disgust. "You drink too much and you work too hard. Definitely type-A behavior, Beau. Typical type A. Heart attack material. You'd best mend your ways, or you won't be around long enough to enjoy your money."

Our conversation probably would have deteriorated further into an all-out quarrel if the phone hadn't rung just then. It was Linda Decker.

"I talked to Sandy Carson," she said. "She told me she gave you the tapes. Did you look at them? Did they help?"

She sounded so eager it was hard to answer her. "We looked at them all right," I said slowly, playing for time, scrambling for the right thing to say.

I was hedging. I didn't want to have to tell Linda Decker that the information she had guarded with her life, the information that had cost her Logan Tyree, her mother, and maybe her brother, was essentially worthless. It's one thing to pay a price. It's something else to discover that the price was meaningless.

"We're still evaluating the information," I said at last.

She sighed. I could sense her disappointment. "What are you doing now?" she asked.

I glanced down at the drink in my hand and found myself wondering exactly how many MacNaughton's there had been in the course of the evening. I couldn't remember exactly, and now, suddenly it seemed important, not because of Ames but because of me. Maybe Ralph Ames was right to be worried.

"Just taking it easy," I said in answer to Linda's question.

"I don't mean right this minute," Linda Decker responded. "I mean what are you going to do next?"

"We're following up on the disappearance of Wayne Martinson."

"Wayne? Do you think you he was involved?"

"Maybe, maybe not," I replied. "And then tomorrow we'll have a look at the pictures of Masters Plaza, to see if those tell us anything."

"That's all?"

"For right now." I heard Linda Decker's sharp intake of breath. For the loved ones, the ones left grieving and waiting, I'm sure the way cops have to work must seem incredibly cumbersome, agonizingly slow.

It's true. It is.

There was nothing more I could or would tell Linda Decker right then, so I changed the subject. "How's Jimmy?" I asked.

There was a long pause before she answered. "I don't know," she said softly. "He may not make it through the night, but at least the sons of bitches didn't get the tapes," she added fiercely. "Thank God for that."

"That's right," I agreed as consolingly as I could manage. "At least they didn't get the tapes."

I put down the phone and sat there looking at it. For a time I forgot I wasn't alone in the room.

"Who was that?" Ames asked.

The sound of his voice startled me, and I jumped. All the potential rancor in our previous discussion faded from mind. It never occurred to me to tell Ralph Ames to mind his own business.

"Linda," I answered. "Linda Decker, wondering how things are going."

"And the tapes?" he pressed.

I shook my head. "They're nothing really, just some accountant's tapes. Angie Dixon, the woman who fell off the building, insisted that they were part of a long-term swindle inside the union—bribes, kickbacks, that kind of thing. The problem is, we've only got the tapes, not the journal entries. Without those, we can't prove a thing."

"What are you going to do about it?" Ames asked.

Pointedly placing my empty glass on the table, I looked Ralph Ames in the eye. "Sleep on it," I said. "Go to bed and see if any bright ideas surface in my subconscious."

Of course, when I finally did manage to wrestle my nighttime demons into submission, I was too exhausted for any inspiration to pay me a nocturnal visit. There were dreams—disjointed, fragmented, ugly dreams in which I almost but not quite found something that didn't want to be found.

There were no flashes of psychic brilliance, no illuminating insights into the problem at hand. When the alarm went off at six the next morning I woke up with a throbbing hangover, no closer to solving the problem than I had been the night before when I fell into bed in a booze-induced stupor.

Hung over or not, I knew as soon as I opened my eyes that something was different. For the first time in weeks, the sky outside my bedroom window was gray instead of blue. Seattle's cool cloud cover was back, announcing that summer had just about run its course. I went out on the balcony. A cool freshening breeze was blowing in off Puget Sound. Sniffing it cleared my head and made me feel better.

Let it rain, I thought. Labor Day or not, Bumbershoot or not, let it rain. I'm ready.

Dressing quickly, I skipped out of the house without bothering to make coffee or waken Ames. I made my way down Second with the other early-morning pedestrian commuters. They were smiling and nodding at one another in greeting. The heat was leaving, the sun was going back where it belonged, and real Seattlites were happy to have their customary weather back.

It was only five to seven when I got to Second and Union, but Paul Kramer was already pacing anxiously back and forth by the empty, drought-dried fountain next to the Arcade Building. Manny Davis, more relaxed, lounged easily against one wall watching Paul Kramer's impatient antics with some amusement.

When he saw me at last, Kramer breathed an exaggerated sigh of relief, turned on his heel, and headed into the building. Manny waited until I reached him. "I figured you'd be on time. Kramer's got no faith."

"He's got all kinds of faith," I corrected, "in all the wrong things."

The temporary Seattle headquarters for Masters and Rogers Developers was on the third floor of the Arcade Building in two small but posh offices that had been sublet from someone else. The woman at the front desk would have made a terrific ice princess. Flawlessly made up. Coldly beautiful. No smile. No discernible sense of humor.

"Mr. Gibson has someone with him just now. May I ask what this is concerning?"

"It's police business, Miss," Manny offered. From the daggered look she gave him, Miss wasn't a term she found endearing.

She sat up straighter in her chair. "Mr. Gibson is meeting with some prospective tenants at the moment. He flew back from Toronto late last night especially for this meeting. I'm sure he'll be glad to talk to you once it's over, but I couldn't possibly interrupt him. It may take several hours. They're on a tour of the building right now."

"Several hours!" Kramer yelped as though he'd been shot. The probability was high that the Masters Plaza pictures would reveal nothing new, yield nothing we hadn't already learned from other sources, but Kramer was young and impatient. He needed to feel like he was doing something, getting somewhere. "We'll wait," he said stubbornly. "However long it takes, we'll wait."

He settled heavily into a chair next to a potted palm. Manny joined him and picked up a recent copy of *Forbes* that was sitting on an end table next to him.

The receptionist shrugged with studied disinterest and turned back to her computer keyboard. "Suit yourselves," she said.

I've seen this kind of corporate guardian angel all too often. They regard themselves as the keepers of all comings and goings. Over the years I've learned you have to get around women like that, because you sure as hell aren't going to get through them.

I made a point of looking at the clock on the receptionist's desk, turning the face toward me so I could see it. "You can wait if you want to," I said over my shoulder to Kramer and Manny. "I've got better things to do." Without saying anything more, I made my way out of the office. When I stopped at the elevator, I glanced back. Paul Kramer was glaring sourly at me through the glass, muttering something to Manny. Suspicions confirmed, probably. Smiling, I gave them a breezy wave and disappeared into the elevator.

I dashed across Second on a flashing DON'T WALK signal

and ran all the way to the construction gate and elevator at the opposite end of Masters Plaza. I managed to squeeze on the elevator just as the door went shut, but the operator pointed at me and shook his head. "Where do you think you're going?"

"I'm with Mr. Gibson's party," I said. "I had to stop and take a leak."

The operator grinned. "Happens to the best of us, but you'll have to go back out to the tool shack and get a hard hat. I'll pick you up on the next trip."

I did as I was told, knowing that if the operator ran into Gibson on the way, the jig was up, but he didn't. He came back for me.

"I dropped Mr. Gibson off on the thirty-seventh floor a few minutes ago," the operator told me. "They said they'd work their way down from there. How about if I drop you at thirty-six?"

"That'll be fine," I said.

As soon as I stepped off the elevator, the wind rushing through the open spaces between the concrete beams caught me and almost blew the hard hat off my head. What was a freshening breeze at street level was a whistling gale on the thirty-sixth floor. Someone had hung a huge piece of heavy plastic along the side of the building, but it was flapping loose in the wind.

Since my suit and tie had been good enough to get me past the elevator operator, I figured I was looking for a suit and tie group. What I saw on the thirty-sixth floor were plumbers, electricians, and carpenters without a pinstripe or knotted silk tie in sight.

I took the unfinished metal stairway and clambered down to thirty-five. Still no luck. I finally caught up with them on thirty-three. There were six men in the group altogether. Quietly, I attached myself to the end of the procession. I figured the guests would think I was with Gibson, and Gibson would think I was one of the visitors.

And I didn't have any trouble picking Gibson out of the crowd. He was the one doing most of the talking, pointing out building features, gesturing this way and that. Periodically, one of the visitors would stop him long enough to ask a question. Trailing at the end of the pack, it was far too noisy for me to hear much of what was said, but there was a good deal of nodding back and forth among the visitors. Gibson was evidently telling them what they wanted to hear.

At last we got back on the elevator for the return trip to ground level. The elevator operator recognized me and nodded, but he didn't say anything. Once we were back on the ground floor, Gibson stood to one side while the visitors headed for the tool shack to relinquish their hard hats.

I sidled up to him. "Mr. Gibson, could I have a word with you?"

He looked startled that I hadn't gone off with the others. "Sure," he said.

Pulling him aside, I discreetly showed him my identification. "My name is Detective Beaumont," I said. "I'm with the Seattle Police Department. We need your help."

Not nearly as cordial once he realized I wasn't a potential leasee, he glanced nervously toward the tool shack. "What do you want?"

"We need to get a look at that film of yours, the one with the lady who fell off the building."

Gibson swallowed. Clearly he didn't want his prospective tenants hearing about a police investigation into Angie Dixon's fatal fall.

Then he frowned. "Is there a problem?" he asked. "I thought that was all settled, that it had been ruled accidental."

"Maybe not," I answered. "How do we go about seeing the film?"

"I don't actually have it," Gibson said.

"I know you don't have it. Camera Craft does, but they won't show it to us unless you give them permission."

The first of the visitors was coming back from the tool shack. Gibson nodded hurriedly. "Okay, okay. I'll take care of it. Come along back to my office."

I did, trailing behind as before. When I sauntered into the Masters and Rogers office behind Darren Gibson and his guests, the look of absolute consternation on Paul Kramer's face made my day.

Gibson paused for only a moment beside the ice-lady's

desk. "Call Camera Craft," he ordered brusquely. "Tell them to show this gentleman . . . What did you say your name was?"

"Beaumont. J. P. Beaumont."

"Tell them to give Mr. Beaumont here whatever help he needs." With that, Gibson swept into his private office with the entourage of potential customers following behind like so many trailing puppies.

"How'd you do that?" Kramer demanded in a startled whisper as he and Manny both stood up.

"Experience," I answered.

We started toward the door. "You're not going to wait then?" the receptionist asked.

"That won't be necessary now," I said, returning her chilly smile with a cool one of my own. "You just be sure to make that call to Camera Craft before we get there. It won't take us long."

Chapter 20

WE were there at nine, waiting outside on the street when Jim Hadley opened the doors to Camera Craft and let us in. "The secretary already called," he said, in answer to my question about Darren Gibson. "She said to show you whatever you need to see."

I was careful not to look at Paul Kramer. That was the only way to stifle a triumphant grin. Kramer was still dismayed by how easily I'd wrested permission out of Darren Gibson to see the film. I didn't want to shatter the fragile truce between us. My ability to keep my promise to Linda Decker depended totally on Kramer's grudging willingness to work together. One complaint from him, and Watty would have pulled me off the case in a minute.

"So when can we see the film?" I asked Hadley.

The owner of Camera Craft glanced at his watch and shook his head. "Not just yet, I'm afraid. Kath doesn't come in to work until almost three. The editing is one hundred percent her baby. If I go into that room and stir things up, she'll raise hell for weeks.''

"Can't you call her at home then?" Kramer asked. "Ask her to come in early?"

Jim Hadley gave Kramer a derisive look and laughed aloud. "Are you kidding? No way. You've never worked with free-lance editors, have you? They're independent contractors, mostly a night-crawler variety, who won't answer telephones or show their faces before mid-afternoon. If I woke her up at this hour of the day, Kath Naguchi wouldn't ever work with me again, and she's damn good.

"Stop by around three," he added. "She'll be on her third cigarette and her second cup of coffee. By then she'll be about half civilized.''

So there we were, stuck again. This job is like that. You get up early only to stand around and wait. Out on the street, Kramer was still in a hurry, still crabbing about finding Kath Naguchi early. His grousing was in direct opposition to Manny Davis' easygoing view of the world.

"Why'd you want to do a thing like that?" Manny asked, shutting off his partner's litany of complaint. "Sounds to me like we'd be better off tangling with a hibernating grizzly.''

In the end, Manny's cooler head prevailed. I made arrangements to meet them back at Camera Craft at three.

"I suppose you're off on your hot date," Kramer noted sarcastically as I turned to make my way back home. I studied him for a long moment, wondering if I had been that ambitious in my youth, that ambitious and that obnoxious.

"Not hot," I corrected. "As a matter of fact, I'm taking two little girls to Bumbershoot. Care to join us?" Turning on my heel, I headed up the street just as the first real raindrops in more than a month began to fall on downtown Seattle.

It wasn't one of the Northwest's customary dry drizzles that you can walk for blocks in and not get wet. Instead of a light, gentle mist, this was a sidewalk-pounding, clothes-soaking downpour. I was completely drenched by the time I'd walked the six long blocks between Camera Craft and Belltown Terrace.

Annie, the building's concierge, was on duty in the lobby. She opened the door to let me in before I managed to get my key in the lock. Rivulets of water coursed down my face and dripped into my eyes. Looking for something dry, I wiped my forehead with the underside of my jacket sleeve.

"You're all wet," Annie observed unnecessarily.

I nodded, matching inanity for inanity. "It's raining out," I said.

"You're not really taking Heather and Tracie Bumbershooting in this weather, are you?"

I've long since learned that living in a high rise gives you about as much privacy as living in a small town. Which is to say, none. Everybody's business is everybody else's business.

"Who told you that?" I asked.

Annie laughed. "The girls did. They were down here just a few minutes ago looking up the street to see if you were coming. As far as I'm concerned, it's a rotten day for Bumbershooting."

"At least it won't be crowded," I replied.

She held the elevator door until I got on. "It won't be crowded because most people have sense enough to come in out of the rain." The door closd before I could manage to think of one more cliché and heave it in her direction.

While I was waiting for the girls to show up at the apartment, I reluctantly took Annie's hint and went searching for an umbrella to take along. Although the word "bumbershoot" means umbrella, it's usually not necessary to carry one the last weekend in August, even in Seattle. I scrounged around in the back reaches of my coat closet and resurrected a broken-ribbed relic that would have to suffice.

At exactly ten-thirty, the girls rang the bell. Mrs. Edwards had seen to it that they were properly dressed in matching yellow slickers that covered them from head to toe. When we stepped out onto the street and I cracked open the ancient umbrella, they both burst into giggles.

"Where'd you get that thing, Unca Beau?" Heather asked, pointing. "It's broken."

She was right. The umbrella, broken and not exactly

waterproof either, was more a philosophical statement than it was protection from the weather. The plastic had torn loose from one of the ribs, and the resulting fold of material dripped a steady stream of water that ran down the back of my hand and up my sleeve.

"It'll be fine," I told the girls. "Let's get going."

The main gate to Seattle Center is only about three blocks from Belltown Terrace. The site of Seattle's 1962 World's Fair, it contains the Emerald City's signature landmark, the Space Needle, as well as eighteen or so acres of park that include exhibition halls, amusement rides, live theaters, a sports arena, an athletic field, fountains, and a building full of shops and fast-food vendors. On any given Labor Day weekend some 250,000 to 300,000 people find their way through the center to see live music and theater performances, hands-on exhibits, arts and crafts demonstrations, jugglers, magicians, and almost anything else you want to name. It's called Bumbershoot.

I've been there when that last bash of summer has been so crowded that it was all but impossible to move. You inched along, carried forward by the crowd, going whatever direction it was moving at the moment. But on this rainy, dreary Friday morning, that was certainly not the case. The place was almost deserted.

The Bumbershoot workers were delighted to see anybody who might be a potential customer. The girls raced ahead of me collecting a batch of goodies—free balloons and two totally unnecessary sun visors.

They darted past a jazz band playing halfheartedly on the steps of the semi-empty Flag Pavilion. I caught up with them just as they reached the edge of the International Fountain and before they could scramble over the low wall.

The fountain is a huge deep basin some two hundred feet across. The bottom is bordered with a matting of rough white rocks while the heart of the fountain is a slightly convex concrete mound studded with pipes and lights. A varied water show, programmed in concert with classical music, erupts periodically from the pipes. Despite the clearly posted DANGER signs, the interior of the fountain is regarded as a children's free-for-all playground on hot summer days.

"Can't we go in, please?" Heather begged. "Just for a little while. We won't get very wet."

"No way," I told her. "Mrs. Edwards would have a fit." Only a promise of immediate food kept them out of the fountain.

The area around the fountain was lined with wooden outdoor food booths. Every year crafts people, musicians, and food vendors bring samples of their ware to Bumbershoot in a gigantic outdoor festival. The food, with its wide variety of tastes and tantalizing aromas, is easily the most popular part of the weekend, and it's usually the most crowded. But not today. There were no lines, no jostling crowds. We were the only customers at a Mexican food place where the girls ordered bean burritos. I paused next door at a Thai booth for some beef *sate* with peanut sauce.

After lunch we sauntered through the arts and crafts display in the Exhibition Hall and on into the children's area in the Center House. While the girls listened to stories, touched the animals in the petting zoo, and posed briefly for a quick charcoal portrait, I watched from the sidelines with a cup of coffee in hand.

I watched, but my mind was elsewhere, restlessly sifting through the tangled web that led from Logan Tyree to Jimmy Rising. I kept one eye on the girls and the other on my watch, waiting for enough time to pass so I could go back to Camera Craft and see if Kath Naguchi's pictures held any answers to the questions circling in my mind.

At two-fifteen, when I announced it was time to leave, there was no argument. The girls were tired and more than ready to go back home. It was still sprinkling intermittently when we reached the main gate.

A ticket taker offered to stamp our hands. "That way you can get back in if you want to," he said.

Fat chance, I thought. I started to say no, but Heather pitched such a screaming fit that I gave in and we all three had our hands stamped.

On Denny Way Tracie walked briskly along beside me, chattering about all she had seen and done. Heather, tired and whiny, trailed along behind. Finally, despite my aching shoulder, I picked her up and carried her the last block and a half. She was sound asleep when I packed her into their apartment and deposited her on the couch.

Mrs. Edwards shook her head. "Looks like you wore her out."

"It works both ways," I told her, rubbing my shoulder while the difference in pressure again made me aware of the tender spot in my heel, the one my doctor jokingly refers to as my middle-aged bone spur.

"Thank you for taking us, Uncle Beau," Tracie said, as I bent down to give her a goodbye hug.

"You're welcome," I said.

I went upstairs and made myself a small pot of coffee. There was just time enough to gulp down one quick cup and to swallow one of my bone spur anti-inflammatories before I had to go meet Manny Davis and Paul Kramer.

Usually, I would have walked that far, but the hours in Bumbershoot had done their worst and my heel hurt more than it had for weeks. I opted for taking the Porsche, parking it at a meter across the street.

With a name like Kath Naguchi, I suppose I expected Jim Hadley's slugabed film editor to be a petite, dark-haired Asian. Wrong. When the owner of Camera Craft led us upstairs into the small, dimly lit editing room with its thick pall of cigarette smoke, Kath Naguchi turned out to be a behemoth of a woman, as tall as she was wide, with short, bright red hair, thick glasses, and the sickly-white skin of someone who shuns the light of day.

"These are the guys I was telling you about, Kath," Jim Hadley said without physically venturing any farther into the room than was absolutely necessary.

Kath Naguchi made a slight face but she didn't bother to look up. She was sitting in one corner of the room in front of a complicated-looking piece of machinery which I recognized from my *Death in Drydock* movie days as a flatbed editing table with a small viewing screen and numerous levers, knobs, and digital readouts. Three separate reels of film were loaded on the table. A long snarl of film rested in her lap and trailed across the floor under and behind her chair. The edge of the table was lined with a fringe of cut pieces of film. Trims, they call them in movie lingo.

"Watch where you step," she ordered sharply. "I'll be through here in a minute."

We waited patiently while she rewound the tangled film in her lap and hung the trims on clips over the trim bin at her elbow. She worked quickly and silently, with such total concentration that she could just as well have been alone. Only when she was completely finished did she light another cigarette, pick up her cup of coffee, and turn to face us.

"So you guys want to see the Masters Plaza film, do you?" she drawled.

"Yes, that's right." I answered for all of us. "The whole series of frames both before and after the one that was in the paper."

She shrugged. "Okay. No problem. Wait here."

Heaving her massive frame out of the chair, she huffed out of the room with the cigarette in hand. She was gone several minutes. When she returned, she was carrying another reel of film under her arm, a full coffee cup in one hand, and the cigarette in the other.

Effortlessly she cued up the film. "I think it's pretty close to the beginning of this one," she said. "I'll just run it."

We watched in fascination on the viewing screen while the building seemed to grow, floor by floor, before our eyes. The four-minute intervals between shots gave the movement of cranes and other machinery a jerky, fast-forward look, while shadows marching across the screen showed the rise and set of the sun. Five or six days must have flashed by like that before Kath Naguchi stopped the film.

"Here it is," she said.

At first all I could see was the building. Squinting, I moved forward until I was leaning directly over Kath Naguchi's ample shoulder. At that distance, I could see Angie Dixon—barely. She was hardly more than a pin-sized figure on the gray face of the building.

"Are you sure this is it?" Kramer asked. "The picture in the paper was lots closer than this."

"I can make it bigger," Kath Naguchi said. "But not here. This table is just for mixing. The blowup was done from a zoom shot we did down at Cine-tron."

"Where's that?" Kramer asked impatiently.

"Just up the street."

Kramer seemed to be antagonizing her, so I stepped in with the voice of sweet reason. "Could we go there? This might be very important."

"Maybe. It depends on whether or not the equipment is free. I don't usually schedule it until late at night."

"Would it be possible for you to check?" I asked.

"All right," Kath Naguchi agreed reluctantly. She wasn't going to offer anything on her own. We'd have to coax her every step of the way.

She picked up the phone and dialed a number. "This is Kath," she announced flatly into the phone. "Are you all booked up at the moment or could I come over and use the machine for a few minutes." She paused. "They're due at four o'clock? We should be done long before then. See you in a few minutes."

Without a word, she unwound the film and lurched out of the chair. She swept out of the room, down the stairs, and out of the building, leaving us to follow. She walked at a surprisingly rapid pace back up Second to Bell and then down to First Avenue where she led us into a derelict-looking building.

Derelict on the outside only. Inside, the reception area was comfortably if not lavishly furnished. Kath waved briefly at the receptionist then led us through an open door into another dimly lit room, one half of which was filled with a huge console complete with knobs, dials, buttons, and monitors, several showing wave forms only. The centerpiece was a massive television screen.

A man was seated on a high stool in front of the console. He turned as we entered. He too was holding a coffee cup in one hand and a cigarette in the other. They must be film-editor occupational hazards.

"Hi, Jack," Kath Naguchi said. "Thanks for working us in."

"What's up?" Jack asked. "It sounded pretty urgent on the phone."

Kath handed him a videotape. "These gentlemen are interested in seeing some of this. It's the Masters Plaza tape."

Jack looked at us questioningly, but Kath Naguchi offered no introductions, and we didn't volunteer any of our own.

He shrugged. "Okay. If you say so. It's not a freebie, though. It's gonna cost you."

"You guys are paying?"

I nodded.

Jack got up and headed into another small room that opened off the one we were in. As the door swung open, I felt the cool rush of air-conditioning and glimpsed several stacks of humming electronic equipment that filled the room with a low-pitched semi-silence.

"Have a seat while we get set up," Kath ordered before she disappeared into the other room behind Jack.

Looking behind me I discovered a raised platform with two short love seats on it, love seats with ashtrays on or near all available flat surfaces. We sat waiting until Kath and Jack emerged from the other room.

For some reason I had expected Kath would be the one actually running the film, but Jack resumed his seat on the stool while Kath stood at his side. Paul Kramer had evidently been under the same impression.

"You mean you're not going to run it?" he asked.

Kath Naguchi laughed, a hoot that was half chuckle and half smoker's rattling cough. "Are you kidding? Nobody touches this baby but the master or one of his authorized disciples."

Jack laughed at that. "Where is it, Kath?" he asked.

"About six minutes in," she told him.

Jack twirled knobs this way and that, adjusting for light and color. At last he was satisfied. "This should be pretty close," he said.

Once more shadows raced across the screen, showing the passage of a day until the same frame was again frozen on the screen. Once more Angie Dixon, a tiny pin of a figure near the bottom right-hand corner of the picture, was an ungainly bird caught in a deadly free-fall toward the sidewalk far below. I tried not to think about that.

"Zoom in on the lower left-hand corner," Kath ordered.

"Like this?"

The figure of Angie Dixon grew larger. "Again," Kath

said. Twice more the process was repeated. Each time
Angie Dixon grew larger, and each time there was a pause
while Jack adjusted the light and colors. As soon as he did
it the third time, I recognized the picture that had been in
the paper.

"Again?" Jack asked.

Kath nodded.

Once more the process was repeated. Now Angie Dixon
filled the entire screen. At that level, there was some
fuzzing of the picture, but not enough to disguise the look
of horror on the woman's face as she plummeted to earth.
Sickened, I turned away. I live with death far too much to
want to see a detailed portrait of it in living color.

"Isn't that what you wanted?" Kath asked with as much
emotion as a saleslady selling a pair of shoes. The picture
was just that to her—a picture and nothing more.

"Can you do the same thing to some of the other frames
just before and just after this?"

"Sure," she said. "No problem." She turned to Jack.
"Let's try just before."

Jack nodded and called up another frame. "This is the
one. See anything you want me to zoom in on?"

Kath moved closer to the large screen and scrutinized
one corner of it intently. "Try up here near the top," she
said.

He did. Once the adjustments had been made for light
and color, it was possible to make out that there were two
small figures standing close together.

"This one would have been taken four minutes before
the other one?" I asked.

Kath nodded.

"Do it again," she said, pointing. "Right here."

Jack zoomed in again. Now there were clearly two
figures showing on the screen.

I could feel the rush of excitement in my veins. "Again,"
I said, not waiting for Kath to give Jack his marching
orders. I had abandoned the love seat and was standing
next to Kath Naguchi. On the monitor two people were
plainly visible, standing side by side near the edge of the
building. There was some distortion in the lengthened

faces, but they were both recognizable. One of the two was clearly Angie Dixon. The other was familiar as well.

"Hey, wait a minute. I know him."

Kramer bounded off the love seat to stand beside me. "Who is he?" he demanded.

"Martin Green."

"Martin Green?" Kramer echoed. "Who the hell is he?"

"The executive director of the ironworkers' local here."

"And you know him?" Kramer demanded.

"He lives in my building."

"What about him?" Manny asked, stepping forward so he too could see.

I tried to quell the rising excitement I felt but I didn't want to blurt out anything more in front of the two outsiders. "Let's take a look at the next frame," I said quickly.

"The one after the fall shot?" Jack asked.

I nodded.

With Kath Naguchi's help, we examined several more frames of film both before and after Angie Dixon's fall, as well as pictures taken at approximately the same time by the other camera.

There was nothing else unusual, only the unmistakable presence of Martin Green.

"Would you like a hard copy of this?" Jack asked when we finally told him we were finished.

"What do you mean, hard copy?" Kramer asked.

Kath Naguchi sighed. "Do you want a copy of the tape or not? It'll only take a few minutes."

"Yes, we do," I answered.

Once more Kath and Jack disappeared into the back room. Paul Kramer rounded on me. "Now tell me. Who the hell is Martin Green?"

"The guy Linda Decker suspects is responsible for Logan Tyree's death."

Manny whistled. "Hot damn! And maybe this one too?"

"Let's don't jump to conclusions," I cautioned, "but it could be. It just could be."

Chapter 21

When you're fighting in the dark, any connection is better than no connection. And that was the way with this. If Martin Green had been on the iron with the doomed Angie Dixon only minutes before her fatal fall, then it was possible he had something to do with her death. However, we had all been cops too long for any of us to accept that premise at face value.

By the time we were back out on the street, we figured there was probably some perfectly legitimate reason for Green's presence on the Masters Plaza job site. Not only that, we'd made a joint decision to go ask him about it. With that in mind, we headed for the Labor Temple.

There was an election of officers going on in one of the union locals, and parking was at a premium. Kramer and Manny parked in a loading zone on Clay, while I pulled into the first floor of Belltown Terrace's garage and grabbed the first available spot.

The weather had turned wet again and it was raining hard by the time I dashed across the alley that separates the Labor Temple from my building. Paul Kramer was just giving his card to the ironworkers' receptionist when I caught up with them. She gave me a funny look as though trying to place someone she vaguely knew.

"May I help you?" she asked.

"I'm with them," I told her.

She picked up her phone and spoke into an intercom. "Someone's here to see you," she announced.

"Who is it?" he asked. "I'm busy."

"They're detectives," she answered.

Her quiet announcement brought Martin Green to the door of his office in a hurry. The broken glass had been replaced. The receptionist handed him Detective Kramer's card. Green glanced down at it and then up at us, his eyes traveling briefly from face to face until he stopped at mine. He frowned.

"Beaumont, isn't it? From Belltown Terrace?"

I nodded. "That's right."

"To what do I owe the pleasure?"

"We need to ask you a few questions."

"You're with these other gentlemen?" he asked, waving Kramer's card.

"Yes, I am."

"What kind of questions?"

"About Angie Dixon."

He frowned again and cocked his head to one side. "All right. Come in. Kim, hold all my calls, will you?"

Green ushered us into his office and then he had to step back outside to bring along an extra chair. "What about Angie Dixon?" he began, not waiting until he was seated before he asked the question. "I thought that was all settled, that her death had been ruled accidental. Has something changed?" Since we knew each other however briefly, his statements were addressed to me.

I took the ball. "When's the last time you saw her?"

"Minutes before she died."

Green answered evenly, without a moment's hesitation. His straightforward manner surprised me. There was no outward show of concern that our placing him at the scene of Angie Dixon's possibly non-accidental death might mean he was under suspicion.

"What were you doing there?"

"I needed to talk to her," he answered.

"You must have needed to real bad, to track her down at a job site on a Sunday morning."

Martin Green didn't respond, but he met my gaze with unblinking indifference.

"Why was it so important for you to see her?"

This time there was a pause, the kind of noticeable, momentary indecision that puts any detective worth his salt on red alert.

"She had something I needed," Green answered blandly.

"And what might that be?" Kramer asked, plowing into the process—the proverbial bull in a china shop.

Martin Green's eyes momentarily flicked from me to Kramer, as if assessing the weight of the interruption. By the time he answered, though, he was once more addressing me, closing out both Manny and Kramer. The two of us might have been alone in the room.

"Some tapes," he answered quietly. "I believed she had some accounting tapes. I wanted them."

The accounting tapes! Linda Decker's infernal tapes again. I tried not to let anything in my voice betray that we knew what tapes he was talking about, that we *did* have copies of them.

"And did she give them to you?"

"She was going to," Martin Green answered. "She said she wouldn't be able to get them until the next day."

"But instead, she died a few minutes later," I prompted.

Green nodded.

"Did it occur to you that there might be some connection between her death and her agreeing to give you those missing tapes?"

"No. The people I talked to said her death was an accident, and I believed them."

"And where were you the night Logan Tyree's boat blew up over on Lake Union?"

"The night Logan Tyree was killed? I was out of town."

The fact that he spat out that detail right off the top of his head alerted me further. Without careful reflection, people don't usually remember what they were doing on a certain day or at a certain time. Unless that time and date have some special significance.

"Where out of town?" I asked.

"Vancouver, B.C."

"Is there someone who can verify that?"

"No."

The abrupt certainty of his answer set more alarm bells clanging inside my head. "You're saying that you went to Vancouver that night, but no one saw you there."

"Why are you asking me about that night?"

"Because I have someone who claims Logan Tyree had an appointment to see you the night he died."

For the first time, Martin Green looked uncomfortable. "That's impossible. I wouldn't have scheduled an appointment with him. That's the night . . ." He broke off suddenly and didn't continue.

"That was the night what?" I prodded.

Green shook his head stubbornly. "I did see someone there, in Vancouver, but I won't bring her into it. She's married."

"To someone else?"

"That's right."

That struck me as ironic. Here was Martin Green claiming to be stuck with an unusable alibi. If the story was true, his reticence, for somewhat different reasons, was still the same as mine with Marilyn Sykes—confidentiality.

"But why would I want to kill Logan?"

"For the same motive you might have to kill Angie Dixon," I replied. "To get the tapes."

"Don't you understand?" Martin Green demanded. "I *wanted* the tapes. I didn't *have* to have them."

"Wait a minute. I thought you said you went to see Angie Dixon on the job because of the tapes."

Martin Green shrugged. "It would be fine to have them, sort of the capper on the jug, but they're not essential. We can nail Martinson without them."

So now the name Martinson had come up. He was the accountant, the erring husband, the ironworkers' bookkeeper who had disappeared on a fishing trip in the wilds of Alaska. Green seemed to be talking about the same puzzle pieces I already had in my possession, those Linda Decker had laid on me, yet there was a slightly different spin to them, a twist, that made them impossible to grasp and utilize.

"What do you mean, nail Martinson? I thought he was dead too. That's what I heard."

Green snorted. "He'd like us all to think he's dead, but I'm not buying it. He and his friends have been looting this local for years. He's got money stashed somewhere, in Canada we think. All of them do. I've got a private detective agency working on finding him right now."

"On finding Martinson? Why?"

Martin Green nodded. "As I said, we believe he's holed up somewhere in Canada. It was simpler for us to hire a private eye and send him after Martinson than it was to get you guys to go looking for him."

A piece of the puzzle finally slipped into place. "So

what our witness told us about bribes and payoffs in the
union was true?''

"Unfortunately, yes. International received an anony-
mous tip about what was going on in Seattle. We put an
independent auditing team on it, and they turned up all
kinds of crap. International sent me out as a troubleshooter
to try to get to the bottom of it, to find out who all was
involved, that sort of thing. It's taken me months to even
start scraping the surface. It's not just one or two guys,
you know. It's a whole clique. They got themselves elected
and then made sure they stayed that way. They've been
real cagey about it.''

Cagey? Green was talking about the problem as though
it was some kind of minor office scandal attributable to
internal politics with no major consequences, no harm
done. It was time for some shock therapy.

"They haven't been cagey at all, Mr. Green. They're
killers, cold-blooded killers. Three people are dead so far.
Another is in critical condition. Why didn't you call us
in?''

Green's chin sank to his chest. He sighed. "International told me not to. They wanted to keep our investigation quiet, out of the media. Unions have enough of a
black eye right now without this kind of scandal being
blown all out of proportion. We're losing membership
right and left as it is.''

"Two of your members died here," I pointed out.
"Logan Tyree and Angie Dixon. Didn't it cross your mind
that the information you had at your disposal might have
helped us solve their murders?''

"But the papers said both deaths were accidental.''

A flashbulb of anger exploded in my head. "What the
papers said!'' I exclaimed. "For Chrissake, you mean
you *believe* what you read in newspapers?''

He nodded. For the first time I wondered if Martin
Green was as smart as I'd given him credit for being. He
was our only solid lead. Suddenly I felt as though we were
leaning on a bent reed.

"Wait a minute,'' Manny Davis put in. "Let me get
this straight. You said a few minutes ago that these tapes

aren't essential to nailing these guys. If they were so important once, why aren't they important now?"

Green got up and walked over to a file cabinet in the corner of the room. He pulled a key from his pocket and unlocked it. My body tensed, shifting into that keen wariness that warned of the possibility of danger. I wondered if maybe he had a weapon concealed in the drawer. Instead of a gun, he extracted two maroon, leather-bound accounting books from behind the files in the second drawer.

"Because we have these," he answered, casually tossing the two books in my direction. "The journal entries. Martinson's so dumb that he left them in his office. It's all right there. The top one is the one Martinson handed in, the legal one. The second one is real. It's the one he kept for everyone else, for the creeps he worked with. None of them are listed by name, only by number. Once we put the squeeze on him, we'll be able to put names on these numbers and nail those SOBs."

He was still standing up. Suddenly, he turned and rushed back to the file cabinet. "Wait a minute. I just thought of something."

Quickly he rummaged through the top drawer and pulled out a file folder. It was jammed full of receipts and copies of credit card transactions. He thumbed through a small stack of onionskin papers. "Here it is," he said triumphantly, handing me one of the receipts. "I have to keep all the receipts," he added. "It's a company car."

The receipt in my hand was from an Esso station in Langley, B.C. The gas had been sold by the liter, not by the gallon, and the date said August fourteenth, the day Logan Tyree's boat had blown sky-high. Martin Green's scribbled but legible signature was scrawled across the bottom of the receipt.

"You see, I got tied up here with a late meeting. By the time I finally headed north, I didn't think to check the gas tank. I almost ran out before I remembered. I realized it while I was waiting in line at the border crossing in Blaine. I got off at the first exit and found a gas station."

"What was the meeting about?"

"Meeting?"

"The one before you left town. The one that made you late."

"With Don Kaplan. I think you know him. He's in charge of our apprenticeship program. A number of women had either dropped out or were threatening to. If we lose very many more we'll be in world of hurt with the EEOC and affirmative action. Federal and state contracts, that kind of thing. We had a meeting to see what could be done."

"I thought Don Kaplan quit."

Green laughed. "He quits every day at least once, but he's always back on the job the next morning."

"And was one of the women who quit Linda Decker?"

"How'd you know that?"

"I'm a detective, remember? It's my job."

"She was the first one to go. It's a shame, too. Hell of a little worker. She lifts weights, you know. Strong for her size. The guys didn't mind working with her. They figured she could take care of herself."

"So why did she quit then?"

"I don't know. She came storming in here one day, threw her union book in my face, and told me I could shove it up my ass."

"That was it?"

"That's right. And that's why I was having the meeting with Don, to try to figure out exactly what was happening, to get a handle on it and fix it."

"Was he able to give you any answers?"

"Not really."

Green had said there was an entire clique involved. For the first time, I wondered about Don Kaplan.

"Is he in on it?" I asked.

Martin Green smiled and shook his head. "You've got to be kidding. Don in with Martinson? Never. He's absolutely straight-arrow."

"What makes you so sure?"

Before I could stop him, Green grabbed his phone, picked up the receiver, and punched the intercom. "Kim, is Don still here?" He waited impatiently for her answer, drumming his fingers on the surface of his desk. "Send him in, would you? I want to talk to him."

Martin Green settled back in his chair. "I've worked with Don Kaplan every single day for as long as I've been in Seattle. If he was mixed up in this business, believe me, I'd know it."

I was still holding the second accounting ledger in my hand. Opening it, I paged through it, noting the precise dollar amounts with single-digit numbers following.

"As near as we can tell, there are only nine people actively involved," Green explained. "At least, that's how many identifying numbers are in the book."

The phone rang and Green snatched it up. "Don?" He stopped abruptly and frowned. "I thought I said to hold all my calls, that I didn't want to be disturbed." He hesitated. "All right. That's different. Put him through. Hello, Frank. How's it going? I'm having a meeting here, so make it quick."

There was another pause, a much longer one, but while Martin Green listened, his face broke into a wide grin. "I'll be damned," he said. "Good for you. I knew you could pull it off. Give me your number and I'll get back to you once the crowd thins out. I think I can make it up there tomorrow."

He jotted a number down on a piece of paper then hung up the phone and sat there looking smug. "We got him," he announced.

"Got who?"

"Martinson. Frank Daniels, my private eye, found him hiding out over in Victoria. He's willing to talk terms."

"Terms? What kind of terms?"

"Money terms, Detective Beaumont. If we had wanted him in jail, I could have turned you guys loose on him, but that's not the point. I want the names of everyone else who's involved. I want *them* in jail. And even if Martinson goes to prison too, he'll have a little nest egg waiting for him when he gets out. International will see to it."

"Wait just a goddamned minute here!" I interjected, not wanting to believe my ears. "You mean to tell me you're going to pay Martinson off in return for squealing on his buddies? You're going to let the ringleader off scot-free?"

"He's not the ringleader," Green assured me. "That's

why we went after him in particular. He's the weak link in the chain. They needed him, and he needed money. One of his kids was sick, died eventually, to the tune of some fifty grand after the insurance had paid everything it would pay. That's how they suckered him in, I'm sure. He was up to his eyeballs in debt, his marriage was in trouble. They made him an offer he couldn't refuse.

"Unfortunately, he's a whole lot better at being an accountant than he is at being a crook. He couldn't stand not keeping meticulous records, even if it meant having two separate ledgers."

Green reached for the phone again. "Kim? Call Chrysler Air Service and see how soon I can get a charter plane to go from here to Victoria. And by the way, where's Don? I thought you said he was still here." Green paused. "What do you mean, he left? Just like that?"

Green slammed the phone into its cradle, shoved his chair against the wall getting out of it, and raced to the window where he stood looking down at Broad. "I'll be damned," he said.

I hurried to his side. "What is it? What's going on?"

"Don was on his way in here when Kim told him about Martinson, that Frank had caught up with him. Kim said he mumbled something about getting a briefcase from his car and left. Look, that's him now, getting in that white T-Bird over there. He didn't forget something; he's leaving."

I looked down across Broad through sheets of pouring rain where a dead gas station had been converted into a temporary parking lot. Don Kaplan was indeed climbing into a white T-Bird.

"You must be right about him," Green said grimly. "If he wasn't involved, he wouldn't take off like this."

"Let's go get him," I said, turning away from the window.

But I was too late. Nobody needed any urging from me. Kramer and Manny were already headed out the door, and I was left bringing up the rear.

Chapter 22

THE good news was it was five o'clock. That was the bad news as well—rush hour, Friday. Seattle's rain-soaked pavements were slick as glass with the oily buildup that comes from more than a month without rain. The roar of traffic was punctuated by the sound of squealing tires as frustrated drivers tried to gain traction on steep, rain-glazed, hillside streets.

From Martin Green's window I had seen Don Kaplan's late-model white T-Bird turn right up First Avenue—a big mistake on his part. Instead of a free-moving thoroughfare, First Avenue between Broad and Denny had slowed to a commuter's-nightmare parking lot. Kaplan pulled into traffic, that was all. He traveled only a few car lengths before he too was stopped cold. Nothing was moving.

Manny, Kramer, and I raced out of the union office, crashed down the stairs, and stopped on the sidewalk long enough to look up the street.

"That's him," I said, pointing. "The white T-Bird in the left-hand lane." Unfortunately, the light on Denny changed. Kaplan's car inched forward.

"Come on," Kramer yelled, heading in the opposite direction. "Let's go get the car."

Manny took off after him, but I didn't. This was my neighborhood, my block. There are times when a car can be far more of a hindrance than a help. Wincing at the sharp pain in my heel, I headed up First on foot. In the snarl of traffic I figured I had a better chance of catching him that way than Manny and Kramer did in a vehicle.

And it almost worked. Kaplan's turbo coupe was stuck in a long line of idling vehicles waiting for the light to change on Denny a block and a half away. I was only three car lengths away and closing fast when Kaplan leaned over and caught sight of me in his rearview mirror. I doubt he recognized me. He was probably looking for any sign of pursuit. A man in a sports jacket jogging up First Avenue in the rain was a dead giveaway.

Laying on the horn, Kaplan muscled the T-Bird across the right-hand lane of vehicles and darted up the short half-block of Warren that reaches across Denny. At the corner of First and Warren I paused for a moment, undecided. Should I continue on foot or wait long enough to signal Kramer and Manny? The problem was, once Kaplan turned right on Denny, he'd have a clear shot at doubling back down Second, Third, or Fifth and eluding us completely.

Hearing the piercing screech of a siren, I turned and looked back. Kramer and Manny were just then turning off Clay onto First. They were on their way, but even with the help of sirens and lights, covering those two and a half blocks would take time—time we didn't have. They would be too late. Kaplan would be long gone.

I couldn't wait. With a burst of speed that surprised me, I sprinted up Warren after him. He was there, less than a tantalizing half-block away, his right-hand turn signal blinking steadily as he waited for a break in traffic.

I snorted and would have laughed aloud but I was running too hard. Driving habits are like that—so ingrained, so automatic, that even driving a getaway car a crook still uses his directional signals.

I was only thirty or forty feet away when he spotted me again and floorboarded it. He plunged into traffic on Denny while the rear of the T-Bird skidded crazily from side to side.

What happened next happened with blinding speed. A driver from the other direction, alarmed by Kaplan's skidding, stepped on his brakes and slid into somebody else. In the fender-crunching melee that followed, two more cars were caught and accordion-pleated. The fourth, an ancient Chrysler Imperial driven by a Mohawked teenager, successfully avoided hitting the other three only to slide sideways into the right-hand lane. The Imperial nailed Kaplan's left fender in a glancing blow that sent the T-Bird spinning up onto the sidewalk.

When the skidding stopped, the street was littered with wreckage and debris. There was a moment of stark silence and then, somewhere, a horn blared.

The Imperial, barely dented, had ended up closest to me, coming to rest with its nose against a fire hydrant which promptly spewed a geyser of water straight up into the air. The driver, unable to open the door, scrambled frantically through the broken window, cutting his hands in the process.

"I couldn't help it," he cried hysterically, running up to me. "My dad's going to kill me, but it wasn't my fault."

His mouth was bleeding, and there was a long jagged cut on one side of his head. I caught him by the shoulders and eased him down on the curb.

"Sit here," I ordered. "Don't move around until after the medics get a look at you."

He sat there, but he wouldn't let go of my hands. "It wasn't my fault," he insisted. "You saw it, didn't you? Will you tell my folks that I couldn't help it?"

"Yes, I will."

That seemed to satisfy him. He let go of my hand and I turned to look for Kaplan. He was gone. The crippled T-Bird, looking like it had been smashed in a garbage compactor, was still sitting half on, half off the sidewalk. Its left rear tire was flat and the driver's door gone. Kaplan was nowhere in sight.

I looked around for help, but it was hopeless. Denny was totally impassible. Kramer and Manny would never make it through the snarl of wrecks in time to be of much help. It was up to me. But at least now Kaplan and I were even. We were both on foot.

At the corner of Second Avenue, I paused to catch my breath and peer up the street. Second is a vast expanse of boulevard and sidewalk that seems to end abruptly in an elbow of skyscrapers a mile away. Through the rain I could see both sides of the street for blocks. There were people gathered here and there at bus stops, but no one was running. Don Kaplan was nowhere in sight.

I looked up Denny just in time to catch sight of him crossing Third in a crowd of pedestrians heading for Seattle Center. Once more I started after him. My breath was already coming in short gasps. The incline there seems benign enough when you're riding in a car, but on foot it's steep. And the blocks are long. And it was crowded.

Labor Day revelers had finally decided against letting the weather spoil Bumbershoot. Finished with work, they were coming out in force, milling up Broad and Denny in a slow-moving forest of open umbrellas that hampered both vision and speed.

Cops learn to think like crooks. I knew instinctively what Kaplan had in mind. Once he was safely inside the gates of Seattle Center, it would be all too easy for him to blend into the crowd and disappear. He was just leaving the ticket booth when I reached the main gate area. Here the crowd was denser, more so now that some people had turned away from the gate to watch the collection of emergency vehicles screaming in frustration as they attempted to reach the accident scene two blocks away.

I tried to force my way through the crowd. "What's the big hurry, Bud?" a man demanded as I pushed past him. "Where's the fire?"

Without answering, I kept on shoving, while fifteen feet and fifty people away, Don Kaplan handed over his ticket and slipped quickly through the gate.

Slowly the crowd gave way, letting me pass. I finally reached the gate and could see Kaplan inside the grounds. He was easy to spot. Except for me, he was the only person there without a raincoat or umbrella. I saw him dash past the fountain with its huge joke of ugly orange statuary near the bottom of the Space Needle.

A woman barred my way. "Ticket, please," she said.

Reaching for my ID, I was already launching into an explanation when she caught sight of the Bumbershoot stamp on my hand, the one Heather had insisted on getting as we left the grounds earlier that day.

"Oh," the woman said. "I didn't know you'd already been inside. Go ahead."

Grateful for small blessings, I darted past her and through the gate. The grounds of Seattle Center were far different from what they'd been earlier in the day. It was more crowded now, although still not as bad as it would have been in good weather. Kaplan had a good lead on me. Just as I cleared the gate, he disappeared around the bumper-car ride some fifty yards or so ahead.

I wanted to catch up, but I didn't want to alert him, to

let him know I was still on his trail. I hurried up the outdoor corridor between the Science Center and the miniature golf course, using the golf concession to conceal my movements. I came out by an open-air stage where a noisy band was risking electrocution blasting heavily amplified rock music into the pouring rain.

If Kaplan had turned into the Center House, I would have lost him entirely. Instead, he turned up through the food concession area with its outdoor booths and grazing throngs. I followed as quickly as I could. I figured he was heading for one of the other entrances where he'd be able to get back off the grounds and maybe call a taxi. I had to catch him before then.

I was closing the distance when suddenly he stopped and turned. Some sixth sense must have warned him. An electric arc of recognition passed between us. He broke and ran.

There was no longer any pretense of stalking him. I still couldn't draw my weapon, though, not in that crowd. My only hope was in actual physical contact. I ran, if you could call it that, pushing and jostling my way through resisting lines of people waiting outside the various booths.

Luckily for me, Kaplan wasn't thinking straight. Desperate to get away, he headed for the relatively open ground by the International Fountain with me in hot pursuit. He would have been better off sticking to the crowds. People around us were becoming aware that something was wrong. They moved aside and cleared a path, giving me the final edge I needed.

As he started by the fountain, I dove for him and caught him by the knees, bringing him down with the kind of flying tackle I hadn't attempted since high school football. He landed on top of me, smashing my face into the muddy grass. My nose started to bleed. Again.

He got up, kicking me in the head, and scrambling away across the rough paving brick that surrounds the fountain. When I got up, he was teetering on the fountain's concrete wall. With dogged determination I went after him again.

By now several uniformed security guards, alerted by the crowd, were converging on the fountain. "Break it up," one of them shouted. I paused long enough to look at my reinforcements. When I did, Kaplan made a break for it and disappeared over the edge of the fountain. I dived in after him.

The fountain has steep sides that drop off abruptly above the border of rugged white rocks. The surface was wet and slick. I tried to stand up, but a sudden burst of water threw me off balance and sent me flying toward Kaplan. I crashed into him and caught him in a crushing bear hug. We both went down, rolling over and over down the incline as the symphonic music around us hit a crescendo. We landed on the rocks, with Kaplan on the bottom.

"Hands up," someone shouted over the music. "Get off him and get your hands up."

"It's all right," I said, standing up, dripping blood and gasping for breath. "It's okay, you guys. I'm a cop. Help me get him out of here."

One of the security guards had splashed down into the fountain beside me. I knew him. He was an off-duty patrolman from the David Sector in downtown Seattle. He recognized me as well. "Hey, Beaumont, what's going on?"

"Help me move him out of the fountain, then call dispatch. Have them tell Detectives Kramer and Davis where I am. Tell them I've got him. And get Medic One here too, on the double. This guy may be hurt."

Together the patrolman and I lifted Kaplan and carried him out of the fountain. We lay him flat on the grass. His eyes were open, but glazed with pain. He made no effort to move or get up. I knelt down beside him. "Are you all right?" I asked. "Can you move your fingers?"

He wiggled them and nodded.

"And your feet?"

He nodded again.

"It's over," I told him. "You guys are out of business."

"Damn," Kaplan murmured and closed his eyes.

The Medic One unit showed up minutes later and loaded Kaplan on a stretcher. They were just getting ready to haul him away when Paul Kramer and Manny Davis arrived on the scene. Someone had thrown a blanket over my shoulders, and I was standing there wet and shivering.

"Where is he?" Kramer asked.

"Kaplan?" I nodded toward the Medic One unit. "He's in there," I answered.

True to form, Kramer headed for the van. He didn't give a shit about whether or not I was hurt. He wanted to be sure Don Kaplan was locked up securely enough that he couldn't get loose.

Manny Davis came over to me then. "Are you all right, Beau?" he asked.

And that was the difference between them. Manny cared. Kramer didn't. It was as simple as that. The son of a bitch might very well end up as police chief some day. God knows he's ruthless enough.

I hope to hell I never have to work for him.

Chapter 23

I JERKED my head in Kramer's direction. "Tell him I've gone home to change clothes. I'll meet you guys back down at the department and we'll finish sorting this out."

Manny at least made the effort to stop me. "Don't you want a ride, Beau? Our car's right over there, just behind the Coliseum."

I shook my head. "No thanks. I need to walk. It'll clear my head."

I limped back to Belltown Terrace. My heel was killing me, sending shooting pains across the top of my foot as I hobbled along. People steered clear of me. It wasn't until I saw myself reflected in the window glass of Belltown Terrace that I realized why. I was still wearing the soaking wet blanket. With two black eyes, my broken nose, and my freshly bloodied face, I'm sure I was mistaken for one of Seattle's more actively unfortunate street people. At least this set of torn and dripping clothing could go on a line-of-duty replacement voucher.

Annie, the concierge, was still on duty. "My God!" she exclaimed when I came into the lobby. "You're a mess, Detective Beaumont. What happened? I thought you were going to Bumbershoot." She must have been at lunch when I brought the girls home.

"I did," I told her. "It's really crowded."

Leaving a puddle of water on the marbled lobby floor, I stepped into the elevator and went upstairs. Within minutes I had stripped off my clothes and was lying in my Jacuzzi.

Good sense said I should have iced my foot, but the steaming water felt good on my chilled body and aching muscles. I should have felt victorious, triumphant. I didn't. I felt broken. Stiff. Old. And filled with a vague sense of discontent.

I guess it was professional pride. I had caught Kaplan, sure. And somebody else had nailed Martinson. But there were seven numbers besides theirs in that leather-bound ledger. That meant seven others still on the loose. Maybe we'd find out who they were if the private eye was right and Martinson was ready to talk, but he had been out of town when the murders started, when Logan Tyree's boat blew up and when Angie Dixon fell off Masters Plaza.

Murder is my bailiwick. Let somebody else deal with the union racketeering. It was the killer I wanted.

With a sudden sense of purpose, I scrambled out of the Jacuzzi, showered, and toweled off. I hurried to the bedroom phone, dialed Manny's number, and got Kramer instead.

"When are you going to question Kaplan?" I asked. "I can be there in ten minutes."

"We're not," Kramer answered shortly.

"What do you mean, you're not?"

"He's in surgery. Ruptured spleen. The doctors are taking it out. They don't know when we'll be able to talk to him."

"Damn. What about Martinson then?"

"Manny's working on it, but right this minute, Green is refusing to press charges."

"So do you want me to come back down or not?"

"I wouldn't bother if I were you. Stay home and take it easy. And keep this under wraps. We're not releasing any names until we see what information Green drags out of Wayne Martinson."

I wasn't dumb enough to believe I was talking to a transformed Paul Kramer, to somebody genuinely concerned about J. P. Beaumont's health and well-being. He was down at the department playing hero, letting the brass know how great he was and how he'd come up with all the answers, and he didn't want me down there gumming up the works.

Let him, I thought savagely as I slammed down the phone.

Pulling on a comfortable pair of sweats, I went on into the living room, poured myself a drink, and settled down in the recliner. Since I wasn't going back to the department, the situation called for a MacNaughton's or two. For medicinal purposes.

I tried to make my mind go blank, to blot the case and everything connected with it out of my head, but it wouldn't stay blotted. I kept coming back to those numbers, those seven people. And Martin Green.

For as long as I'd known him, I had thought of Green as a problem, first in the building and then later, after I'd talked to Linda Decker, in the case. He was supposed to have been the villain of the piece, but now for the first time I began to think seriously about him as an ally, as someone who had come to Seattle to put a stop to the skullduggery in the union that had caused the deaths of Logan Tyree and the others.

What was it he had told us? Something to the effect that after months of work he was finally beginning to scratch the surface. Obviously Don Kaplan had blindsided him. Green hadn't expected Kaplan to be part of the conspiracy, but I wondered if maybe he had identified some of the other scumbags and was playing his cards close to his chest while he waited to bag Martinson and force a private deal.

I had picked up the phone to call him when I remembered that Martin Green had an unlisted phone number. Instead, I dialed the doorman in the lobby.

"I've lost Martin Green's number. Do you happen to have it?"

Pete Duvall sounded a little wary. "I do, but I'm not supposed to give it out. It's probably all right to give it to you, though. Oh, and by the way. When Mr. Ames went out earlier, he said to tell you not to bother to cook. He'll be home around eight, and he's bringing food back with him.''

As if I would have cooked anyway. Ames must have been choking with laughter when he left that message. He knows I don't cook. His sense of humor and his self-sufficiency are two things that make Ralph Ames an enjoyable houseguest. He was being so goddamned self-sufficient that in my preoccupation with the case I had completely forgotten he was still in town.

When I got off the phone with Pete, I tried calling Martin Green. There was no answer. I found myself fuming that the man didn't have an answering machine on his phone. I've come a long way from the time when I didn't have one and wouldn't use one on a bet. I have Ralph Ames to thank for that, among other things.

He showed up right on schedule, bringing with him a selection of delectable carry-out Chinese food which he served with suitable ceremony. "So how did your day go?" he asked.

"Medium," I said, filling him in on the details as we worked our way through sweet-and-sour prawns, ginger beef, and pork-fried rice.

"And how's Jimmy Rising doing?" he asked, when I finished.

"I don't know," I said, "but it won't take long to find out." I went over to the phone and dialed Harborview's number from memory. When the switchboard answered, I asked to be connected to the burn unit.

"This is Detective Beaumont," I said. "I'm calling about Jimmy Rising."

"Are you a member of the family?" the woman asked.

"No," I replied. "I'm a detective. I'm working on the case."

"Hold the line. I'll see if I can put his sister on."

"This is Detective Beaumont. How's it going?" I asked Linda Decker a few moments later when she came on the line.

When she answered, her voice was strained and weary. "No change," she said. "He's no better and no worse."

"How are you doing?"

"I'm plugging," she answered, but it sounded like she was hanging by a thread.

I wanted to tell her about Don Kaplan. I knew how much she needed to hear some news, how much of a boost it would give her to know something was going on, but I kept my mouth shut. Kramer was right. We couldn't afford to let word leak out to any of the other conspirators before we were ready with our fistful of arrest warrants.

"I'll stop by and check on you tomorrow morning," I said.

She hung up. Long after I heard the dial tone I continued to stand there, holding the receiver in my hand, staring at it.

"What's the matter?" Ames called from the kitchen, where he was putting away leftovers.

Slowly I put down the phone. "I didn't tell her about Martinson, Kaplan, any of it."

"Of course not," Ames said. "Especially when you're operating under strict orders to act like a team player."

"But what if the team's screwing up?"

"That's not your problem," Ames said.

"The hell it isn't!"

Slamming my half-finished drink onto the table, I slipped on my holster and headed for the door to retrieve my shoes.

"What do you think you're doing now, Beau?" Ames demanded.

I stopped long enough to try dialing Martin Green's number. There was still no answer. "I'm going to Renton," I said.

"Renton," he echoed. "Why Renton?"

"Because there's somebody down there who may know something about all this and I'm going to ask him."

"You shouldn't be driving," Ames said. "You've had too much to drink."

"You drive me then, because I'm going, and I'm going now!"

During the twenty-minute drive to Renton we spoke only when it was absolutely necessary. I gave Ames terse directions, telling him to turn here or turn there. I was steamed, but I knew Ames was right that night, the same as he had been the night before. I was in no condition to drive and was surprised by how quickly the booze had snuck up on me. My mind was fuzzy as we started out, but it cleared as we drove, as I concentrated all my physical and mental energies on what had to happen.

When we pulled into the yard of Katherine Tyree's house, the television set was going in the living room. Ames got out of the Porsche and followed me into the yard.

Fred McKinney answered the door and recognized me as soon as he opened it. He didn't seem startled to see me. "We heard," he said.

"Heard what?" I was almost afraid of his answer, afraid someone had leaked the Don Kaplan story to the press.

"About Linda's mother," he answered. "It's a crying shame."

I breathed a sigh of relief. "And did you hear about her brother?" I asked. "He's in the hospital. Probably won't make it."

Fred nodded bleakly. "Will it ever stop?"

"That depends," I said.

"On what?"

"On whether or not someone finally has balls enough to come forward and say what's really going on."

"Who is it?" Katherine Tyree called from in front of the television set.

"It's one of those detectives," Fred answered. He looked at me, his eyes narrowing. "What do you want with us?"

"Do you have balls enough, Fred?"

"What do you mean?"

"You told me you came up here as a boomer. I want you to answer just one question. How did you manage to get to work on Columbia Center?"

McKinney dropped his gaze. As soon as I saw it, I knew I had him. "I bought my way on," he said quietly.

"How?"

"Five grand. Cash. I took out a second mortgage on my boat. I paid the second off when Logan bought *Boomer* from me."

"So you bribed your way onto that job?"

McKinney nodded.

"Who to?" I asked.

"You mean who'd I give the money to?"

"That's right."

"The guy who used to be in charge of book transfers."

"Who's that?"

"His name is Harry Campbell."

"Harry Campbell. Harry Campbell. The name sounded familiar, but I couldn't place it right off. "You say he used to be in charge?"

McKinney shrugged. "That's right. When Green came in he kicked him back in the gang."

"Do you know where I can find him?"

"The last I knew, he was working in the raising gang down on Masters Plaza."

And suddenly I realized why Harry Campbell's name was so familiar. I *had* seen it before. In the newspaper. He was Angie Dixon's partner. The one who had sent her after the welding lead.

Leaving a puzzled Fred McKinney standing in the doorway, I wheeled and charged back toward the car with Ames right behind me.

"Where to now?" Ames asked.

"Back home."

As soon as we were back in my apartment, I dialed Martin Green's number for the last time. His mother answered. "I think he's down on the jogging track," she told me. "He said he couldn't sleep and that he was going for a walk."

I found Martin Green smoking a cigarette on a bench at the far end of the building. It was almost eleven. The rain had stopped. The gardens next to the jogging track smelled fresh and moist. Green was sitting with his back to me, looking at the same cityscape Don Kaplan had been looking at when I first met him at Martin Green's party.

When he heard footsteps approaching, he turned and glanced at me over his shoulder. "Did you get him?" he asked.

"He's in the hospital. They're removing his spleen."

"I never thought about Kaplan being involved," Green

said. "It irks me that he suckered me that badly." Then he was quiet, taking a long drag on his cigarette.

"When do you go to Victoria?" I asked.

"Chrysler Air was all booked up. I go first thing tomorrow morning."

There was another brief silence between us. "Aren't you going to hassle me about not pressing charges?" Green asked after a pause. "Your friends were ripped about it."

"I don't give a damn what you do with Martinson," I said.

"You don't?" Green sounded surprised.

"I'm a homicide detective," I told him.

"So?"

"So Kaplan and Martinson are only two of the nine. One or more of those other seven is a killer. That's who I want. Have you identified any of the others?"

"Only one. I caught him red-handed and fired his ass."

"Who was that? Harry Campbell?"

Martin Green looked at me, startled. "How'd you find that out?"

"How doesn't much matter. Think back to when you were up on the building with Angie Dixon," I continued. "Is there a chance that someone up there could have overheard her agree to give you the tapes?"

For a moment Green said nothing, then as the realization dawned on him, he nodded, his mouth hardening into a grim line. "He was her partner, wasn't he?"

I nodded.

"Right off-hand, I'd say the chances are one hundred percent that he must have been listening."

"And is that crew working overtime again tomorrow?" I asked.

He nodded. "They start at six-thirty. If you want me to, I'll be only too happy to go along and point him out."

Chapter 24

I DIDN'T want to give Watty any ammunition about my not being a team player. Martin Green and I walked over to the Labor Temple and picked up Harry Campbell's address. When we got back to my apartment, I called Manny Davis at home, told him what was up, and gave him Harry's address in Edmonds just north of Seattle proper. He said to hold tight, that either he or Kramer would get back to me.

As soon as Ralph Ames caught wind of what was going on, he went into the kitchen and started a pot of coffee. He brought the pot and three cups on a tray into the living room.

"Looks like it could be a long night," he said, handing me a cup.

I accepted it gratefully, but I was watching the phone, waiting for it to ring. Willing it to ring.

It did. Finally. Two cups of coffee later. But it wasn't Manny or Kramer. "Sergeant Watkins here, Beau. How's it going?"

"How the hell should I know how it's going? I've been sitting here for forty-five minutes, cooling my heels, and waiting for someone to get back to me."

"There wasn't time."

"What do you mean, there wasn't time?"

"We had to get a warrant and negotiate a peace treaty with the Edmonds Police."

"Wait one fucking minute here! Do you mean to tell me Kramer and Davis have gone up to Edmonds to pick him up?"

"Kramer was still here working. He took off as soon as we had the warrant. Said he'd pick Manny up on his way north."

"What about me?"

"I already told you, Beau. There wasn't time. We were afraid Campbell might get wind of what had happened to

Kaplan and take off. Besides, the doc says Kaplan should be coming out of sedation about now. I thought I'd send you up to Virginia Mason to talk to him.''

"Talk to Kaplan!" I sputtered. "You mean . . ."

"Look," Watty interrupted. "I'm giving this one to Manny and Kramer. And if you know what's good for you, you will too. I had a chat with Kramer while we were waiting. You let them take credit for this and he won't file a grievance on the other.''

"In other words, blackmail.''

"Let's just say tit for tat," Watty responded. "Kaplan's up in Virginia Mason. Go see him, Beau. And let this be a lesson to you.''

I flung down the phone. Ralph Ames and Martin Green had been chatting quietly on the window seat. They both looked up. "What's the matter?" Ames asked.

"I've just been screwed, blued, and tattooed. Without a kiss.''

"What's that supposed to mean?''

"I'm on my way to Virginia Mason.''

"Want me to drive?" he asked.

"No thanks. Believe me. I'm stone-cold sober!''

It was almost two o'clock in the morning when I walked up to the door of Don Kaplan's room in Virginia Mason Hospital. A police guard was standing by outside.

"He's awake," he told me. "One of the nurses was just in talking to him.''

I pushed open the door. Don Kaplan lay in the bed, his eyes fixed on a flickering screen of television set on the wall at his feet. He glanced over at me, and then turned back to the old movie.

"I want to see my lawyer," he said.

"You'll need one, you son of a bitch. By the time we finish talking to the prosecutor, we're going to nail you for murder every bit as hard as if you'd pulled the trigger yourself.''

Kaplan turned and looked at me. "I want my lawyer.''

Turning on my heel, I stalked out of the room. The threat had sounded good, but I wondered if we'd be able to make it stick.

There was an ambulance coming up Boren and I waited

for it to pass. It was headed for Harborview. After a moment's hesitation, I followed it. There was no longer any reason not to tell Linda Decker what was happening.

The nurses' station was empty when I got to the ninth floor. I could see a flurry of activity down the hallway a door or two. The folding chair in the hallway outside Jimmy Rising's room was empty. With an eerie sense of foreboding, I stepped to the door and pushed it open.

The room was dimly lit. The thermos and the lunch pail sat on a table near Jimmy Rising's head. He seemed to be asleep. I started toward the waiting room, thinking Linda might be there, when I ran into the guard. He was coming out of a rest room, zipping his fly.

"Where's Linda Decker?" I asked.

"Who are you?"

"Beaumont. Detective Beaumont from homicide."

"She left just a few minutes ago."

"Where'd she go?"

"The chaplain came and got her. I guess they were going to his office."

A nurse came bustling down the hall. She had to walk around us. "Excuse me," I said, "but where's the chaplain's office?"

"On the first floor. Why do you need to know?"

"I'm looking for Linda Decker. According to the guard here, she just left with the chaplain. They went down to his office."

"His?" the nurse asked, frowning.

"His," I repeated. Maybe she wasn't awake. "The chaplain's office."

"But the night duty chaplain is a woman," she said.

A hard knot of fear lumped in my gut. I turned on the guard. "What did this guy look like?"

The guard shrugged. "Fairly tall. Well-built for a minister, I thought."

"Did he say anything?"

"Something about her kids. I don't know exactly."

The nurse had gone on into the nurses' station and was studying a chart. "Can you call the chaplain's office?" I asked.

She looked annoyed, but she picked up the phone,

dialed a number, and handed the receiver to me. A woman answered. "Lucille Kenmore. How may I help you?"

"You're the chaplain?" I asked.

"Yes, I am."

"Did you just send someone up for Linda Decker on the ninth floor?"

"No, I certainly didn't. I'm involved in a conference right now. If you could just leave your number . . ."

I handed the phone back to the nurse. My mind was racing. If the person who came for Linda Decker wasn't from the chaplain's office, then it was someone who had lied to the guard to gain access.

I turned to the guard. "How long ago did they leave?"

"Not that long ago. A few minutes maybe. I'm surprised you didn't run into them in the elevator."

The nurse was looking at me. "Is there a problem?"

"Do you have a phone number for Jimmy Rising's sister?"

"Yes, but . . ."

"No buts. Get it for me and get it fast. She may have been taken out of here against her will."

The guard shook his head, looking skeptical. "I doubt that. She knew the guy. She called him by name."

"What name?"

"Harry."

Harry Campbell. Shit! A wave of gooseflesh washed down my legs. My guess was that somehow Campbell had tumbled to the fact that we were after him and he had decided to buy himself a little insurance. If one hostage was good, three would be better.

I wheeled on the nurse, who still hadn't moved. "Get me that number and get it *now*!" I barked.

"This is highly irregular."

"Look, lady, don't you understand? Lives are at stake!"

That finally jarred her loose. She took a metal-covered chart from its place on the counter and ran her finger down the first page. "Here it is," she said. "Would you like me to dial it for you?"

When she handed me the receiver I could hear a phone ringing at the other end. It was on its sixth ring when someone finally answered, a woman's voice still thick and groggy with sleep.

"Is Linda there?" I asked.

"No. Oh, wait. Maybe she came in and I didn't hear her."

"But this is where she's staying?"

"Yes, but she's been at the hospital most of the time."

"Are her kids there?"

"Yes, but . . ."

"Listen to me, and listen very carefully. My name's Beaumont, Detective J. P. Beaumont with the Seattle Police."

"Oh, I remember you, Detective Beaumont. I'm Sandy. Remember? From micrographics."

That was almost more than I could have hoped for—someone I knew. I wouldn't have to start the explanations from scratch. "Sandy," I said, "you've got to get those kids out of there."

"But they're asleep."

"Listen. I only have time to say this once. Wake them up. Get them out of the house. Where do you live?"

"On the back side of Queen Anne Hill just a few blocks from Northwest Center," she answered. "I usually walk to work."

"Load those kids into your car. You do have a car, don't you?"

"Yes."

"Take them somewhere, anywhere. My place. Do you know where Belltown Terrace is at Second and Broad?"

"I've driven past it."

"Take the kids there. Now. Call my apartment. A man named Ames will answer. Tell him I told you to come there and wait, understand?"

"But what's the rush?"

"I can't explain now, Sandy, but hurry. Please. Give me your address."

Sandy Carson's street address was on 13th. I took it down and then dropped both the phone and the note into the mystified guard's hand. "Call 911," I ordered. "Have them send a squad car to this address. No lights and no

sirens, got that? Tell them to wait for me there." I headed
for the elevator.

"Yes, but . . ."

"And get hold of Sergeant Watkins. Give him a mes-
sage for me. Tell him that if Kramer and Davis are still in
Edmonds, they're barking up the wrong goddamned tree.
That's where they need to be. The address in your hand."

The elevator door slid shut behind me. The ride was
surprisingly quick. It went all the way from the ninth floor
to the bottom without stopping for anyone else. I couldn't
believe my luck. As soon as I got on the street, though, I
realized I'd screwed up. I had no idea what kind of car
Harry Campbell might be driving, and I had no way of
finding out. Once more I wished I had taken Ames' advice
and installed a cellular phone in the 928.

The engine of the Porsche roared to life when I turned
the key. Pulling a fast U-turn on Jefferson, I headed back
toward Boren. The lights ahead of me turned green as I
started down the hill. Fortunately, there weren't any stray
pedestrians. And no traffic cops, either. I was doing sixty
when I had to slow down for the Y at Stewart.

There was a car ahead of me, and I just made the yellow
arrow onto Denny Way. The lights had been with me from
the top of the hill. I knew I was making incredibly good
time, but all the speed in the world would be meaningless
unless Harry Campbell was going where I thought he was
going.

On Denny Way my luck with the traffic came to an end.
There was a car, an older-model Datsun, poking along in
the left-hand lane ahead of me, and a Chevron gasoline
tanker tooling along at my side. I flashed my high beams
at the Datsun. Instead of moving to the right out of the
way, it slowed, swerved toward the left, and straddled the
yellow traffic divider in the middle of the roadway without
leaving enough room between it and the tanker for me to
pass.

Just then the driver's door flew open and a body fell out
of the front seat of the Datsun, rolling over and over into
the oncoming lane. My steel-belted radials smoked to a
stop as I stood on the brakes, and the driver of the tanker
blared his horn. Suddenly the body on the street rose to its

feet and came scrambling toward me, arms waving frantically. I recognized Linda Decker's face as she grabbed
desperately for my door.

"Please help me," she gasped, wrenching my door
open. "Help me. He's got a gun."

"Get in, quick," I told her. "He won't get away."

She stopped and stared at me. "It's you!" she exclaimed. "How did you find me?"

"Never mind. Get in the car, goddamnit."

The truck driver had stopped half a block away and now
he too came dashing up to the Porsche. "Lady, are you all
right? Is something the matter?"

By then Linda was finally moving toward the rider's
door. I leaned out the window and called to the truck
driver. "Do you have a CB in that rig?"

He nodded. "Sure."

"Notify Seattle P.D. There's a fugitive in that Datsun
up there. His name's Harry Campbell. He's armed and
dangerous. What's your license number, Linda?"

She was crying, but she managed to choke out an
answer. I started to relay it to the driver, but he waved me
on. "Got it," he said and started back for his truck while I
rammed the gas pedal to the floor and we shot forward.
Ahead of us, the taillights from the Datsun bounced back
over the median and into traffic. Campbell was still heading west on Denny.

"He said he had my kids, that they were down in the
car. That's why I went with him. He wanted me to drive
him to Canada, using us as cover. He took me down the
stairs," she added. "He was afraid we might meet
somebody in the elevator."

"He was right," I said grimly. "You would have."

"I thought he'd done something to the kids, but when I
found out they weren't in the car, that he wanted me to
drive him to the house, I decided I'd try to get away from
him before we got there."

"You did great," I told her. "And the kids are fine. I
told Sandy Carson to take them to my place."

"Thank you," Linda murmured.

"Glad to be of service."

The Datsun was a few blocks ahead of us, but I didn't

try to close the gap. Instead, I concentrated on maintaining visual contact. That was enough. No heroics. Not with Linda Decker in the car. Patrol cars were on their way. I'd let some Joe Blow patrol officer bring the guy to ground. At least it wouldn't be Detective Paul Kramer. Let him put that in his pipe and smoke it.

"But how did you know what was happening?" Linda Decker asked. "How did you know where he'd go?"

"I got lucky for a change," I told her. "For once in my life, I flat got lucky."

Chapter 25

A ROOKIE fresh out of the academy actually made the arrest. That was fine with me. As long as it wasn't Paul Kramer putting the cuffs on Harry Campbell's wrists, I didn't much care who did.

Ralph Ames had been far more right than he knew when he said it was going to be a long night. The sun was already up by the time Linda Decker and I left the department to go back to Belltown Terrace. And it was after five when she and Sandy Carson packed the two sleeping kids down to Sandy's car for the short ride home.

I was sound asleep at six when the phone rang. It was Linda Decker. The hospital had just called her. Jimmy Rising was dead.

He had been so badly burned, and the road back would have been so tough, that I couldn't help thinking he was better off, but I felt sick just the same. If there was anyone Upstairs keeping score, the good guys had lost big in this particular skirmish.

The next time I saw Linda Decker, it was the afternoon of Jimmy Rising's funeral at a cemetery somewhere in the wilds of Bellevue. She came over and stood beside me as they lowered Jimmy's simple casket into the ground.

"They're in there with him, you know," she said softly.

"Pardon me?"

"The thermos and the lunch pail you gave him. If

heaven's perfect, Jimmy will have a job to go to every day. He'll need them.''

Linda Decker walked away from me then. Her kids wanted her for something, and I was glad she left. I wouldn't have been able to talk for the lump in my throat.

As I started back toward where the cars were parked, Martin Green fell into step beside me. I had seen him in the funeral chapel, but we hadn't spoken.

''She's a gutsy little thing,'' he said, nodding toward Linda's retreating figure. ''Did you know she's coming back to work at the hall?''

''No. I hadn't heard.''

''It took some selling. I finally talked her into it. The union needs women like her,'' Green continued. ''The good ones. The ones with some backbone.''

''She's long on backbone all right,'' I said, remembering how Linda Decker had looked in Pe Ell when she'd been staring down at me over the barrel of a gun. ''I wouldn't cross her if I were you.''

Martin Green chuckled. ''Don't worry,'' he said. ''I already figured that out.''

So maybe Ironworkers Local 165 will turn out to be a more perfect union after all. Good for Martin Green. Good for Linda Decker. I'm sure she'll do a fine job of raising those kids no matter what kind of work she does, but it'll be easier to do it by herself on the kind of money she'll make working construction than it would be on what she'd earn tending bar in some backwater like Pe Ell.

About that time I caught sight of Linda's two kids standing together next to the funeral parlor's limousine, waiting for their mother. Jason was holding his little sister's hand protectively. As I got closer to the children, I could hear they were arguing.

''Is too,'' Jason insisted.

''Is not,'' Allison responded. When I walked across the parking lot to get in the Porsche, they followed at a respectful distance.

''See there?'' Jason announced archly as soon as I opened the door to the 928. ''It is too him. I told you.''

When I turned on the ignition, the cellular phone let me know I'd had a call. The readout didn't tell me who had called, but I knew. Ralph Ames was the only person so far who had the number. I called him back and told him to meet me at the Doghouse for lunch.

There wasn't much traffic on the bridge, and Lake Washington was as still and blue as the sky above it. I drove along and thought about Harry Campbell. He had turned out to be a wormy shit. As soon as he saw the writing on the wall, he spilled his guts, thinking that by naming names first and by agreeing to turn state's evidence, he might be able to work himself some kind of deal. That remains to be seen. It's up to the prosecutor's office. Once we turn creeps over to them, it's out of our hands.

According to both Campbell and Martinson, Don Kaplan had been the brains of the outfit, all the while seeming to be working the problem right along with Martin Green. Which just goes to show what a hell of a good judge of character I am. Martin Green wasn't the only one snowed by Don Kaplan. So was J. P. Beaumont.

It was Kaplan who had discovered the leak and sicced Harry Campbell on Logan Tyree and Angie Dixon in a futile attempt at damage control to cover up disclosure of those worthless tapes. In the state of Washington, conspiracy to commit murder is as good as doing the job yourself. In a year or so, maybe Don Kaplan and Harry Campbell will be occupying neighboring cells on Death Row in Walla Walla.

Ames was waiting when I got to the Doghouse. He had already ordered—for both of us. Wanda brought me my bacon and eggs, accompanied by a knowing smile. "I saw your friend's picture in the paper this morning," she said.

"What friend is that?" I asked.

"You know. The movie star."

"What about him?"

"He got married in Las Vegas yesterday to some woman he met while he was here in Seattle."

"Derrick Parker got married?" I asked incredulously, not quite trusting my ears. "You've got to be kidding!"

Wanda shook her head. "Hold on, I think I can find the picture.

Sure enough, when she brought it, there was Derrick

Parker, grinning from ear to ear. Next to him stood a radiant Merrilee Jackson.

I didn't say a word. Who the hell am I to criticize whirlwind courtships?

When we got up to leave, there was a man waiting for a table. Somewhat oversized, he was wearing a black-and-white T-shirt. I'M FAT BUT YOU'RE UGLY, the shirt proclaimed. I CAN GO ON A DIET.

I'm sure Ralph Ames thought I was crazy when I burst out laughing.

"What's so funny?" he asked.

I nodded toward the shirt. "It reminds me of Detective Kramer and J. P. Beaumont."

"How's that?"

"Kramer's probably still down at the department sopping up every bit of glory he can muster."

"So?"

"So maybe I am a playboy cop, and maybe Kramer will turn out to be Chief some day when he grows up, but I'm like that fat man who can go on a diet. I can always quit. Anytime I want to."

Ralph Ames looked at me speculatively. "Anytime," he agreed, nodding. "It's up to you."